Wordless

and Other Stories

By Robin Scott

For

L

Table of Contents

Introduction

It all started as a practical joke.

One of my best friends was out on a date, and it wasn't a date she particularly wanted to be on. I couldn't resist! I decided to have a little fun, hoping to distract and amuse her.

While she was at dinner, I began sending text messages to her cell phone, and before I knew it, I was spinning a story – a story designed to make her blush, in front of her date. And it worked! She made it through the evening, and even asked me to write another one.

So I wrote another, and another, and before long a theme was emerging. I wasn't just writing Make-Me-Blush stories, I was writing about what goes on in the minds of women and men in encounters of every kind. Most are erotic, to some degree, but the eroticism is more about what happens in the mind than below the waist.

I made the stories intentionally sparse, using no proper names, just She and He, to make space for the reader to substitute herself, if the story rang true. To leave space in her imagination, I also made an effort not to clutter them up with unnecessary detail.

Before long, I was writing four or five stories a month, and I had several hundred subscribers.

Another feature of these stories is that every one of them is based on an event in my life, or (more often) from the experience of a friend. Those real events have been fictionalized to some degree, of course, and in some cases separate events have been combined into a single story – but the truth of each comes from the real world.

Sometimes we communicate best when we use unspoken languages, replacing words with touch and gesture, expression and offering. The gulf between woman and man often seems unbridgeable; so many times we seem unable to hear one another, despite all our efforts, especially when it matters the very most. Relationship, ultimately, *is* communication, in the long run; if we love, we find a way.

Wordless

They had talked three nights in a row, and gotten nowhere.

He said he had forgiven her, and she said she had forgiven him. Somewhere in the words and the tone of voice and the hurt and hope and mixed signals, she chose to believe they both meant it, and that they were only a step or two away from ... well, from whatever they were becoming.

She'd spilled, at lunch with her BFF, venting her frustration and trying to convey how earnest she was, how certain, how ready to take things to the next level. Her BFF knew the whole story – about the mixed messages, the stupid mistakes, the near-misses – and expressed a belief that they really were good together.

It's like trying to catch my own hand, she complained. *It's that way for both of us! I just don't have the right words. And I don't blame him for being on his guard, after the mess I've made of things.*

Her BFF reminded her that he, too, had contributed to the mess.

I know, she had answered. *And I really believe he's in the same boat. He's not exactly Shakespeare at his best, let alone under this kind of pressure. But I know he wants this to work, as much as I do. We just don't have the right words.*

And her BFF had sipped her Chardonnay, smiled that little smile of hers, and said, *Who needs words?*

She had gotten to work, preparing the most ambitious undertaking of her romantic life. It took her several days to work out what she wanted to say, and several more days to work out how she could say it without words.

Her rough draft was over-the-top, dramatic and flamboyant and, in the end, not very real. Her second pass, she thought, brought everything home.

He came through the back door too tired to be apprehensive, not quite distant but also not quite fully there. He didn't notice the vast spread of raw materials and cooking utensils spread across the kitchen countertops. She intercepted him before he could get to the living room, easing off his jacket, hugging him warmly.

He started to speak.

Shhhhhhh …

She touched a finger to his lips. He frowned, amused. She waved a hand at the food that waited to be prepared.

He smiled, and started to speak again.

Shhhhhhh!

She smiled, too.

He started to speak again, caught himself before she did, and indicated that he would be back in a moment.

Returning to the kitchen in jeans and a t-shirt, having washed his hands and face as much to draw energy from warm water as anything, he grinned at her playful body language – she was clearly eager for him to get back, and almost bouncy with excitement over the evening that lay ahead. He put his own finger to his lips, at this point on board with the game.

No words tonight!

She handed him a bowl and a wooden spoon, and set him in front of an assortment of ingredients. She herself picked up a small saucepan and turned on one of the front burners on the stove.

They were going to fix dinner together.

We're a team …

Not quite an hour later, the meal was spread out before them, a happy banquet with way too many calories and numerous amusing imperfections. She handed him two fresh candles, having him hold their wicks together. She held up a lighter, and lit both at once, then took one candle from him.

We share the fire …

They ate in playful silence, feeding one another bits of food, making a mess, licking each other's fingers, sipping each other's wine. Wordless was even more fun than words, as she managed to silently tease him over the vegetables she knew he only pretended to like. The dessert – decadent, messy, and eaten very much with fingers – was sensual.

The messages were many, until finally the meal was done.

Ordinarily the dishes would have waited. Leading him back in to the kitchen, she set him before the sink and started handing him dishes.

We clean up our messes together …

He dried his hands off with a dishtowel and she took one of them, interlocking fingers, and they left the house. It was a clear, cool summer evening, with lightning bugs and kids making noise in neighboring yards and streetlights just beginning to come on. They walked hand in hand throughout the neighborhood, till the stars were out and the crickets could be heard. Walking back toward their own home, they passed window after window, each glowing with the soft light of family.

This is our journey …

When they got back to their house, she led him to the porch swing, lighting a candle on the plastic table next to it. She brought out wine glasses and an already-open bottle from beneath the table, and poured them both a second glass. They sat quietly in candlelight and starlight, listening to the soft sounds of evening around them, the occasional noisy child not yet in for the night, the dog-walking neighbor running late, the moon drifting into view.

She gave him a wine kiss and nestled into his arm.

I want to grow old with you …

They lingered on the porch, the steady rhythmic creak of the swing blending with the staccato chirp of crickets, as the candle flickered and the wine disappeared. The peace was almost indescribable, and she felt so safe, so far removed from the terrible argument that had shaken them so badly last week, the awful things that had been said. She hoped he felt as comforted as she did – and, realizing that she could hear his heart beating, she searched it for signs of the same security she was drawing from their unique dialog.

She eased away from him and leaned over to the candle, blowing it out. Handing him the empty wine bottle, she took the glasses in one hand and his hand in the other and led them inside.

The walk-in shower had always been a luxury to her, but tonight more than ever. A single candle on the bathroom sink lit the room, and she undressed him slowly, encouraging him to undress her, and they took a long, slow shower together, each bathing the other … she led, with slow, deliberate movements, encouraging him into a sharing that was more intimate than erotic, reaching not into the depths of sex, but of bonding. They lingered until the hot water began to wane, and then she dried him off slowly, luxuriously, and he did the same.

We take care of each other …

… and it was again a single candle that lit their way as they eased into their bed. The usual frantic rush was absent tonight; in its place was a steady, certain pulse, working its way through them both and bringing them closer. She straddled him, her body glowing, and leaned down, taking his face in her hands, looking deeply into him, stroking his cheek, running her fingers along his neck. She reached down and kissed him long, finally surrendering to the fire …

I can be myself with you …

Their bodies merged again and again, with the tireless abandon of teenagers, and she wondered where the energy was coming from. It hadn't been like this in a very long time … but the answer became clear, as they moved together firmly, fiercely, but slowly, not for ecstasy but for the oneness. In the back of her mind she knew that the rarity of these moments was more her fault than his, the usual rush, the need to be needed … and this deeper connection went unexplored, all too often. Tonight, there was nothing else.

In the continuous exquisite tangle, her rewards came in gasps, not shouts, and he was unsure of her satisfaction, as she drew more and more from their bonding. He paused and reached for the nightstand, where they kept her favorite playthings, hoping to bring her whatever she was missing. She stopped him with a firm hand, sinking into their deepest kiss yet …

You're all I need …

Tears welled up, and she was on the edge of breaking her own rule. She rolled them both, with determination, putting him above her, wrapping her arms and legs around him firmly ... her eyes wet, she dug her fingers into him, encouraging him with every move, every muscle, opening herself completely to him, to all that they were. She let herself become lost in the quickening rhythm, the force of his movements, her need enfolding them both like a shroud. Their common surge was like a cliff falling away beneath them, warm currents lifting them both into evening sky, and as they both trembled with shared joy, she was truly wordless ... she couldn't have spoken if her life had depended on it.

He held her long as the candle burned low, and all the things they'd said without speaking lingered like incense. Peace and calm slowly enfolded the moment, though her eyes were still wet. They sparkled as she looked up into his eyes, one final message passing through the stillness.

Forgive me ...

Need to Know

There are a handful of perfect days in every spring and every fall, on either side of summer – warm but not hot by day, cool but not cold by night, and perfect weather for walking hand in hand.

And they did, playfully, with no romantic intent – *he would never…!* – along the very populated, noisy beach, among the stores in the shopping center, through the park. It had started when they were throwing coins into the fountain, and then hair pins, and then an expired library card, and he'd jumped up on the concrete ledge of the fountain and pulled her up behind him, circumscribing it far too quickly for her comfort (acutely aware of what she's look like, soaking wet, in this already-skintight outfit!).

And they'd just kept doing it …

They had laughed over old memories, and exchanged funny stories about this or that romantic adventure in recent years. He was as much fun as he'd ever been, and it was food in famine for her. She'd told him about her life lately. But not really. Not even close.

They'd had dinner at a hot dog stand, where she'd inwardly fretted over how completely unhealthy it was, and he'd threatened to squirt her with ketchup. He had fed her French fries, one or two at a time, amused at how much she seemed to enjoy it. At least the drinks had been diet!

And the sun had fallen to the sea, casting the most glorious sunset she'd ever seen in all her years of living here, and the ocean breeze was both warm and cool, and the glow all around her mirrored the glow inside.

And they talked and laughed and the moon came out, and they'd walked back to the parking lot where they'd left both cars, and he told her how great it had been to see her after all this time, and how much he enjoyed their daily emails, and …

… he'd taken her into his arms, in a heartbeat, and kissed her, and it was one of those I-really-mean-it kisses, and she had pulled back, almost recoiling … shocked … taken totally by surprise.

I'm so sorry ... I didn't mean ...
She stood there, stunned, unable to say anything.
And his eyes changed, and he moved away, toward his car.
I needed to know there wasn't any chance ...
And he was gone.

She dropped her keys and purse on the dining room table and stood in silence for a moment, trying to take in what had happened. Had this been a date, and she hadn't realized it? Had he thought it was a date? Had they somehow miscommunicated so completely? Reviewing the evening, the day, the week before, she really didn't think so. There was nothing in any of their emails, phone calls or conversation that led her to think that this had been anything other than old friends reconnecting. If she'd had any inkling, all her alarms would have gone off. She was just in *no* shape for...

She took her cell phone from her purse, briefly considered calling him, decided not to. What in the world would she say?

Not a date ...

But *what* a date!!!

Up until that moment, it had been a *perfect* evening, the best time she'd had with a man since, well, since ... hmm. Nowhere to go with that. She couldn't pull anything at all out of her memory.

Knowing what she knew now... well. She wished the night had continued, *as* a date, and yet, not really. Was she ready for that? It had been months and months, and she had gone out of her way to avoid...

She'd have brought him back here, and they'd have put music on...

And she did.

And we'd have turned the lights low...

And she did.

She lit incense, and began to sway to the music, there in the dark living room. Not a drop of alcohol in her, and yet she felt sleepy-drunk relaxed, warm, and... yes. Sexy. It had been months and months...

Eyes closed, she imagined she was dancing with him...

... and he would hold her close...

And she embraced herself, swaying in the dark...

... and his hands would roam...

And she caressed herself, swaying in the dark...

... and things would fall away...

17

She stepped out of her jeans without breaking rhythm, and her fingers loosened buttons slowly, one at a time, as he would do, and a hand slipped into her open blouse, as his would...

The song on the CD changed, and there was a pulse, a powerful thump from the stereo's sub-woofer, and her blouse fell to the floor... and a strap came down; that's how men did it, they weren't at all practical... and now he's dancing behind me... pressing up against me... and I can feel how aroused he is, and with a quick flick of fingers, no more bra...*one hand on my breast, the other caressing my stomach, as we sway...*

... a finger teasing elastic...

... lips on the side of her neck...

And she would take him by the hand, and lead him into her bedroom, where she would light a single candle...

... and stand with him at the foot of the bed, lifting off his shirt, then pulling his bare chest to hers, kissing him slowly, while her hands went to work on his belt buckle... pulling him onto the bed with her as he shed his pants...

She lay sprawled across the bed, candle-shadow flickering all around, lost in the fantasy... nagged by a distant voice that this was too far, a place she couldn't go now... but these feelings were truly him, not just need, not just relief. She could still feel his fingers locked around hers, still hear his laugh... which she reworked into a moan, as she imagined stroking him through his briefs...

Her own remaining undergarment was soaked, and she bisected it with a firm fingertip --- *his* fingertip --- which proceeded to creep through the side, teasing, emerging wet and warm...*his*, and he hovered over her, and brought the wet fingertip to her mouth, tracing her lips... then he kissed her, allowing his body to press down, their cotton-bound arousal thwarted as he ground slowly against her...

Her hands slip down along his back, fingers easing into his drawers and pulling them down, and he kicked them off as he eased back and did the same for her, gazing at her naked body beneath him in candlelight for a moment... lying beside her again, he took her hand in his, reached down, immersed her own fingers in her warm wetness, intertwined his own... then licked them lightly, and - with erotic abandon, fed them to her...

She took each fingertip into her mouth one at a time, warm and slow, her tongue excited, her breathing hot... and heard a whisper...*chocolate*...

... and reached into the nightstand for her stash, breaking off a piece, feeding it to him, imagining him holding it in his mouth, bending to hers, sharing it... she felt the hard fragment on her lips and tongue, taking it in, letting it slowly melt... fingers exploring as she focused on the warm, sweet taste, her mouth filling with the rich, lingering softness...

Chocolate just makes everything better...

She was going to make this last. Oh yes.

Kisses along the insides of her arms... a grazing of lips on her shoulder... and then another piece of chocolate, melted slowly, shared in a long, warm, sensual, slightly messy kiss... and a chocolate-covered fingertip, warm and wet, began tracing the borders of her nipples, causing her to shiver. Strong hands, kneading her breasts firmly, a little rougher than she herself normally would... a finger tracing her lips again, slipping into her mouth... emerging with chocolate...

His name, written across her stomach... his tongue, then erasing it...

She reached into the nightstand drawer again and pulled out a toy, the seriously-man-shaped one, the thick one that took "C" batteries... she stroked it, then wet it with her mouth slowly, taking her time, taking in the familiar shape, and attaching optimistic imaginings to the act...

And then imagined him about to enter her, teasingly slow, hovering...

She took another piece of chocolate into her mouth for another slow-melt, then eased him in, her senses heightened, her nerves screamingly alive...

And she did not flip the switch. Not this time. She wanted him, that sense of fullness, maleness, not a buzz, not a novelty. She moved slowly, rhythmically, deliberately, feeling the shape of him, tensing and releasing along with him, as her mouth filled once again with sensual, sweet warmth...*slow and steady... that's who he is...*

This way, it would take awhile... she was determined to savor every second. The music ran out, in the other room, and she could only hear breathing, and sighs, and moans... he found that spot, that one spot, that *oooooooo* spot, and he started working it - *how many men bother?* - pulsing against the happy place without as he probed the happy place within... slow and steady, relentless... and she rewarded his patience with strong caresses from her inner muscles, determined to make this as ecstatic for him as it was for her...

In the past, the very best moments had been like a damn bursting...

This one was a step up... to *volcano erupting...*

She let herself cry out, and she wasn't at all quiet about it. The neighbors might well have heard, and it went on and on... and on and on ...

It had been months and months...

In her reverie, he followed her in seconds, and she played it out, imagining his continued motions, after her release... when her hands finally stopped, she began to caress herself again, as he would, and hold herself...

She lay quiet, still shaken by the intensity of feelings she hadn't known were there.

It was clear to her that she'd been carrying these feelings around for awhile, and keeping them even from herself. That wasn't surprising; she had a lot of healing yet to do, and she'd closed off this part of herself for many months, like rooms in a house in the wintertime when most of the family is away. Still ... there were little things ... the way she'd dressed this evening...

She lay quiet as the candle burned, aware of the cell phone in her purse on the dining room table.

I can call ...

Yes, she could call ... and what had just happened, here in her bed, could happen for real. And be even better.

Or ... I can take some time and pull myself together.

In her heart, she knew the first option wasn't really an option. *I'm not ready ... and it wouldn't be fair to him.*

She needed to take some time and get herself back on track, to heal, to grow, to get back to the woman she knew she was. She couldn't subject him, or any man, to the expectations of a growing relationship, while she was still in the process of rebuilding.

Or ...

I can call, and meet with him, and tell him how I feel ... and ask him if he is willing to give me some time.

Yes.

The candle was burning down. The bed was a bit of a mess, and so was she; she touched the toy, laying beside her on the bed, realizing she'd need another round or two to truly purge the pent-up tension she had been carrying. And she would think of him, again, and again, and want him even more ...

… and much later, completely spent, she lay in the dark, a single sheet cocooning her.

She thought of the cell phone.

And she decided.

Addicted

It had been public and it had been embarrassing.

The very, very loud music from the stage, the laughter and sing-along and general buzz of the crowd has surely kept anyone from hearing the ugly details - except when he had shouted at her, at the end - but no one could miss the way he stormed out, drunkenly pushing and shoving as he went. One of her friends had tried to comfort her, but you couldn't hear yourself think in the place, let alone talk - so she fought back tears and smiled it away.

Brave face in place, she turned to the stage. The band was just roaring, blasting into "Addicted to Love," take-no-prisoners, at ear-bleeding volume. The dance floor, already well-populated, flooded to overflowing.

Even so, she knew that up there on the stage, rocking his ass off, he hadn't missed it. He never missed anything. Over the years, she had counted on that. Plus, he knew the history here. He'd have been watching.

The volume was so high the band sounded like a spaceship landing, and the lights were psychedelic insanity. As soon as she sought him out, his eyes were on her, and despite his stage-smile and his aggressive attack on his guitar, she knew he'd seen the whole thing.

Your heart sweats... your body shake...

He held her eyes as the lead vocalist blasted out the verse, then looked down at the floor and motioned to the closest dancers with the neck of his guitar. A space cleared, and he jumped from the stage, to loud cheers. Wireless on both his guitar and microphone, as always, he was free to go where he wanted - and he playfully waved a path clear with the neck of his guitar, all the dancers in his vicinity playing along, clearing a path.

Your throat is tight... you can't breathe...

At the bridge before the chorus - a keyboard spot lasting a few seconds - he whipped off the guitar and loosened the strap as far as it would go, and motioned for her to stand. She did, and he was in front of her in a heartbeat, grabbing her with one arm and pulling her completely against him as he dropped the guitar back over his shoulder with the other, around them both...

The dozen or so dancers immediately surrounding them all watched, pointing them out to others, as he started playing again, his sleeveless arms around her, pulling the guitar right up against her, in the best-of-all-possible places. It was as close as she'd ever been to a man in public, tighter than most embraces, and tighter still because of his pull on the guitar. Every chord was a very intimate pressure, and he began singing on the chorus, their faces almost touching...

You're gonna have to face it, you're addicted ...

As their audience grew, he began swaying, dancing with her, and her balance was suddenly a problem. She put her arms around him, but there were bumpy, sharp boxes on the leather guitar strap - wireless transmitters? - and she was afraid she might accidentally turn one of them off.

There was only one other place to put her hands.

The immediate crowd roared their approval of that choice, and she suddenly realized that she was having the time of her life - less than two minutes after being on the edge of a breakdown.

Even so, the question of balance made her nervous - *what if I make us fall down in the middle of the song? Is he out of his mind?* - but he was tall, and maybe not fireman-hunky but muscular enough, with a runner's body toned from hauling heavy speakers and amplifiers all the time. He didn't seem worried about it - and it's not like she had any choice in the matter...

He pulled his head back just enough for their eyes to meet, and smiled his best smile. He slammed chords with erotic gusto, fully aware of the effect.

The lead singer was into the second verse, so he didn't need to sing, and he pulled her close as the pressure of the guitar eased off some. Their audience was cheering them on, but as they swayed forcefully along with the song, she began to tune everyone out. The leather in her hands was warm, and sweating slightly, and she was even more aware of the vest and the half-bare chest underneath it. He was sweating, too, and he smelled like he always smelled - he had hugged her a thousand times - but somehow he was more *him* this time.

Might as well face it...

The song heated up again as the second chorus blasted across the dance floor, and he sang again, his face alongside hers, warm air tingling against her ear. They rocked harder, and the guitar pressure increased, and suddenly the other guitarist, up on stage, tore loose.

But the spotlight wasn't on the stage anymore. Suddenly their too-private space lit up like the fourth of July, and they were the center of attention. The hole in the dance floor that they occupied had grown, and so had the number of dancers watching them, and now they were immersed in blinding light. He cranked everything up a notch, swaying harder, pulling her closer, and -

Ohdeargod!

Their southernmost contact was as close as all the rest, owing to his pull against his guitar, and with his shift of position - leather pants notwithstanding - it was now unmistakable that he was, ah, inspired. *Fully* inspired.

It must have shown on her face, from the reaction of their onlookers.

He pulled back and met her eyes again, grinning roguishly, and as the lead break ended, he bent close, and their lips brushed together, and again, and -

Might as well face it, you're addicted ...!

Back into the chorus, and he was singing *into* her, and it was like nothing like it in anything she'd ever done. Her nipples had long since popped, and her fingers were pretty well dug in as he swayed even harder.

The entire crowd was singing as the band ploughed back into the chorus one last time. They ground together in perfect rhythm, one swaying body, and she went in all the way, singing with him, oblivious to the fact that she was now singing into his wireless microphone - and she wasn't the world's greatest singer. The crowd was, in any case, having too much fun to notice.

The song came crashing to a volcanic finish, and she realized that she was about to do the same, when his lips found hers again, and this time it wasn't a light tough. For the first time in their years of knowing each other... and his hands wailed on the guitar and the drums and lights just went berserk. She made a sound, right into his microphone - and the crowd roared even louder.

A heft of those sweaty arms, a split-second eye contact and smile, and he was sprinting back onstage as the next song started up. Turning, she saw her friend beside her, and the two began dancing. Off to the side - her boyfriend, who had seen the whole thing - *ex-*

boyfriend! - and she felt an incredible rush, as if the jerk was being flushed out of her system.

Turning to the stage, she saw him wink. She winked back.

Your heart beats in double-time... another kiss, and you'll be mine...

The Toy We Left Behind

She snapped her suitcase shut and looked around the small cabin.
Do we have everything?
He likewise looked around the cabin, his own suitcase in one hand and a bookbag in the other.
I think so, he nodded.
They finished loading the van. Then they hugged and kissed on the cabin's porch, climbed in, and drove into the week ahead.

It had not been their first trip out of state, but it had been the first that had been just the two of them. At the San Diego conference five months earlier, they'd been part of a group, and his daughter had come along. This weekend they'd kept for themselves.

It had begun with a rock concert in a city near this cabin, followed by the adventure of getting lost in the dark 40 miles from anywhere, thanks to bad directions from a cellphone map app. They'd arrived at the cabin very late. It was very small, very cozy, and pretty much perfect for the weekend they were needing. That first night, they'd just crashed.

The following morning, they woke up, fixed coffee and stepped outside – and realized they had stumbled into heaven.

Standing on the porch, they looked out at a beautiful sunrise over a vast field, stitched with pasture fencing and surrounding a pond glowing orange, with misty Tennessee mountains on the horizon. There were houses not too far away, but no people to be seen. This was as beautiful a solitude as they had ever shared.

A big breakfast and a long walk filled out their morning. He loved walking with her, talking about nothing, how her hand felt in his. He loved the beauty of their surroundings, and how her presence made it perfect.

After a lunch of sandwiches and an afternoon movie on the couch, they thought about the evening. Chicken and corn-on-the-cob, grilled on the cabin's back porch, with side salads and wine would require a grocery run to a nearby town.

That took almost two hours. They didn't know the area and no longer trusted the map app, so tracking down a market meant asking directions. A couple of times. But they made it back in time to fix dinner together and pour a second wine, just as the sun was setting.

And as the stars softly began emerging, he dug around in his suitcase for a little something his adult son had scored for him: a small handful of weed, unfortunately very damp. He'd also brought along a weed pipe. They meandered down to the pond in the moonlight and lit up, but the dampness of the product and his inexperience with the pipe made it more a laugh than a high. Neither of them had touched the stuff in decades.

They soaked in the cabin's hot tub for a while, then settled into bed.

Did you bring it? he asked.

But of course! she replied.

She reached into the nightstand on her side, where she'd already stowed the toy, that magical wand that pointed them into the end zone every time they made love. And with that, she was in his arms, as nightshirts and undergarments fell away.

The toy facilitated a number of wonderful unions, but tonight they assumed her favorite: he looked up at her as she moved above him, swaying in ecstasy, the toy doing its part. This was the two of them at their best, sharing a passion that not only satisfied but fulfilled them. He was grateful that they had something to share that worked so well for them both – and, of course, was deeply appreciative of the visual.

As she moved on him, haloed in moonlight, he was struck with awe; that he loved her more deeply than he'd ever loved anyone before had long been clear to him, but in this moment, he was swept up in understandings of *why*.

She was magnificent. Beautiful and sexy, certainly, but more importantly, brilliant and principled, with deep values he shared and a sense of humor that meshed perfectly with his own. On their west coast trip, they'd learned that they traveled well together – always a good sign! - and this weekend was better still. They fit together perfectly, and in his admiration of her he was discovering new facets of himself, a new potential for love that he'd long since stopped searching for.

She came with a loud cry, giving her passion a long moment, then cast aside the toy and leaned down onto him. He encircled her with his arms as they rolled together, as she urged him toward his own moment.

On the drive home, he reflected on the joy of their brief weekend, and felt a discomfort nagging at him. She was, indeed, a magnificent woman – and he worried about being worthy of her. He was prone to saying the wrong thing at the wrong time, and there was a train wreck or two in his romantic history to forever remind him of it. He had done some work on himself to combat that problem, but at this point it was more about the train wrecks themselves.

He hadn't reconciled himself with his past. He hadn't confronted his failures. And he hadn't realized how this might trip him up, in being the man he could be.

He hadn't yet grieved for what he'd lost.

Omigod...

He was in another room when he heard her, and the urgency of her tone was alarming. He hurried.

She was in the bedroom, unpacking. Tossing clothes here and there – very unlike her – she was clearly searching for something.

What's wrong?

I can't find it!

Find what?

And before she answered, he knew what the answer must be.

He opened his own suitcase and began searching for the toy.

They searched again. And again.

She was mortified.

We must have left it behind! There's no place else it could be!

That thought both embarrassed and horrified her. The cabin's owner would send someone to clean it for the next visitors – or, worse yet, clean it herself – and discover the toy, wherever it had ended up. She was deeply grateful she had washed it after use, as she always did.

Finally they gave up, and he tried to reassure her past her embarrassment. Surely BnB owners and cabin providers found such left-behinds all the time? They laughed, and began picking up clothes.

And as they did, he thought some more. The toy, which she required for her fullest self-expression in bed, made him conscious of his own need and desire to make her happy - his capacity for which he felt uncertain about.

And in a flash of insight, he saw the paradox of the toy: if he was going to make this wonderful woman happy, he was going to have to leave some things behind.

28

That would take a great deal of work on his part, and he knew he would make mistakes along the way. But their time in the cabin this weekend had strengthened his resolve. He would be the man she needed him to be.

As for the toy – well, there was always the spare in the nightstand...

Backrub

She could tell he was exhausted. More than exhausted, he was completely wiped out.

Things had been so tough lately. He'd been working three nights a week, and Saturdays, in addition to his day job – and even with that, and her part-time income from the school, there wasn't enough. She couldn't work more, because of the kids' schedule and the rising cost of daycare – so it was up to him. And it was just wearing him out.

She had actually been feeling kind of sexy tonight, and had embraced the desire, since it seemed as though neither of them had been in the mood much lately and some rekindling was in order. But after he'd kissed the sleeping kids and taken out the trash and retrieved the dog, she'd stolen a glance at him coming through the back door, and he had sagged for a moment, almost too weary to stand.

He'd lingered in the shower for the relief of hot water, and she had fixed them both a drink. He scarcely noticed, taking the glass from her mechanically, without really looking at it, downing it in a few seconds.

She had lit candles in the bedroom, and she saw a flicker of concern in his face, that she might have expectations on this, a night when there was no chance at all of a decent result. She'd already thought of this, and had changed from her most incendiary lingerie into her frumpiest, most frightening sweatshirt, the one she usually wore to signal that she was too tired. That, she figured, would at least somewhat offset any mixed signals.

He had wandered out of the bathroom in a clean t-shirt and boxers. Pulling him gently down onto the bed, with no pretext, no innuendo, she rolled him belly-down and eased herself down onto him like a blanket, covering him and warming him, intending to telegraph comfort. She could sense fatigue rolling off him like summer heat off pavement, and imagined herself absorbing it, putting herself into the space he was in.

After several long moments, she pulled back gently, sitting up, astride him. She ran her hands over his back, fingers firm but not pressing hard. She felt him sigh slowly, and knew that he understood where she was headed.

She began to knead his taut shoulders, gently at first – then, realizing how knotted up he was, she increased the pressure slowly but steadily, beginning to dig in, surprised and a little embarrassed that she hadn't fully realized just how stressed out he had become. Understanding just how wrung-out he was, she resolved to do everything she possibly could to give him peace.

She grasped his neck firmly, where she found the muscles along the back to be as thick and hard as leather. She realized he must have a headache, and began to dig in with her thumbs, pressing hard but adding gentle circular motions, to spread out the sharp twinges she knew she was causing. It wouldn't feel so good at first, but after a few moments he'd have some relief. She stayed with it, and soon felt relaxation in the hard flesh, along with steady heat. His breathing was slowing.

She returned to his shoulders, where she knew there was no easy way, wrestling the pent-up tension with an almost violent grip, squeezing muscles behind collarbone with fierce energy, pressing out the stress and pain without mercy. He moaned, and almost cried out, but remained submissive, welcoming the relief.

This is silly, she thought, and she reached down and pulled up his t-shirt, tugging it over his head and tossing it aside without making him roll over. Before returning to her task, she did the same, shedding her ghastly sweatshirt with one swift, efficient motion.

Back to his shoulders, lower now, and there was more artistry and less brute force in her motions as she squeezed and pressed and caressed his tired flesh. She could feel him yielding underneath her aggressive touch, surrendering, accepting twinges of pain for the warm trickles of relief. She bent low as she scooted down, sinking hard fingertips into the middle of his back, smelling his hair, his warm, tired skin, feeling aroused but feeling even more sympathetic. Her awareness of all that he did for her, for their kids, surrounded her and filled her like the air of a summer night, enveloping her in certainty and safety. Whatever desire was teasing at her was a small thing compared to her deep appreciation of his commitment to her, to their family, to the effort that enabled their lives and left him so very tired, so in need of her comfort and compassion.

She found the small of his back, where pain came to live and stayed, and knew that this was no place to slack off. These muscles were hardened steel, cold and fierce, and she felt twinges of pain in her now-tiring hands as she dug in hard with her thumbs and began to work the pain out of them, feeling him wince, hearing him moan, knowing that it hurt but that he would feel better if she stuck with it. He actually cried out at one point, but he remained passive, willing to go through the tough stuff for the peace and comfort on the other side.

And she realized, on the edge of tears, that this truth represented their whole life together.

The candles burned and so did the bourbon, and he began the slow, sleepy movements of peace, at ease with her forceful ministrations, and ready for whatever else she could do. Determined not to spin the moment to her own wants, she slowly slid away his boxers.

Completely aware that she had made this move a hundred times before with utterly different intent, she resisted those spots she knew would inspire desire, electric lust that would come back to her as pay-off, and focused instead on the tension, the fatigue, the collapsing energy in the muscles there, working them with the same patient, steady rhythms she had applied above. It had never occurred to her that he could be so keyed up, so tense, so tired – but there it was, written into his muscles, written into his skin, and all she cared about was giving him relief. It was a massage like no other, and all the erotic overtones of her motions evaporated into a sheltering canopy of shared release. The tension dissipated slowly, cordlike muscles eventually becoming easy, his skin releasing heat as earth into evening air.

The candles had burned low when she finally returned to her original position, spreading herself over him like a thick comforter – but now skin on skin, no longer hot but soothingly warm, and she sensed that he was on the edge of sleep. She herself was still aroused, but gave this no serious thought; her hard nipples would barely register with him now, and it was with deep satisfaction and gratitude that she stretched forward and blew out the candles on the nightstand, pulling the blanket over them both.

She nestled into him, pulling his arm over her, and felt the rhythm of sleep in his breathing on the back of her neck. This was a peace that transcended sex, surpassed celebration, a connection so deep there were no words to describe it. Her senses were filled with him, her heart sated with the assurances and truths of a life so completely shared, and she felt indescribably rich and utterly treasured, all at once.

He was gently snoring, but he was also just a bit … firm.

Ah, well … there's always tomorrow morning …

Low-Carb Mexican

The issue was condoms.

She felt very strongly about it, and had high hopes for the committee the school had put together: herself, girls' phys ed teacher and counselor; her male counterpart; the assistant dean of students; a progressive pastor who was mother to two teenagers in the school, and who had a medical background; and the owner of the house she had just located.

Pulling into the circular driveway, her thoughts about the availability of condoms at the school and their upcoming presentation to the county board of education went into the back seat, as she surveyed the house. It looked like something out of very-Olde England, all thick, dark beams and large, shuttered windows. Flowers grew in neat patches below the windows and along the stone walkway.

I thought he was single?

She immediately set the thought aside with self-scolding - of course men can grow plants! One or two men, surely - and parked, wondering where the other cars were.

It was very much the home of a college professor. He was a sociologist who taught at the local branch of the state university, had a son in his sophomore year at the high school and a daughter in junior high. His son had been in her health class; the younger sister would be in her gym class in the upcoming term.

A laptop slung over her shoulder, her arms laden with thick envelopes filled with xeroxed sheets, she approached the big wooden doors. IT'S OPEN, COME ON IN, a hand-scrawled sign instructed her.

The door actually creaked, which was sort of charming, and she stepped into a lazy cloud of acoustic rock. The house was exactly what she had expected - all books, comfortable mis-matched furniture and eccentric artwork - and smelled like one big glorious kitchen. There he was, across the open living-dining area, putting something on a plate, and humming along with Crosby, Stills and Nash.

"Anybody home?" she said, a little louder than the music.

He turned and smiled - "Hey!" - picked up a remote and stabbed at thin air with it, taking CSN's volume down three notches. He nodded toward the coffee table that sat between two big stuffed sofas, where another stack of similar materials already sat. She put all of her materials down.

"The reverend has already been here," he said as he opened the refrigerator. "She apologizes, she has some kid emergency. She dropped her stuff off and said she'll tag up with everybody by phone this weekend."

"... and the dean is out of town."

"Looks like it's just you, me, and your doppelganger." That sort of remark was common; her phys ed colleague had the same hair color and same last name that she had.

"You want something to drink?"

He fixed her iced tea, and one for himself, and they sat on opposite couches, talking about nothing, until the phone rang.

"Guess who?" he said, hanging up after a brief exchange. She could tell from the conversation that Doppelganger had just canceled.

"Just us, I guess," he said, returning to the kitchen. "Wow, I hate for all of this to go to waste."

He walked back into the living room with a tray of wonderful-smelling snack food: pan dulce, rolled tacos with wheat tortillas and turkey meat, homemade salsa.

"All very healthy, I promise," he said. "Low cal, low carb." She could tell by looking that it probably was, and was uncertain from his tone of voice whether or not he was tweaking her. She was the faculty health nut, and everybody knew it.

But he probably was, too, now that she thought about it. All of this food was made from scratch, and for the first time she noticed that he was in really good shape for a man with kids as old as his - mid-40s? The only way to eat Mexican and know how to cook Mexican and still be that lean and muscular -

He was speaking to her.

"I'm sorry?"

"I asked if you like Mexican."

She *loved* Mexican, but almost always denied herself, because she *was* a true health nut and couldn't cook worth a damn and almost never had healthy Mexican food offered to her.

So she had a rolled taco or two, and sipped her tea, and told him about the data she'd meticulously gathered on teen pregnancy and STD vectors in their state and the total failure of abstinence pledges. And he listened, actually looking at her when she spoke, and nodded here and there.

"Listen, are you in a hurry?"

Caught off-guard, she frowned as though she didn't understand the question.

"I mean, it's Friday, and that's why we all agreed to only meet for an hour, because people have things to do on Friday night - "

"We just couldn't find a night during the school week that would work for everyone."

"If you have somewhere to be, that's cool, but I'm really hungrier than this, and if you have some time I thought I could fix us something a little more substantial."

She actually had absolutely nowhere to be. Home with her cat. She was two years divorced and when she had finally started to date again, she'd found it too crushingly disappointing to continue.

And had he actually just said *that's cool*?

"I could probably move a couple of things around... "

"My kids are with their mom this weekend," he said. "All I have waiting for me right now is a stack of reading I'm behind on, and a few hundred weeds that need pulling tomorrow."

She felt a little, well... she didn't know, exactly, being here in his home, saying Yes to a home-cooked meal, and the pan dulce was really, *really* good, and -

"Great!" he said, and bounced back into the kitchen. She pretended to send a text message.

Carne asada fajitas, filled with lean flank steak, sprinkled with chili powder and grilled in cumin-spiced lime juice, in multi-grain tortillas, took shape as she sat at the breakfast bar, sipping the sangria that had appeared in front of her. She ran her entire condom-distribution case past him, arguing from facts and figures with passion and strong articulation as he stuffed the chilis he had roasted with no-fat Monterey Jack.

I like your case, and I agree with your numbers, he countered, but I don't think they'll go very far with the Fundies on the board.

She defensively underscored the accuracy of her data. These statistics aren't partisan, she insisted, and they aren't refutable!

They don't need to be, he replied; the minds we're trying to change aren't interested in facts. They're interested in preserving the feeling that they get from defending what they see as social order.

But we'll have *more and better* social order if we offer these alternatives, she said.

Yes, we will, and we have to make that case in some way that isn't about the numbers, some way that preserves the feelings they derive from their beliefs, he continued, stirring black beans into red pepper flakes and tomatoes, then splashing them with lime juice and a sprinkling of cilantro.

He served it all there at the breakfast bar, sitting on the end at a right angle to her. Harmless enough - except that he then lit a candle and changed the music to Julio Iglesias.

They continued to argue, she for her numbers, he for his theories of social groups, and she grew a little exasperated.

"If you *didn't* have access to condoms anywhere else, wouldn't you take advantage of it when you could?" she blurted out.

"You mean, me, personally?" he said, his expression dead-pan.

She was momentarily horrified. The conversation seemed suddenly, crushingly inappropriate.

Before she could answer, he proceeded, "Not interested. Never touch the things."

The conversation had lurched sideways so suddenly that she couldn't construct a reply to that.

"The way I see it," he continued, "other methods make more sense. What happens in intimacy between a man and a woman is a metaphor, I think."

"A... metaphor."

"Physical intimacy, the sharing of genes, the mingling of our essence, creates a baby," he said, quietly and thoughtfully. "Emotional intimacy, the sharing of our spirits, the mingling of our selves, creates a marriage. The same magnificent act of creation, totally shared, in different domains that are really the same. There should be no barriers."

She could think of absolutely nothing to say.

"... but that doesn't apply to teenagers, of course." And he smiled, and the tension lifted.

He then refilled her glass again, and she realized it wasn't the first time.

"Are you trying to get me drunk?" and she giggled a little bit, and immediately regretted it.

He grinned."I figure if I get you drunk, I'll be able to get you to laugh more."

And he looked at her, with eyes that reached right into her isolation and her incessant busy-ness and her detachment from herself and her life, isolation and detachment that had been numbing her for two years now, and smiled a little.

"And I have a feeling you really need that."

It was not at all what she expected him to say, nothing like the lame lines she'd heard during her brief dating disasters. And she was suddenly self-conscious of her own seriousness, the self-absorbed manner that she was afraid others could too easily see... her need to throw herself into causes, because her life was so...

And he was so, well...*not* what she had in mind, so unexpected, so kind, so at ease with himself, so interesting, so...

No one was saying anything.

"Well, bottoms up," he finally said, raising his glass to her. "I mean, I have, you know, eight more bottles of this stuff... "

And she laughed.

... and woke up more than ten hours later, wrapped in his slumbering arms.

This cannot, *cannot* be happening...

Bright sunlight poured into a bedroom she could only describe as spacious, onto a bed that was more spacious still. She gave herself a moment to get oriented; she was wrapped in him, and they were both wrapped in a comforter, and he was, as nearly as she could determine, still sound asleep. They were spooned, and she could feel his warm, rhythmic breathing on the back of her neck.

She was wearing - well, something (thank god!) - but her legs were bare. She couldn't see him because everything but his arm was behind her, and she desperately hoped he was wearing something, too.

Her head buzzed faintly - not so faintly - damn sangria! - and she reached back into her memories for some sign of how she'd gotten here.

Nothing.

Could I possibly have had that much? She hadn't gotten drunk enough to lose her memory since college. Well, no, that wasn't true, there were two or three nights, just before and during the divorce...

He *had* gotten her drunk, and it had been for the obvious reason!

She felt a sharp flush of anger, which only brought her descending hangover into harsh relief.

Mercifully, she was facing away from the window. The sunlight wasn't making it worse.

Had they...?

She had never, ever in her life had a one-night stand. Such a thing had never interested her and never would. If anything, she viewed sex as a merging of souls, more than bodies - an idea expressed as recently as yesterday...

... expressed by the sleeping man who was now draped over her.

Until she untangled herself from him, she couldn't search for any clues. She was wearing panties, but they may or not provide evidence of her earlier arousal or activity, and -

She realized suddenly that she was mildly aroused, right then and there.

What the hell? She was certain he was completely asleep. This man who had gotten her drunk, who had taken advantage of her, who... was holding her so tenderly, and whom she felt so increasingly comfortable around, and who had such strong arms and searching eyes and such a kind smile, who smelled so *good*, so masculine yet so benign... yeah, no reason I would be aroused right now.

She honestly couldn't tell. Maybe there had been sex. Maybe there had just been cuddling. Maybe she had just passed out and he was only looking after her, and this entanglement had happened in their sleep. Nobody's fault. Maybe...

If there had been sex, how had it been? How *much* had there been? Had he been any good? Had *she* been -

She felt stupid for even wondering.

She didn't know whether to be angry with him or appreciate him.

One thing was certain, she reflected as her hangover became more insistent - I can't blame him for the sangria. I'm a big girl. I know better.

Which left her the question, why had she gone so far overboard?

Very slowly, she eased out from under his arm, being as careful as she possibly could be not to wake him, letting her legs slide clear of the comforter, not even breathing...

She was wearing an oversized t-shirt, clearly one of his, and wondered what *that* was about. Her bra was in place. Nothing down south but panties. No sign of her other clothes in the room.

She tip-toed toward the door, determined to escape undetected -

"Morning!"

Dammit!

She turned lazily and smiled, arms swinging, totally uncertain how to play it.

He tossed back the comforter. She fought hard the impulse to close her eyes. He was, thank god, wearing something.

Gonna invite me back in for another romp?

No, he slid to the side of the bed and sat up on its edge. He, too, wore a t-shirt - and his fit much better than hers. She was suddenly grateful that the one she was wearing went down to her thighs.

He was also wearing shorts - boxers, but that was way better than briefs. Under the circumstances, anyway. She felt relief that he was not wearing socks, and suddenly questioned why in the world she would have expected him to.

"Well, that looks way better on you than it does on me!" he said, meaning the t-shirt. She looked down at it, uncertain of what to say next, but certain she didn't want him to know that she had no idea why she was wearing it.

"Well, maybe this is not my best look in general," was all she could think of to say.

He blinked, amused, as though there were so many possible comebacks that he just couldn't choose.

"How about some breakfast?" he said invitingly. How could any man be this agreeable thirty seconds after waking up?

And how could she refuse? An offer of breakfast was appropriate no matter *what* had happened last night. She was trapped, she had no choice: she smiled and nodded.

Stepping off the limb, she smiled a bit more weakly, "Um... ?" and indicated her state of dress.

"Oh, yeah," he said, wiping his face apologetically, "bathroom's over there." He pointed. "I'll use the one down the hall, and get breakfast moving."

It had gone completely past him that she was asking where her clothes were. On the other hand, if he stands up and moves this way, he might hug me... he might kiss me... there was nothing but retreat. She vanished into the bathroom with the speed of a cat.

Emerging from the bathroom, she felt somewhat better. Her investigation of her recent sexual state had been, maddeningly, inconclusive. She had felt too self-conscious to use his shower, had taken a quick sponge bath and washed out her panties, drying them quickly with a blow-dryer from the bathroom closet. There had been Tylenol on the bathroom counter; she had taken a handful. And there had been a new, unopened toothbrush lying there.

Even so, she still had only her bra, her panties, and his t-shirt. His bathrobe hung from the back of the bathroom door, and she tried it on, but she looked too goofy to even consider it.

Slipping into the hall, she smelled coffee, and found that she was on the second floor. She located the stairs and descended hesitantly, scanning for her clothes. She saw him on the far side of the living-dining area, chopping something up in the kitchen. He looked up and smiled. He was still bed-headed, and in the same t-shirt, but had pulled on a pair of jeans.

The Tylenol was kicking in, giving her nothing else to focus on but her missing clothes.

"Can you do eggs, as long as they're healthy?"

She nodded absently, hoping it wasn't obvious what she was looking around for.

"Last night's black beans, mixed into egg whites, with low-fat cheddar and a spoonful of the salsa," he announced, "plus turkey sausage."

"That sounds great," she said, her eyes darting around.

"Well, that was quite an evening," she said hesitantly, in as neutral a voice as she could manage - pitching her tone so as not to imply either enthusiasm or regret. Let's see what he says to that...

He nodded, and it was a big nod, a profound nod. "It sure was!" His eyes widened thoughtfully, but he didn't take them off his cooking.

Dammit!

As she tried to think of some other way to coax a clue out of him, she scanned more intently for some sign of her clothes.

"I can't remember the last time I had so much -" She stopped, suddenly feeling horror, realizing how many bad ways there were to finish that sentence.

"- Mexican food," she finished.

He smiled, slightly, knowingly. This was only making things worse. Now she was afraid she'd made a pig of herself, on top of everything else.

"A memorable evening!" he said as he stirred something in a pan. From across the room, she studied his face. No amusement or mockery, his expression was earnest. But... "memorable?" Was he making fun of the fact that she couldn't remember? Can he tell? Surely he can! His eyes and his voice were neutral enough that she couldn't tell what he meant by "memorable."

At this point she had wandered all around the room at this point, looking for clothes.

It suddenly dawned on him. He didn't look up.

"Family room," he said, "during the movie."

Movie???

"Thanks," she said, trying to keep her voice casual. Family room?

He expects me to remember the movie, she realized, and to know where the family room is. Looking back at him, she determined that he was busy pouring something into something, as something else sizzled. She quickly surveyed the room.

Bedrooms upstairs, even the master bedroom. Family room on this floor? An open door opposite the kitchen revealed what must be his office - she'd seen that yesterday. No other doors, open or closed, that weren't so small they must be closets.

Under the stairs - another staircase. There's a basement, and the family room must be down there. Hoping he wouldn't turn her way, she quietly went to the stairs and descended.

Dark. She fumbled around for a light switch, and -

Oh. My. God...

The big-screen TV was still on, and the menu of a DVD was displayed - appropriately, *The Hangover.* The sound was down. A mostly-consumed bottle of sangria sat next to an empty one on the carpet in front of the couch.

Her blouse was draped over the back of an easy chair. Her jeans were behind the couch.

One sock was partially embedded in the couch. The other one was nowhere to be found. Her shoes were on opposite sides of the room.

Her mind was almost frantic as she methodically reassembled herself. *Two bottles of sangria? How much of that was me and how much was him?* From experience, she knew that more than three or four glasses would have resulted in very bad judgment - but completely memory loss would have meant it had been more.

And her clothes? Had she done the flinging or had he?

"Breakfast!" he called from upstairs.

She had to know. Then, it dawned on her that there was a way.

Ascending the stairs, she walked calmly back into the living-dining room. He looked up and smiled again. She was holding the not-quite-empty bottle.

"Um... " She held up the bottle.

"No thanks," he said, grinning. "A little early in the day for me."

"How much... " she started, and he opened his mouth to say something dismissive - "... did *you* have?"

For the first time, she saw him truly hesitate.

"Really." And she met and held his eye. She suddenly noticed that, bedhead or no, he had shaved.

He seemed to argue with himself for an instance. Then he replied, earnest and respectful.

"Only the one glass."

She nodded, scooped up her purse, and leaving everything else on the coffee table, she fled.

Only the one glass...

She gripped the steering wheel with white knuckles, just furious. She realized she was speeding, and backed off. But not much.

Only one glass meant getting her drunk so he could use her as he pleased, letting her go completely off the rails so he could jump completely on. He'd fed her sangria till she lost all judgment, then stripped her down in the basement and...

...removed her clothes, one piece at a time, tossing them any which way... hauled her into his bed, and...

... and...

Why had her underwear not been in the basement? Sure, pull a t-shirt onto me, so I won't be totally humiliated in the morning... but put my underwear back on?

My underwear and *a t-shirt?* It didn't make any sense.

And why hadn't she woken up on the couch in the basement? Why had he even bothered taking her all the way to the master bedroom? She knew her very-drunk self, and there's no way she climbs two flights of stairs after two bottles of...

It all made sense at once.

He hadn't limited himself to one glass so that he could take advantage of the situation.

He'd limited himself to one glass to avoid exactly what she was imagining... to make sure he *wouldn't* behave as he'd assumed he had.

He'd let her go off the rails... because somehow, he was smart enough and compassionate enough to realize that she needed to.*I have a feeling you really need that.* Yes, she had needed release - but not the kind she'd assumed he'd wanted from her.

She had let months and months of emptiness and pain numb her into darkness, and she had needed to unleash all of her stored-up hurt and need and anger and confusion. And she had. She'd released it all.

Released... heaven only knows what she might have said, what she might have blurted out, what rant she might have gone on... what tears she might have shed...

But forget what she'd said... dear god, what had she *done*? The sangria, the family room... her *clothes*!

She had, at some point, taken them off and flung them any which way. She had tried to...

... and he had stopped her from going too far, and calmed her somehow. And... she had somehow gotten from the basement all the way to the second floor, leaving her clothes where they had fallen, forgotten...

He had carried her up two flights of stairs, her underwear still in place, her honor still intact...

... and had taken the trouble to put a t-shirt on her, to shield her from the embarrassment of waking up in her underwear. She could almost imagine the tenderness with which he had done it. And then he'd made the bathroom ready for her.

And he had placed her in his own bed, bundling her up and letting her sleep, and had kept watch.

And fallen asleep next to her...

... and, in the quiet of the night, instinctively gathered her close to him.

Only one of the two explanations could be correct.

Only one was consistent with the man who had spoken so honestly and earnestly about the meaning of intimacy at dinner the night before.

She found her way home, drew a hot bath, and thought long about what had happened, as her cat waited patiently.

Walking past piles of pulled weeds, she noticed that the COME ON IN sign was still in place, and took the liberty. Everything was as it had been, except for an open book on the coffee table. She ventured in, carrying two big bags, and heard him above.

He stood at the top of the stairs, hair still damp from the shower - of course, he had just cleaned up after an afternoon of landscaping - and his face was pure surprise.

She held up the two bags.

"Really bad Mexican," she said, "I mean, really *good* Mexican, but really bad for us. At least twice the calories from last night... "

He grinned, and descended the stairs.

"Five hundred twenty-five calories," he said, "not counting the sangria."

"I didn't bring any sangria," she said, "You have seven more bottles, right?"

"Well... five, now."

She closed her eyes and struggled not to blush.

"That's... ah... another twelve hundred and eighty calories?"

He shrugged and grinned. "More or less."

She looked at the two bags she was holding up. "Are you into, what, running? biking? roller blading?"

He grinned. "All three."

She waited at the top of the basement stairs as he retrieved a bottle.

The second dinner was even better than the first, calories aside, and they never once discussed condoms.

With an inner smile, however, she felt certain the subject would come up very soon.

Karaoke Night

It was in moments like this, when she was playful, that he enjoyed her most.

The party was in full roar, as increasingly-drunk would-be rock stars stepped up to the mic, one after another, blasting out Aerosmith and Styx and the Eagles and Madonna and Skynyrd and Kenny Chesney and Lady Gaga and Foreigner and Keith Urban and Aretha Franklin and Ed Sheeran and the Beatles. She'd been up once, and had belted out some Carly Simon; he'd been up once, and had asked the DJ for "Sharp-Dressed Man"; but the DJ had answered with "Open Arms" - not just a Journey song, but a Journey song with high notes written for Mariah Carey.

But there she was, watching from a couch in the back of the room, and he wasn't about to back down. As the words "Lying beside you..." emerged, he shot the DJ a dirty look – bastard! - and all the lighters came out and flickered. He put on his best castrati and made it through the high notes, drawing applause from the swaying crowd.

He felt self-conscious, not because he had failed to impress her, but because he realized he had been seriously trying to.

They both sang along, sitting on the couch, as some poor schlub butchered "More Than a Feeling". The DJ soon took a break and approached them with a grin, handing him a Mason jar of some unidentified pink inebriant and high-fiving him by way of apology. And when the DJ called for the next round of tunes, she leaned over and whispered in his ear.

Are you crazy?

Come on! she persisted, *It'll be fun!*

Their turn came, and she tugged him into the middle of the floor. As it happened, they were the first duet of the night, and the room urged them on with applause as the opening notes of the song spilled out.

> *Don't go breakin' my heart...*
>> *I couldn't if I tried!*
> *Honey, if I get restless-*
>> *Baby, you're not that kind!*

It was all the more fun because they were facing each other; they didn't need the lyrics on the screen, they both knew all the words.

She wasn't just singing, she was acting out the song, pointing to him and throwing in all the right expressions. He started hamming it up too, matching her gesture for gesture and half-dancing as he sang.

> *Ah honey, when you knock on my door,*
>> *Ooo, I gave you my key!*

It hadn't been long after they'd gotten together that their mutual love of Elton had risen to the surface. But even though Elton had been his inspiration for becoming a rock musician himself, he'd never give this particular song a lot of thought.

Suddenly, singing these words after a year of loving her, it was a whole new song.

> *When I was down,*
>> *I was your clown!*
> *Right from the start,*
>> *I gave you my heart!*

It was a little-known fact that when Elton had first written the song, he'd only given Kiki about four lines, and his producer had insisted Elton make it 50-50, a real duet. But little-known facts were kind of his thing, and he was grateful for the perfect back-

and-forth of the song – like the old Motown duets, a lover's dialog – and the equal footing it evinced. It perfectly reflected his feelings for her: partners in song, partners in love, partners in life.

> And nobody told us
> > 'Cause nobody showed us,
> Mm, now it's up to us, babe,
> > Ooo, I think we can make it!

The lyrics, which he'd never thought all that inspired in the past, described them utterly. And the hamming-up they were doing – well, it didn't feel like a performance anymore.

> So don't misunderstand me,
> > You put the light in my life!
> Ah, you put the sparks to the flame,
> > I got your heart in my sights!

> So don't go breakin' my heart!
> > I won't go breakin' your heart!

They sounded great in harmony. They sounded great in unison. Whatever impulse had put this in her head, her instincts were spot-on: this truly was their song.

He air-guitared the Davey Johnstone licks, and when the song ended, the crowd went nuts. They held hands and bowed.
And kept holding hands as they returned to the couch and the Mason jar. And his heart pounded as the song started replaying in his head.

> Right from the start, I gave you my heart...

Sleepover

Midnight had slipped away when the second bottle ran dry, and she was all talked out.

And he had listened. She had so needed to talk about it, and he was her go-to, and he had listened, all evening, into the night. Since dinner, which he had whipped up on the spur of the moment, after she showed up unannounced on a Friday evening. And *what* a dinner! – scallops in a butter-and-white-wine sauce – being there for her, giving something extra.

As he always did.

Her best friend.

Lots of her girlfriends rolled their eyes ("oh, this is some kind of Paul Rudd thing" … "you *know* he's secretly into you …"), but they didn't get it, they didn't know … not one of them could take his place. He was always there, always giving something extra, always …

… her best friend.

For two years now.

It suddenly occurred to her, as he smiled through the lateness of the hour, that he might have had plans – but if he had, he'd have discreetly canceled them, without telling her. She almost asked. But she knew it would embarrass him.

I'd better let you go to bed! she suddenly said.

He stood, she stood,

You are so-

She swayed.

He caught her.

I don't think you're driving home! he laughed.

He steadied her. They steadied each other.

I don't think you're driving me home, either, she giggled.

They hugged, warm and affectionate, with that extra tightness that says … something.

You take the big bed, he said. *I got the couch.*

No no no! she protested. *I would never kick you out of bed!*

'That's what she said …'
No, I don't want to put you on the couch –
You want the couch?
She paused. His bed was *luxurious*. King size, with all the frills. He took the physical side of relationships very seriously.
We can share! There's plenty of room.
He paused, for a long moment.
Are you sure?
She leaned into him. *The Dallas Cowboys could fit in that bed!*
And wouldn't you just love that!
Giggle.
Go sleep, he said. *I'll clean up.*
Any other night, she'd have helped. But if they were both going to sleep in his bed, better if they didn't climb in at the same moment.

Later, as he tip-toed into the darkness, he could tell from the stillness that she was already out. He stepped on her blue jeans, laid out on the floor at the foot of the bed, and retrieved his warm-ups from the back of a chair. He quietly slipped out of his own jeans and into his jogging pants.

Moonlight was pouring through the window – the moon was full – and a spring breeze cooled the room. He preferred open windows to air conditioning, and found that it helped him sleep. Clearly, it helped her, too. Her face glowed, and she was dead to the world.

Woozy himself, he watched her sleep for a few minutes, thinking of all the things she'd said … and before long, he too was out.

A surge of cool breeze caressed her face, and she blinked in the moonlight.

The scent in the air, the light-blue shadow around her told her she was somewhere else. Blinking again, she realized she was a little tipsy, and it took her a minute or two to remember where she was and what was happening.

His scent …

It wasn't the first time she'd been in this bed. Once, she'd been very sick, and she'd spent a weekend here, while he fed her and mopped her hot forehead. Once, she'd napped on a Sunday afternoon.

The sheets smelled like he did. He –

50

He was two feet away, breathing slowly, sound asleep. She lifted up, turning to him. He was facing the other direction. His shoulder and arm –

He'd shed his t-shirt. In his sleep, it seemed, it was lying on the comforter between them. His shoulder and arm ... were more muscular than she would have expected. He tended to wear loose t-shirts and jeans.

She almost touched him.

Settling in, facing away from the moon, she gathered the comforter around her shoulder and fluffed up the pillow, sighing. She needed this space, this distance from her life, this warm refuge. The blue glow bounced off his skin.

She almost touched him ...

Rolling over, he drifted out of sleep, opening his eyes to shadows on the ceiling. *Full moon ...* bright blue glow, which he had always loved, and whispers in the window with the flutter of curtain. And ...

The gentle sigh to his left.

He rolled over.

She was facing him, her face in shadow, her hair silhouetted in the moonglow. Their noses were inches apart. She hadn't stirred, as he had moved, and he was suddenly mindful not to disturb her. He remembered what had happened, why she was here, and noted with satisfaction the depth of her slumber. He relaxed. If she was that far gone, he was unlikely to wake her.

He wondered over her dreams. Heavy, most likely, open-ended too much.

Wine sleep. Wine dreams.

After all that she'd said tonight, downstairs ... too much.

He felt a wave of almost unbearable tenderness sweeping over him, and felt her breathing lightly on his cheek. Her right hand lay on her pillow, between them.

Ever so slowly, he brought up his own hand, to cover hers ...

Her dreams had gone tender, from echoes of the hurt she'd carried into his home tonight to gentle scenes of something else, and there was a warmth, a firmness, a strength ...

... a hand, holding hers, and she blinked in the darkness, feeling the soft –

They were breathing the same air.

He was holding her hand.

His face was only inches from her, but it was lost in deep sleep, peaceful and shadowed.

She had never seen him asleep before.

He had seen her sleeping before, she felt certain. There was that time she was sick … and once she'd taken a nap in the middle of a picnic they'd had at the state park …

But this was a first. This was his sleeping face. Even more gentle than his waking face … eyes totally closed, able to completely wink out … a slight smile on his lips.

He must have happy dreams … much happier than mine …

Tempted to touch his face, she looked it over, all the more closely – difficult, since she herself was blocking the moonlight – and imagined that his beard was growing.

Suddenly he rolled away from her, onto his back, releasing her hand. He stirred slightly, then settled back into deep breathing. Shirtless, sprawling slightly, he had shifted the comforter off his chest.

Very slowly, desperately careful not to disturb him, she nestled into him …

A tingling tugged him from a dream.

The sensation commanded attention, rippling across his chest. He felt cool-warm, breeze over … warmth? The negligible weight of … her arm.

He came to his senses, and realized the scent of her hair, almost tickling his nose.

Her face lay on his shoulder. Her arm and hand lay across his chest.

He was careful to control his breathing, to remain calm. Her breathing was slow and deep. She was asleep.

He was her pillow.

Again, an unbearable surge of tenderness swept over him like a tidal wave, and he wavered between acceptance and uncertainty. Surely, this was just … circumstance? *I didn't plan this … she didn't plan this …*

The stirring …

He was suddenly grateful beyond expression that he was wearing the jogging pants.

Suddenly her chest heaved, and he fought hard to suppress the impulse to flinch.

Is she awake?

Oh shit … are we both lying here awake? Are we both in this incredibly awkward situation, trying to not be awkward? Dammit! What do I do?

What do I do if she says something? Do I answer? Do I pretend to be asleep? What am I supposed to say? What if she says-

Her deep breath settled back into the regular rhythm of sleep, and he calmed down.

He thought about the moment.

He thought about the evening, of all the things she'd said.

He thought about the fact that she'd sought him out, to say them all to him.

He thought about these past two years.

He thought and thought, until his thoughts became dreams.

Her dreams were … intimate …

… and she began to stir, her hand moving -

her hand on –

Her hand lay on his warm, firm skin, amid the hairs of his chest, and she felt his arm under her neck, his hand and forearm against her shoulder.

They were nestled together, and she vaguely remembered crawling up against him.

He seemed to –

Is he asleep?

Does he know I'm … cuddling with him?

She froze, but managed to do so without consciously tensing up. She shallowed her breathing.

This moment, this closeness, this … whatever it was, this was exactly what she needed. He was sound asleep, oblivious, unaware, but even in this disconnected state, he was everything she wanted. Comfort, support, presence, togetherness. *My best friend?*

She realized, with a touch of embarrassment, that she couldn't even remember what all she had babbled to him this evening, when she'd done her venting and her complaining and unpacked her insecurities for him once again, knowing he'd really listen, and really care, and really understand what she was going through, and be there for her anyway.

Lying there in his arms, it suddenly occurred to her that the details of what she'd said didn't really matter to either of them. What mattered was ... this.

With sudden horror, she realized that she wasn't breathing deeply enough, and she was oxygen-starved, and she was going to –

She suddenly took a deep breath, unable to take it anymore, almost gasping, sucking in as much air as she could,

Oh shit

and was terrified that she would wake him. Then she was even more terrified.

Is he already awake?

Does he know I'm cuddling him, does he know I'm laying here almost on top of him? What is he thinking? Is he trying to think of a way to ease out from under me? What must he think of me?

Does he regret letting me sleep over?

Have I put him in an awkward situation?

The thoughts flashed through her in a heartbeat, and she rallied, no longer wine-sleepy, controlling her breathing instantly. She returned to the steady bellows of deep sleep, suddenly realizing that if she focused, she'd feel his heartbeat.

It was steady ... not fast ... but not slow ... somewhere in between? In the face of uncertainty, she chose to believe he was as asleep as she was pretending to be.

Only ...

Part of her was wide awake. *Wildly* awake.

She was suddenly grateful that part of her was not in contact with his leg ...

It was a whisper of breaking dawn, or the whisper of bacon and coffee, or both, that brought her into the morning.

She blinked, and found herself looking toward the window, and realizing that there really was bacon and coffee.

Blinking again, she saw a small tray on the nightstand next to her. A plate, a warm breakfast, a cup of coffee.

And she smiled.

Always giving something extra ...

Steam rose from the coffee, and the food glistened with heat. He'd set the tray down only seconds ago ...

His voice came from behind her on the bed.

Good morning!

As she rolled over, into his smile, his eyes, the stubble of his beard, a joyous thought swept over her.

More so than if they'd spent the night naked, impassioned, having sex again and again, more so than if they'd discussed it and decided it and chosen it ...

... everything had changed.

Feather Bed

Cold droplets splattered off gray stone, and she hugged his arm fiercely.

Mommy and Daddy standing behind, just as cold, just as gray. Blackness above, a tent, thumping with heavy raindrops, and the dark black sleeve of Poppy's old suit. Dark, noisy sky. The preacher in black coat. Her own very ugly dress, which she would never ever wear again.

A single, slow tear on Poppy's cheek. She reached up and wiped it away. He turned to her, away from the preacher, looking down on her in love, through his unbearable sorrow ...

Are we close?

She had been dozing, and came awake at his voice. The bluegrass farmlands slipped by outside the car window. He had slowed, afraid of passing the farm. She got her bearings, saw the creek ahead.

Just a few more miles ...

The welcoming blue skies she remembered were obscured. The old farmhouse lost all its charm in the gray Kentucky rain, and with a horrified shiver she realized that she now faced that wonderful haven of her childhood with dread instead of joy, realizing that in place of its charms and treasures, there were now nothing but ghosts.

Holding his hand tightly – too tightly - she led him into the empty, shadowed rooms of her past. The kitchen, with its antiquated fluorescent lights and bacon-grease smell and pots and pans twice as old as she was, Coca Cola bottles that dated back decades ... the dining room, with its wall of family pictures, including about thirty of herself, through the years ... the living room, with its pot belly stove; the creaking sofa, where countless quilts were made, where her great-grandmother had passed; and Poppy's old oak desk, and his makeshift shelves, groaning under the weight of the old newspapers and magazine he had saved ...

... and the bedroom, with its familiar scent of mothballs trickling from the closet, the dresser with a mirror as big as a tabletop - and the ancient four-poster bed.

The feather bed. Grammy and Poppy's bed.

A tear slipped down her cheek as she let go of his hand and touched the bed. Pressing gently, it responded as it always had, almost swallowing her arm. Infinitely soft, infinitely comforting, Grammy and Poppy's feather bed ... how many hundreds of times had she jumped into it, hopped out of it, been chided for bouncing on it, been lowered onto it late, by Poppy's strong arms?

A sob escaped her, and she felt his hands slipping around her waste, gathering her in. She turned and buried herself in his shoulder, but rallying, holding back the tears, being strong.

I miss her, Poppy!

I know, Honey Bear.

Do you miss her? Poppy? Do you miss her?

I miss her every day, Honey Bear. I miss her every hour.

Oh Poppy ... how can we go on without -

Honey Bear, look at me. Look at me. That's my girl! I wancha to listen, listen good. On the other side of every night, there's a tomorrow. Missin' her feels like night, but there's a tomorrow, I promise ...

(sob)

I've had all my tomorrows, Honey Bear ... but your tomorrows, yours are just beginning. I need you ta listen now: when these dark times feel like they're gonna swallow you up, you need to remember something. I want you to promise me you'll remember ... when what we've had has passed away, all that means is - it means ... everything is new again.

Everything is new again! You'll remember that? Promise me, Honey Bear.

Promise me ...

I promise ...

Oh, Honey Bear ... you look just like her ...

Cold droplets splattered off gray stone, and she hugged his arm fiercely.

Her mother stood behind her, just as cold. Her father had sent flowers from the coast, and left a cell phone message. Dozens of neighbors and vague aunts and uncles and cousins surrounded them.

She hugged his arm fiercely.

Her mother had hugged her briefly, said very little, and vanished.

Oh, Poppy ... how can I go on without you now?

Suburban abundance, half-grown trees; harsh orange skies. Noise. Shouting. Droning television. Slamming doors. Solitude. School. Sex. Escape ...

Grammy, when I was younger I remember going to sleep in the feather bed and waking up in the attic room.

That you did, child! Your Poppy knew you'd go to slumber faster in the feather bed.

Ooo, I love the feather bed!

I know, child. Me too!

Did you and Poppy always have the feather bed?

Oh, no! When we were young, it was lean times, and your Poppy, it took him awhile to become easy with words. That feather bed cost a bit and it took him a lotta savin' to buy. And when he brought it home, he didn't say much ... the bed said all he wanted to say.

I don't understand?

Your Poppy is fine with words now, from all his readin' ... but when we were not much older than you are now, he needed other ways to say what was in his heart. The feather bed ... how would you describe it?

Hmmm, it's warm ... it's comfortable ... it's ---

It's ... what?

--- safe.

Do you see?

See what?

Think a bit. In time you'll see. Your Poppy, child, he's ... well, Poppy is my feather bed.

The dining room table was stacked with well-meaning leftover food. Cousins and neighbors, numbering in the dozens, had finally, mercifully, departed. Her mother was on a plane, headed elsewhere.

He had found a quilt in a chest and wrapped it around her, and sat her in a chair in front of the pot belly stove, where he left her while he put all the food away.

Then he watched her from the doorway, thinking of all that she had been through, all that he had seen, all the things he'd wondered about and pondered. He watched her face, in the glow of the fire, a mash-up of loss, confusion, anger, despair ... and considered the uncertainties in her world that he himself had unwittingly cultivated. He remembered many things ... the phone call, her eyes as she'd stared out the car window, leaking tears; the painful, vice-like clench of her hand ...

He reflected on his own uncertainty, his lack of clarity about what he needed to do, what he needed to give her in this moment. But there was certainty too, and he was clueless as to how to express what he felt.

He walked hesitantly into the living room, took the big reading chair, and pulled her onto his lap as the fire burned, encircling her in his arms.

After a long moment, she spoke.

When I was very small, she said quietly, *Grammy told me a story about Poppy.*

Over the years, with all of his reading and studying, Poppy became very wise ... kind of a Will Rogers, plain-spoken but really poignant. When he was our age, he didn't have that in him. He found other ways ...

He held her tight.

When Poppy knew that he wanted Grammy to be his wife, he had no way to ask her, she went on. *This house, this whole county ... it was in the days when they were just beginning to string power lines this far back. Even though most houses had power, they only used it for refrigeration.*

So Poppy brought his own candles over to Grammy's house, and he said, when her parents weren't around, 'Love and marriage, they need candlelight ...', and he left it at that. And that night, she wakes up, and in her window, outside, there's a candle burning ...

That's how he asked her to marry him. That candle burning in the window, that was Poppy saying, 'Will you marry me?' How beautiful is that?

He kissed her forehead.

'Everything is new again ...' That's what he said when she passed ... how can anyone be that brave? How could I ever be that brave?

A long moment passed, and she lifted herself out of the chair, and he followed her into the bedroom, to the feather bed.

There was no light, only the glow of the stove fire from the living room, and he found her kneeling by the side of the bed, her arms stretched across the comforter, sinking helplessly into the softness.

She began to sob, and his arms enfolded her, and all of her grief and loss came welling up, endlessly. No longer able to hold it in, no longer able to be strong, she cried out in the night. He gathered her up, rocking her, kissing her forehead, absorbing her sorrow and her longing, as her pain echoed through the wooden halls of the old, empty house.

He held her and rocked her and kissed her and stroked her hair and her wet cheeks for an eternity, until her shuddering subsided into exhaustion, and she drifted into tormented sleep. Then he lifted her in his arms, gently lowered her onto the feather bed, and wrapped the comforter around her. He bent down, and kissed her softly on the lips.

In the middle of the night, a warm glow flickered across her face, stirring her from saddened sleep, and her eyelids fluttered.

She opened them, and sought out the light.

Her heart leapt.

Everything is new again ...

Beyond the feather bed, in the window, a candle glowed ...

Two Rooms, Full Bath, Walk-In

He'd known her since she'd been in college, but that was an eternity ago. She was past thirty now, with two small children and no husband. And he was older still —late forties, and his kids were both in college.

He'd met her through a mutual friend, who knew he was a writer and that she wanted to be - and they'd struck up a friendship, all those years ago, when she was nineteen and he was thirty-four and freshly divorced, and helping her get published made him feel young again.

Now she sat across the table, a deep-dish pizza between them - also divorced, back in town, a six-year-old boy and a little girl not yet a year old... and not a penny to her name.

Her own father had rejected her when the first baby had come and the baby's father had gone, pre-wedding. He was a pastor, as fire-breathing and intolerant as they came, and that was when the emails had started. The second man had married her, two years ago, and they'd made a daughter, but he hadn't been good to her boy, and as the months wore on, he hadn't been good to her, either. So she'd filed the papers, packed up her old clunker of a car and headed home, with two kids, no money, and very little hope.

When she hit town, he was her first call. A pizza was the least he could do.

She was staying with friends, she told him.

How did that work? with two kids? He couldn't imagine.

We're living in the basement, there's plenty of room, she said. *We're fine for now - until I save up enough for an apartment.*

Do you know how much a two-bedroom apartment is going to cost? he asked her.

About six-fifty a month.

He motioned for the waiter to refill her drink.

My house has two empty bedrooms, he told her, *and two bathrooms. Since the kids went to school, that's just empty space. Why don't you just use them until you get on your feet?*

On top of that, he had his own software business, he mostly worked from home - he could look after her kids, to save her money on child care.

She looked at him for a moment without saying anything.

How much?

He started to say 'nothing,' but then he realized that this would be insulting to her, and would send a *very* wrong message.

Three hundred a month? he suggested.

She stared at him for another long moment. Her eyes changed several times; he saw desperation... suspicion... rapid calculation... and, finally, gratitude.

She slowly nodded. *Okay...*

He spent the week cleaning up the bedrooms, clearing out the walk-in closet between them, straightening up the upstairs bathroom. He bought sheets and blankets for the beds, plenty of supplies. New towels for the bathroom. It would be their own corner of the house, private, comfortable.

He stocked the kitchen and pantry with things young kids would like - not all that far distant in his memory - and bought a box of children's movies on DVD.

They arrived the following weekend, and he'd been deliberately low-key. Her little boy and girl, already painfully uprooted and wary from weeks in someone else's basement, were hesitant. He'd been nonchalant, presenting them casually with their new quarters, corn dogs and chips, chocolate milk - too much for the little girl, who defaulted to mommy's tits - and *Toy Story 3*.

He'd broken a date to free up the evening.

When they'd fallen asleep on the living room couch, he had carried them up the stairs and helped her tuck them in. She'd hugged him fiercely, and thanked him, and they agreed they would talk in the morning, to start working out details.

It was then that he realized that she and the little girl were basically sharing a single bed.

Listen, he said early the next morning, when she'd stumbled into the kitchen in a t-shirt and warm-up pants - *Why don't you take the master bedroom? I can put a mattress in my office...*

He saw her actually consider it before shaking her head. *I couldn't do that to you,* she said, *you're already doing so much for us.*

I hate to see you so uncomfortable... and it can't be very comfortable for your daughter, either.

She smiled. *I'm sure we'll do just fine,* she answered. *It's only for a few months...*

Then he watched her face, and saw her eyes go through those same stages... desperation, calculation...

Here's an idea, she offered. *That bed of yours is huge...*It was king-size, from an earlier time. *Maybe we could share it?*

*Share...*he was careful to keep his face neutral. *You mean, share the bedroom?*

Plenty of room... then I wouldn't be putting you out.

She met his eyes squarely, bravely, unassuming, with a slightly-forced innocence.

It was his turn to do some calculating. Was she coming on to him? *Surely not...*

Okay, he told himself. This was a delicate situation, and he needed to handle it in the right way, for both of them, but it was a matter of getting some details right. This could work, there was no reason it had to get complicated. This could work.

Okay, he told her.

The kids were sound asleep. She lingered in the bathroom.

He had started using the downstairs bathroom, with the shower, exclusively. He had long since gotten ready for bed and climbed in. The lamp on the other side of the bed was still on. His was out. He closed his eyes, simultaneously shutting out the awkwardness.

He heard her quietly enter the room, and pretended to be asleep. He listened as she moved through the room, shed her robe, and slid into bed.

It was so big that he scarcely noticed her settling in. He'd been meaning to get rid of it for the very reason that so much of it went unused, wasted.

He smiled to himself. This wasn't going to be a problem. In this huge bed, with all this space, they were hardly going to notice each other.

The light went out.

Her son had started the first grade. He could already read, but math puzzled him. While she fixed dinner for the kids, he sat on the couch with the boy, working thru the math worksheet that had been sent home. His baby sister played on the living room floor.

After she fed the kids, they watched a cartoon on cable TV. Then she hustled them upstairs for their baths, and he insisted on cleaning up the kitchen.

It was mid-evening when she came back downstairs and announced they were asleep. He fixed her a drink and she talked about her day, describing the restaurant where she was serving - a job she knew well - which led her back to sharing her aspirations of writing.

He had always encouraged her desire to write. He'd done very well as an author of technical books, and had published some non-fiction about famous people in culture and politics. She was hoping for a new media sort of position, writing for a website.

It wasn't yet late, but he could tell she was tired. He didn't prolong the conversation, and soon vanished to take a shower.

It was shortly past midnight when he awoke, aware of... something. He wasn't sure what.

He could hear her breathing, and it was quick - a soft panting. The bed wasn't exactly moving, but he could tell she wasn't still, and -

Omigod!

He suddenly realized what she was doing.

At first he was captivated. How often did he - or anyone else, for that matter - find themselves in a situation like this? Waking up next to someone *masturbating*?

His instinctive response was insuppressible - he was immediately both fascinated and aroused. Very careful not to move, or let his breathing change in any way, he simply listened.

Her breathing shifted, and he could sense that however she was touching herself had increased. There were subtle sounds, wet sounds, *squishy* sounds, along with her breathing, and her body eased into a different position. He could tell she was going to great effort to remain quiet.

Suddenly her motions ceased, her breath caught sharply, and she shuddered, causing a tiny tremor in the blanket. She was having an orgasm, and he realized it was excruciating, doing that undetected.

Like so many guys before him, he'd experienced the Married Man's Dilemma: how to get off when you're dying to, and you're in bed with a woman who just wants to sleep? Men, in general, need more release than women, and muscular men - which he was - more still. How many nights during his marriage had he been dying for sex, while his wife, unresponsive, had just drifted off to sleep?

Every married man is faced with a choice: suffer in silence, or try to rub one out, undetected. The latter is often so difficult that the former becomes the default.

And now, having heard what he'd just heard, he found himself facing exactly that dilemma.

Okay, he hadn't thought of this. Two healthy adults, each without a partner - yes, self-pleasuring was not only something they were both used to, it helped keep them sane. And yet - now they were in each other's way.

This was going to be a problem.

The weekend arrived, and he'd gone on an early-morning run, leaving the house before anyone else had stirred. The leaves were turning and the air was crisp, and he felt wonderful as he walked up the driveway and through the back door.

He walked into happy pandemonium, both kids racing around the kitchen floor to their mother's mild annoyance as she tried to pour pancakes. She stopped and handed him coffee, motioning that it was barter, not free - would he please get them out of here? With a smile, he herded them into the living room until breakfast was ready.

As she left for the restaurant, she thanked him again for watching them during her shift. He planned a trip to the park until their nap times, with lunch at Mickey D's. As he listened to the rattle of her old clunker of a car easing out of the driveway, he set the kids down in front of a cartoon and gathered up the breakfast dishes, suddenly very aware of how much fun he was having.

It was Saturday night, and tomorrow was a sleep-in day. The kids were tucked in, and they shared a bottle of wine and watched a movie. He had once again canceled a date, and his date had been angry. He had agreed to meet and discuss it.

The movie wasn't long, a romantic comedy that left them feeling a little silly. No, it was the wine - and half an hour later, she lay against his shoulder in the bed.

They're going to give me more hours at the restaurant, she told him, and that meant more money sooner, which was good - but there was the problem of the kids. One of her friends could take them maybe two nights a week, but still -

He cut her off. *Don't be silly. This is their home, for now, anyway. I don't go anywhere - and if for some reason I need to, then we'll ask your friend to help.*

She kissed him on the cheek. There was a long silence.

You heard me the other night, she suddenly said.

He was so caught off guard that he didn't know what to say.

You could tell I was whacking off.

Women say 'whacking off?'

You know how I know? You didn't move at all, or make any sound at all, the whole time I was finishing.

She propped her head up, in the darkness next to him.

Usually you move a little, here and there, and you take deep breaths every so often when you're asleep. But you went completely still, the whole time. You gave yourself away.

He smiled. There was no fighting it.

Yup, you caught me, he admitted.

Oh, I think you *caught* me, and she laughed a little.

Did you think it was hot? she asked, playfully.

It... got my attention, he admitted.

Seriously, though, we should talk about it, she said. *We're in this weird situation, and I don't know about you, but I need to do that. A lot, actually.* She poked his chest hard. *And I'll bet you do, too, Mr. Gym Rat!*

You have to see it from my side, he said. *I mean, technically, I'm your landlord, and we're already doing something very... unconventional.*

That's why I'm the one bringing it up, she said. *This is coming from me. So it's okay.*

And he realized she was right. He could never have broached it, it would have been inappropriate. And they were already pushing 'appropriate' to the limit. But she was free to bring up whatever she pleased.

She sat up and pulled off her nightshirt.

What the hell???

Just go with it, she said, tossing the nightshirt aside and pulling off her panties.

It wasn't like the other night. She wasn't under the covers, she was on top of them, naked, only a hand's length between them. He wasn't under the covers, either, and there was no retreat.

Just be here with me, she whispered, and her hands began to explore her body, with no trace of embarrassment.

There was enough moonlight in the window that he could see what she was doing. She arched her hands to make the stroke of her fingertips very deliberate. She didn't zero in immediately on any one body part, but ran her fingers over neck and shoulder, across her stomach, along her outer legs, awakening her skin completely before getting down to it. She sighed deeply, enjoying the freedom to pleasure herself without restraint, and when she let one hand drift to her breast and the other between her legs, she turned her head his way and opened her eyes, looking into his as she began to touch herself.

He could smell her.

That was trouble. She was wet and getting wetter, and her scent was arousing him far more than the event itself, but there was nothing he could do. She was trying to acclimate him to a practical reality, and this was an act of honesty, not titillation. Her face went from playful to intense as she crossed a threshold, and a soft moan escaped her.

She rolled over, in his direction, and he had to back off a bit to give her room. Stomach down, she slid her fist between her legs, her ass slightly elevated, and began the thrusting motion of a man. In a burst of insight, he realized she was sliding her clit over the knuckles of her hand, back and forth - a move he'd never seen or even heard of before. He watched her body's rhythms in the moonlight, entranced, and her moans increased as she suddenly rolled back over and began to rub furiously, sliding the fingers of her other hand inside as she hit the home stretch.

She gasped, suddenly stopping, and one hand slapped down on the blanket and grabbed in firmly. Her body trembled, and a small sound escaped, and he could tell she was struggling to hold back. She wanted to cry out.

There were children in the next room and down the hall.

She lay there, breathing deeply, wallowing in the glow of her climax, serene.

He could do or say nothing. He was mesmerized.

67

She suddenly rolled over, propping her head next to his.

Thank you, she said, although he didn't know what for. *Now it's your turn.*

Oh, no, not a chance -

Come on, she said, pulling his shirt away. *We can't be embarrassed by this. We have to be comfortable with each other.*

I don't know if I can -

You'll be fine, she said casually. *There's nothing to be embarrassed about.*

She wasn't taking No for an answer. She rose to her knees and pulled his warm-up bottoms away. He was a deer caught in headlights, unable to protest, but desperate for some way out.

He was naked. She was naked. This was wildly surreal. He was aroused, and she could dimly see that, and whether he liked it or not, he was deeply embarrassed by that alone.

Lucky guess! she said playfully, and he felt unbearably self-conscious.

She was aware enough to realize that he was backed into a corner. He couldn't quite see her face in the darkness, wrinkling into that calculating look.

She eased back down beside him, kissed his cheek, then his mouth. *This will work,* she whispered.

Kissing him again, she reached down and took him in her hand, squeezing gently. He almost pushed her away, but he worried that would make things even worse. She squeezed again, then began to rhythmically stroke him.

She said nothing, just distracted him from his anxiety with the softness of her kiss. Her grip on him was firm, her strokes strong and sensuous. She backed off from the kiss to let him breathe, and he surrendered to the inevitability of the moment. It had been a very long time since he'd had any intimate contact with a woman. She pulled him over the edge in only a few minutes.

A man mess is untroubling to a couple, but they weren't a couple. The awkwardness started rising to a whole new level when she massaged his receding member, then slid her hand over his stomach and chest, indifferent to the masculine moisture, making it all seem part of the moment. Out of nowhere, a damp washcloth appeared, and as she cleaned him up, he realized...

... she planned this!

Things had changed between them - and yet they hadn't. Whatever this was, it wasn't a relationship, and it was only intimacy in the sense that it was shared. This was not the consummation of pining and longing, no romance, no mutual pursuit. It was just mutual need, shared and met, in a way he would never have imagined or expected.

Now, she said, lying on her back again, and placing his hand between her legs, *my turn...*

As she began picking up longer and longer shifts, his mornings included letting her little girl play on the floor of his home office until lunch time and nap time, his afternoons including the retrieval of big brother from the bus stop, after-school snack, and a walk around the neighborhood in the autumn air, after supper. A few of his neighbors had stared, and he'd found it hard to explain to the one or two who actually asked.

Homework on the couch with the boy, then bath time, bedtime story, and they would be asleep by the time she got home. She would kiss them in the dark and stumble into the bathroom for a hot shower. He would have a drink waiting and lavender incense burning. During the first week or two, the stress had her needing the release of climax - *I need my finger buddy tonight*, she'd say, and he was afraid to ask where she'd picked up that term.

She gave the kids every free moment of her days off, and he did all he could to support their time together and make it carefree and fun, joining in when appropriate, giving them space as she needed.

And on one of her days off, he met the woman he'd been dating for coffee, to tell her about the refugees he'd taken in, to explain the cancellations -

She'd stormed off with some very harsh words.

By the end of the first month she was a wreck. He came back from his morning run and heard her in her bathroom, sobbing quietly - but the kids were awake, so he went back downstairs and started breakfast.

There on the counter sat $300 in cash.

He briefly considered not accepting it, especially given the nature of their recent nights. But he quickly realized that not taking it would be far worse than simply accepting it. It would be more than an assault on her dignity; it would change the nature of the private exchange they had both accepted.

That night he texted her to know exactly when she'd walk through the door, and she found a hot bubble bath waiting, lavender candles burning around the bathroom. She took a long time, and when she entered the candle-lit bedroom wrapped in a towel, he gently removed it, then eased her onto the bed and gave her a long, deep massage.

It wasn't long before she was sound asleep, and he wrapped his own blanket around her, holding her close for a long moment, kissing the back of her neck, and blowing out the candle.

She had let him spring for Halloween costumes - Iron Man for the boy, a pumpkin suit for his little sister - and she'd gone to effort to make sure she'd be off work to take them trick-or-treating. She was crushed when the co-worker who'd agreed to cover her had a sick child, and she'd had to go in anyway.

He hesitantly offered to take them. Would that be okay?

Sure, she said, smiling through her disappointment. She met his eyes with the smile. *I trust you.*

And with that, he suddenly understood all that had happened so far.

Her father had abandoned her. Her son's father had abandoned them both, and the man after that.

He was probably the first and only man in her life whom she knew would not abandon her. *Trust...* all of this, all that had happened, came down to trust. It explained everything. That she had even one person she could have that feeling for must be all she had left, at this moment in her life.

As she pulled the old clunker out of the driveway and he gathered the kids up for trick-or-treat, he resolved to be worthy of it.

Many mornings he went on a pre-dawn run, compensating for the drop-off in gym time that this new life had caused. He was surprised, on one of his mornings when he just slept, to find her quietly putting on running clothes in the dark.

As she laced up her sneakers, he sat up in bed.

You're a good influence, she said in a cheerful voice, and she was out the door. From that day on, they alternated running mornings, with the one at home getting the kids moving.

She came home angry. Kids already in bed, she kissed them, then dropped onto the couch next to him and unloaded about work.

The general manager hadn't kept the promise he'd made when he'd hired her, she ranted. He mostly needed day workers, he'd said at first, nights were covered by his servers who attended classes at the community college by day.

That had changed as the semester had progressed, with a number of kids dropping out and going to full-time work in other jobs. The manager needed her on nights now, that was how it was. For weeks, she'd been missing her kids at night. She appreciated his help, of course, but the situation had to change. She was going to give her boss an ultimatum.

Always take what you need, and don't apologize for it, he told her. *Nobody is going to just give it to you.*

Nobody but you, she thought, looking into his eyes.

That night, they stopped being finger buddies.

That night, she took him into her hand, then took him into her mouth.

Then she took not his hand, but his head, and placed it between her legs.

It took them far longer to get to sleep.

The sound of the bedroom door opening brought him awake, and the first thing he saw was the numbers on the alarm clock. It was past midnight.

A small figure in Captain America pajamas shuffled to the bedside, finding his face in the clock's digital glow.

I had a bad dream...

Without a word, he lifted the boy into the bed, placing him between himself and his mother. He wrapped him in his own blanket, kissing the top of his head, and covered himself with the sheet. Both were back asleep in seconds.

From the outside, they looked like a family. On the inside, they functioned like a family.

In his heart - and, he was certain, in hers - they were something else.

Their nighttime intimacies aside, this was a practical partnership, not a romantic one. Affectionate, certainly, and, yes, loving - but not a romance.

All the same, they became more a family still when the holidays arrived. Her father still wanted nothing to do with her, and her mother was half a continent away. His daughter was off to spend the time with her new boyfriend's family, and his son - disapproving of his new arrangement - was headed west for a holiday with his boyfriend.

He suspected that neither of his kids were comfortable with what he was doing, or with seeing their old bedrooms turned over to small children.

She brokered a compromise at work, agreeing to help with management grunt work on weekends in exchange for two weeknights off. Realizing that her new penchant for jogging was keeping her energy level up for her day-to-day challenges, he expanded his YMCA membership to 'family' status, passing her off as his sister. She began doing early mornings at the gym, three times a week.

A new ritual emerged. She called it their 'alarm clock,' and it basically amounted one awakening the other, on running/gym mornings... orally.

As Thanksgiving approached, she had been placed in charge of the restaurant's local web pages, and although not in the management program she was given managerial duties. She jumped at the chance to handle Thanksgiving day at the restaurant, for double pay, at the relief managers' rate. The restaurant was closing at 4 p.m., so she'd be home for a turkey dinner with the kids.

He agreed, of course, and rose early on Thanksgiving Day to start the turkey. By the time she got home, the house was filled with wonderful scents. It was a traditional dinner, with both pumpkin and apple pies for dessert. The girl, still nursing from time to time, wanted only mommy for dinner (Mommy must have tasted really interesting.) The kids went to bed stuffed, and the two of them got drunk on wine and spiced rum.

He let her sleep in the next morning.

He went all out at Christmas, sending only checks and cards to his own kids, but playing Santa lavishly with hers. He knew she wouldn't object, and it was largesse that she wouldn't consider charity over and above what they already enjoyed.

Every month, her $300 would be sitting in an envelope on the kitchen counter, and since he didn't really need it, he'd squirreled it away for just such occasions.

He went all out.

The bike for the boy was top-of-the-line, and would have been enough; the game console and the dozen games that went with it were over-the-top. His little sister would have an entire toy box full of new fascinations, age-appropriate and enough to take her well into her third year.

Amazed that her noisy junk heap wouldn't last the winter, he wanted to buy her a car. But he knew she'd refuse it, and there was no point in causing them both the embarrassment. He settled for a gift card, enough for a new wardrobe, at her favorite store, and a laptop computer, loaded with office and web authoring software.

On Christmas Eve, he read "The Night Before Christmas" to the kids and tucked them in, along with their mother. He followed her in kissing their foreheads.

They retired to the living room, where they placed all of the children's presents under the tree for Christmas morning. Then he poured them each a glass of very good wine he'd bought just for the moment, and put on quiet Christmas music. He gave her both gifts, and she cried.

She had two gifts for him, too. The first was a thumb drive, with screen-savers she'd made on a computer at work, collages of her and the kids, and some shots of both of them.

She gave him his other present a little later, upstairs, peeling away his t-shirt and boxers and taking them both into the night. She made love to him wildly, without reserve, mounting him from above, riding him with out-of-control passion. As she'd straddled him, he'd reached for the nightstand, when she stopped him, passively reminding him that she was still lactating - baby-proof.

She did things to him he'd never imagined, and encouraged him to write his own fantasies on her body. He let himself go, pouring himself into her without reservation, accepting all that she was offering, enjoying it to the limit, and offering everything he possibly could in return.

In a relationship defined by a powerful and final boundary, they were - in this moment - without boundaries. All of her gratitude, all of her respect for him, all of her appreciation - all of her trust - went into the ministrations of her hands, her fingertips, her tongue. He responded in kind, expressing all of his admiration, affection, protectiveness, with a passion and aggression and masculinity that would have been unlike him, six months ago. Responding to her on-top display, which brought her to a thundering climax, he grabbed her and rolled her over, thrusting into her powerfully, with unprecedented force, bringing her off again before he exploded into her, crying out helplessly.

It took them ten minutes to calm down, and then they giggled, with whispered jokes about how much they *didn't* sound like Santa, and they were amazed he hadn't awakened the children.

She bit his chin.

Lick me, she whispered.

Whatever had been before, it was far, far more in this moment. All inhibitions removed, all boundaries erased, she adopted an entirely new vocabulary, and the very free mutual satisfaction they'd enjoyed for months became the stuff of dreams...

Put your fingers in me...

Make me wetter...

GOD, you taste good!

Don't stop!...do it again...

I love your cock...

I need you inside me...

Harder! harder!.

Harder... faster... higher... lower... faster... slower...

A six-word vocabulary, merged with quiet sighs and moans and panting, and as winter moved to spring, they would utterly master it, entering into a level of intimate partnership that no married couple even dreams of.

It was a happy Christmas morning, filled with laughter, squeals of joy, many cell phone pics, and bouncy Christmas music. He slipped away and put together a Christmas dinner he'd had in the wings, with country ham, sweet potatoes, honey-buttered rolls, pecan pie. And wine. Once again, baby sister preferred Mommy's treats.

He could not identify the feeling that overwhelmed him when he watched the child at her breast.

When the kids napped, they did, too. He cradled her in his arms.

It was a wonderful new year.

The late nights were fewer; her computer skills, which he augmented with tips and training, made her all the more valuable at the restaurant, but when offered management training, she had refused; she had her sights set higher.

One night when she was working, baby sister did another of her wobbly stands in the middle of the living room floor, while he and big brother watched a Disney movie from the couch.

She didn't collapse. She wobbled, steadying herself... and he whipped out his cell phone, easing off the couch to a position in front of her, catching her eye, smiling, cooing her name, encouraging. Big brother was wide-eyed as she shifted, lurching, thrusting a foot forward... and didn't fall.

They gently cheered her on, caught up in the magic, getting it all on video. She managed four steps before tumbling over, and big brother hugged her and they both giggled uncontrollably.

That night, she came home and saw the video... sobbing that she missed it, and deeply grateful that he'd been thoughtful enough to capture the moment for her to share.

Winter had descended, but their life rolled forward with joy and energy. They continued to alternate running/gym mornings. The general manager gave her a raise. His business thrived. The school sent home a letter, noting her son's academic accomplishment. By Valentine's Day, she had lost all of her baby weight. Not that he had ever noticed any.

They ignored Valentine's Day. This wasn't a romance. The night was... wild and passionate and special, but...

They ignored Valentine's Day.

Spring dawned, and they began weekend picnics, taking the boy's bike to the park, where he quickly learned to ride, strapping baby sister onto his back for long, laughter-filled hikes... they were both up for it, after months of running and gym time and healthy eating, and either of them could carry their worn-out boy for a mile or more...

... and their nights... almost every one was filled with passion, rich sharing, easy and free expression of need. They made love constantly, a dozen hours a week and more, effortlessly expressing themselves, bluntly asking for more, for this, for that... constantly surprising each other, inventing entirely new ways of encountering each other, meeting needs they'd never known they had.

He came to her admire her body as more than exemplary womanhood, but a work of art that stood apart, from her baby-chewed nipples - glorious in their post-nursing pride - to her glowing face, her shining eyes, her firming muscles, her hungry arms, her passionate womanhood.

He himself had always been fit, but the stirring of their private nights had inspired him to Herculean efforts in the gym, and the more he pushed himself, the stronger he became... he set new records for himself on the early-morning road, running with energy and freedom and a sense of self-discovery, becoming more fit and powerful day by day, and bringing it all home to her. To them.

As her son brought home worksheets from school, he made a point of never missing a moment of the boy's learning adventures - reading with him, reviewing every worksheet, offering hints - and when the science project came along (for third graders, not first graders, but he'd expressed an interest, and received permission to participate), they'd gone to the home improvement store for supplies, and built it together.

Either of them took the other, in bed, with power and unfettered need and no apology on any night, when the babies were down and the door to their sanctum closed, and the candles burned and their muscles tensed and their juices flowed and their voices resisted - there were children in the next room! - and almost every night, they collapsed in each other's arms.

And here and there, she would come home exhausted, and there was a back rub and a kiss, and nothing more... and from time to time, she'd come home and he'd be worn out, because the kids had been a handful, and there was a back rub and a kiss, and nothing more.

And she cuddled in his warmth, and wondered, with a tear he never saw, how she would ever do without him.

They sat in the auditorium with all the other parents, trying to keep little sister quiet - hard to do, as her vocabulary expanded! - as the awards were handed out.

They called little brother's name, and he proudly stepped forward, accepting the science award for his project - an award he'd won in competition with kids two years older.

He stepped to the microphone.

I want to say thank you, to my mom... and my dad...

And they both sat there in shock.

Two weeks later, she announced to all three of them at dinner that she had applied for a position in the county clerk's office, writing for the county website. Though she didn't have a journalism degree, she'd gotten the job, which included maintenance of the website - skills he had taught her.

They never talked about it. They just knew that it was time.

Ten months had passed, since that lunch, that deep-dish pizza.

On a Saturday in the early summer, his son and his son's boyfriend were in a nearby city, and he drove to meet them for the day.

When he came back, they were gone. Bedrooms empty, the walk-in closet devoid of all her clothes.

It had been ten months, far longer than they had originally planned. Ten long, wonderful, magical months. She had managed to save almost nine thousand dollars, and had never failed to pay her rent.

A handmade card, written in crayon, expressed deep thanks and love from a boy now seven and a little girl approaching two.

Another card, containing a very lengthy handwritten note, expressed far, far more.

Tears came.

Leave Saturday open, the text said. It surprised him, but he sent an acknowledgment.

6 pm, came another on Friday, with an additional note - **Dress up**.

He wore his best sport coat and the shirt that was her favorite, and his puzzlement was set aside by the sight of her pulling into his driveway in a used SUV, a pretty nice one. Her old clunker was gone, along with the other vestiges of her brush with hardship. And then she stepped out of the car.

She was beautiful. Not just young and pretty, not just nice to look at, not just toned up, but *beautiful*.

She'd had her hair done up, and it was only now that he was realizing how long it had grown over the past year. She wore a new curve-hugging dress with floral print, very summery, and it dawned on him that her breasts, which he knew intimately but mostly horizontally, were magnificent; no longer full of milk, they were a perfect accentuation of what he now saw as strong, stunning femininity.

Her face glowed.

I was thinking pizza, she said, tossing him her keys.

He burst into a smile.

Hours later they pulled back into his driveway and made their way into the house. He started to fix drinks, but she took his hand and led him straight upstairs to the master bedroom, wordlessly lighting a candle, kissing him, and retreating into the bathroom.

He partially undressed, waiting, not quite sure what was going on.

She slipped back into the room in a new silk nightgown, her hair down, and slid straight into his arms. She was the most beautiful sight he'd ever seen, soft in his embrace and yet stronger than ever. She always smelled wonderful to him, but tonight there was something extra, and it left him dizzy as she eased them onto the bed, in flickering candleglow.

They made love for hours, long past the candle's life, revisiting all their favorite memories, inventing new ones. They went new places, pouring into each other far more than the affection and accommodation and intimacies of their unique friendship they'd shared so long. This was a moment they needed to give all that there was to give.

This is goodbye.

But there was one other unique feature of this magical night...
There were no children in the next room.

The stillness was almost unbearable.

He'd slept later than he had in years, and when he'd finally stirred, she was gone. He realized that had been wise, on her part; for the first time ever, it would have been awkward.

He walked into each empty room in the gray of the late morning, an ache spreading through him slowly. In the back of his mind, he'd known this would be hard, but he had no idea...

But something was different now. On this side of those ten months, he was beginning to realize he could hear more, see more, feel more, and in the stillness he began to hear echoes... little giggles, small voices... her sighs in the darkness.

He wasn't alone. He was among happy ghosts.

This was loneliness, but it was a rich, well-earned feeling.

He smiled.

To ease the transition with the kids, there were some picnics together in the park, tapering off as the weather turned. It was hard not to touch her. Emails and pictures continued, and a year later, she married a young man only a little older than himself - quiet, strong, kind, and generous, from her descriptions. He had not attended the wedding, and she had been disappointed, but she understood.

And a year after that, he, too, remarried - an empty-nested woman only a little younger than himself, and they went off to see the world.

Each carried into the new marriages all that they had learned, discovered, and invented together, all the growth, all the courage, all the respect and love of self that their exploration had brought to life. Two happy families, where none had been before. They thought of each other often, without regret.

The emails and pictures never stopped, and of course there were birthday cards and Christmas cards. And for a long time, every year, on the anniversary of that first lunch, he sent her a pizza coupon.

Birthday Present

They were destroying their clothes, making *way* too much noise, and her legs were cramping.

But *oh*, was it *good!*

He was a powerful, aggressive lover, but skilled and generous, confident in his masculine role but hungering for her satisfaction. That in itself was really satisfying, and she loved the things he did. He was creative ... passionate ...

Invested.

He was also a little rough. And she *liked* rough.

With her usual timing, she did her long moan, and he proceeded with his. Hers wasn't real, of course – it never was, except when she was alone – and she suspected that he suspected it.

As they disentangled – and he took his sweet time, which she liked – she briefly appreciated what she could feel of his body, as deeply middle-aged as hers, but firm, gym-hardened, much better maintained than her own. She just *hated* her boobs. And her butt. And compensated by doing extreme things to her hair, which must look particularly frightening right now ...

He made a joke about fogged windows and cops. She felt a flush of embarrassment when it occurred to her how old that joke was. She briefly worried that she wouldn't be able to find her panties.

Back-seat love. Ah, the memories.

Far too many.

She awoke the next morning to find that she had indeed destroyed the blouse, and this pissed her off a little bit. He called a little later to tell her that he actually had found her panties, and this pissed her off even more. Fixing coffee, she found herself resenting the whole back-seat thing. She suddenly felt cheap, and her resentment began flaming into anger, anger that he would see her that way, that he would demean her that way,

Except …
The back seat had been *her* idea.
Oops.

He had cooked dinner for her — he loved to cook — and not just dinner, but an over-the-top gourmet extravaganza that was pure calories, sure to make her fatter. They went through a bottle of wine, then half of another bottle, and when she cut loose on him, she was pretty over-the-top herself. He was deer-in-headlights stunned, suddenly having to defend himself, unprepared; and he staggered out into the night, badly shaken, but with a look of understanding and determination that she, in her emotional storm, didn't see.

I do this every time.
She didn't want to tell her best friend. Or her cousin. They'd give her that look, and she really didn't need that again. Her sister, well, she really didn't care much either way. She had an even worse track record with men, and that was saying something.

Mother, of course, knew, and was already rattling in her brain across the years: "You just run off all the good ones! Threw away a perfectly good marriage! What's wrong with you?"

And he *was* one of the good ones.

Text messages, little notes, picnics, long walks …

He was one of the good ones.

She was too embarrassed to call him. She was certain he'd never call her.

When she was with him, she felt … *better.*

Better than she really was.

Special.

Which she certainly wasn't.

She was back online that night, browsing through dating-site men, bored and irritable. An almost-empty glass of Chardonnay sat next to the keyboard, scolding her. Journey songs bounced off the walls behind.

A text bleeped into her cell phone. For a heart-stopping instant, she thought it might be him.

Party next weekend, don't forget. Her cousin.

Blah blah blah, she answered. This was a birthday she wasn't anxious to celebrate.

Once again, the Ritual, and she forced herself not to think about how many times she'd been through it.

Step One, carb-heavy carry-out meal, decadent Chinese. *Bad for me. Yummy.* Alcohol.

Step Two, long long hot hot bubble bath. Candles. Pity music. Alcohol.

Step Three, an hour of really filthy porn, the DVD hidden under the shoe boxes in the closet, reserved for just such occasions. Alcohol. Get *completely* horny. Imagining herself doing things she would never, ever do with an actual man. Or woman. Or both. Idle fingers ...

Step Four, retire to bed, more candles, The Mega-Toy. Extra batteries. Grind and grind till I pass out ... let it all loose, all the pent-up ...

She made it to the beginning of Step Four, began missing him, and cried herself to sleep.

Weekend. Facebook. He'd friended her cousin! And her best friend! *Oh, God ...*

She inquired. They claimed not to have noticed.

Mother.

Just as well ... You're too old to be acting this way!

Age has nothing to do with it, Mother.
Running around like a teenager! You are making a fool of yourself!

You said the same thing when I was *a teenager, Mother.*

You'll never find a decent man, and if you do, you'll run him off, behaving like one of those *girls! You've already ruined one perfectly good marriage –*

82

Perfectly good marriage, Mother? Like yours? You were colder to Dad than you were to me, if that's even possible ...

Sister.
Tell that boyfriend of yours I'm not going to friend him on Facebook. I thought you broke up?

She stared at her cell phone.
Over a week.
No call, no text. Her insides felt cold and hollow.

PARTY!
They'd invited most of her office, half of her old school friends. Her sister and brother-in-law were there and not particularly happy about it. Her daughters even drove in from college.

They'd spared no expense, even springing for a male stripper.

She allowed herself to have a good time, but for once, she carefully measured the alcohol.

Mother hovered.

Gift time, and it was an outrageously fun mix of gags and generous affection. She laughed and laughed. And teared up twice.

And then she came to *his* gift, which her cousin had brought.

It was a medium-sized box, obviously wrapped by a man. There was a card attached. She had enough presence of mind not to open it in front of everyone.

She tore at the paper, and had a sudden horrified thought.

Oh God ... please, please let it not be my panties!

Then an even more horrified thought. *Christ, let him at least have had the sense to wash them!*

What was she thinking? *He's a man. OF COURSE he didn't wash them!*

The room had fallen quiet by the time she opened the lid of the box
...

!!!

Chutes and Ladders. Her favorite childhood game. And a very old one, at least 30 years. eBay?

Her favorite doll.

An ancient copy of her favorite storybook – which she'd taught herself to read, since her parents hadn't.

A pair of the pants she'd defiantly worn in junior high school, under Mother's scathing disapproval, in the exact size she'd worn them all those years ago …

And a scrapbook, which she opened tentatively, almost holding her breath.

An arm slipped around her shoulders … her cousin … and she turned the pages, pulled into one long-past scene after another, happy times with her cousin and friends unforgotten, the dog she'd loved … happy times long since locked deep in an impenetrable vault, a place to store joys of which she felt unworthy.

Page after page! …pulled from her cousin's online albums, her best friend's collection, along with the memories that had uncovered all these beloved artifacts.

And no Mother, in any of the pictures.

He knew!

And this was his response, this gift, this unbundling of so many years of repressed joy and warmth and self-love, to tear away the door of that awful vault and allow all the buried happiness back into the sun.

It wasn't enough, of course. Opening up these old pockets of happiness could not make her happy.

But he had given her a path back to loving herself. It would take a long time. But it could happen.

She tried so hard not to cry in front of everyone. She didn't succeed.

It was appropriately cold and cloudy.

She stood alone before the dark granite, reading the dates again and realizing how long it had been.

Don't speak, Mother!

This time, I will do the talking.

And she did, at long last. She released all her rage, all her old longings, all the disappointments …

I needed to be held … you wouldn't touch me …

I needed your smile …

I needed your kiss on my forehead at night … I needed your voice …

Hot tears …

I was able to give those things to my girls, Mother! Those things aren't hard to give! God builds them into us! What was so wrong with me, that you withheld them?

And the answer is …

Nothing!

I am a good woman, and I have been a good mom, and I want to be a woman – really be a woman - with a good man!

And I will.

She had been standing, and now she knelt, laying the box before the stone.

This is who I am, Mother. These toys, these clothes, these pictures … this is who I am. This is what you missed.

I love you, Mom. Now, be silent!

And before driving away, she opened his birthday card. And laughed, for the first time in ages.

You don't think you're getting rid of me that easily, do you?

The Curtains

Dark, blue, cool summer wind in suburban heat, windows open, save on the electric, no air conditioning … past two a.m. with soothing sighs and flutter, no hum, and quiet flutter across the bedroom …

Sweetheart …

Drowsy turbulence, ending some inane dream and she breathed in deeply, warm-cool and tingly, a little annoyed.

Sweetheart …

She expected his fingers, creeping sensually around her waist – *he still could make her shiver!* – with that *I-need-more* intrusion that once thrilled and impressed her, but now seemed excessive …
No fingers?

Sweetheart … Listen to me …

Her eyes opened to the rude glow of red digital figures, **2:47**, and she fought down an inner groan. Three hours since they had drifted off, and they'd made love, and she'd done all the work – as usual, lately – and could still feel where the moisture had trickled down her thigh … *he can't be serious …*

Listen to me …

Why is he whispering?

There's so much I haven't said that I need to say …

She clutched the sheet.

I remember that first night … when we were kids, in high school. The station wagon … our first night together …

2:48

I know I wasn't your first … but you were mine. I don't know if I've ever really told you this … but that night, I knew … I knew we'd be together always … I knew we'd have a home, and our babies, and make a family …

Suddenly the breeze was cold, and she felt herself curling up.
She expected him to pull closer, expected the warmth of his breath on the back of her neck. She felt only the coolness easing in through the window.

You've given me more than I ever thought this life could offer … I am so lucky, the luckiest man who ever lived …

Why is he saying this???

I have this picture of us, many years from now, sitting on a porch swing … and a car pulls up and our grandkids pile out of it and run up and jump in our laps …

Omigod!!!
The curtains swelled, flapping …

That boy and his little sister are so beautiful … we made them … we made them, you and I …

She thought of the pictures above them on the shelf behind the headboard. She started to speak, to respond, to agree, and felt wetness on her cheek. *Why is he saying this?*

Every time I felt weak, you made me strong … when I doubted myself, I looked in your eyes, and knew I could do it …

She was fighting hard, resisting the sobbing that she knew was welling up in her breast. *What is going on?*

When I got sick, I felt so embarrassed … so ashamed … I was afraid you wouldn't see me as a man anymore …

She was suddenly aware of the many pill bottles on the headboard, the moaning, the fevers, the weakness, and felt deep shame at the irritation and impatience and resentment she had let loose within herself, these past few months. The tears, freely flowing now, felt cold.

Why doesn't he hug me? He usually puts his arm around me when he pillow-talks …

The curtains sighed, flowing like angels' wings.

2:49

His whisper softened.

I wouldn't trade a day of our life together for anything … Our life together, our babies, our days, our nights …

She thought to turn over.
Fear.

I have to go now …

Terror!

Thank you for loving me …

The curtains fluttered.
He was long since cold. Her screams woke all the neighbors.

The West Coast Conference

In the elevator, she always smelled so good. At first he enjoyed it, looked forward to it, but the more he got to know her, the more he forced it out of his mind.

She was married.

He had been, once. A too-young adventure that began with a bang – many bangs, actually - and ended without a whimper.

He admired her mind, her energy, her enthusiasm. He enjoyed the projects they were assigned, appreciated her insights, easily overlooked her weaknesses, valued her support.

She was married.

Once she didn't come in to the office, without explanation ... and was out the next day, and the next. Two weeks. And he got on just fine, handling the workload, and worked up the courage to step into her cubicle, afraid someone would see him. As if anyone cared.

He knew the pictures, had seen them out of the corner of his eye on the many occasions when he'd stood there, talking to her about this project or that ... the pictures of her with him, their smiles, the exotic backgrounds. Her and him. No kids. They'd been married for years, he knew ... the vacations explained it, they enjoyed their travel and their adventures too much to be tied down with kids.

None of his business.

She was married.

It was he who got the department together to celebrate her fifth anniversary with the department. She'd been totally surprised, and the lunch he sprang for had been fun for everyone. She had hugged him fiercely ...

... and disappeared, without explanation, for days.

We need you to fly out to the technical conference next month, their boss had told him. *Both of you.*

So many thoughts assaulted him. He set them aside.

She was married.

It was late spring, and the weather was wonderful. Arriving the night before the conference, they had grabbed a bite to eat in the hotel restaurant. She had been polite but formal, somewhat apprehensive, a little distant.

The conference sessions were intense, and they went their separate ways, to different meetings, each taking copious notes. They met briefly for lunch, but she'd gotten a cell phone call, and vanished.

The day ended. Would she like to grab some dinner, take a walk? No, thank you, she smiled, a little distant.

The next morning, they met for coffee. She dropped a pair of rectangular mint chocolates onto the table, and they discussed the ridiculousness of hotel mints on freshly-made beds. For a moment, she seemed like herself.

More sessions. Her focus was intense; when they met up, she almost babbled, preoccupied with technical details that could certainly wait until they were home ...

He worked up his courage.

Dinner?

No, thank you, she smiled, a little distant.

She was married.

The last full day ... more sessions ... more details ... more notes. He waited for her mid-day in the lobby, and she didn't appear.

And didn't answer her cell.

And didn't appear for the afternoon sessions.

And didn't respond to his knock, at dinnertime.

As before, back home, she just vanished.

Three hours of mindless cable TV, an overpriced bourbon, and he was drifting off to sleep when there was a knock on his hotel room door.

It didn't even occur to him that it would be her.

Opening the door in sweatpants and a t-shirt, he found her dressed in even less, her eyes wet and desperate.

She tumbled into the room, into the dark, into his arms. Confused, he held her as she broke into deep sobs.

The golden-blue light of the television lit the room as her sobbing continued, and her anguish grew so deep that he found her beginning to collapse, sagging in his arms, and there was nowhere to go but the bed.

He had never been so confused in his life.

She always smelled so good...

He started to speak, but didn't.

He tightened his arms around her, and she responded, clutching him as if holding on for dear life, releasing some pain deeper than he could fathom. There was nothing to do but hold her, to absorb the anguish, to give the only thing he could … his presence …

Her sobbing continued, for almost an hour … when it faded, it was only because she had drifted away, in exhaustion.

He continued to hold her, to envelop her in whatever warmth he could offer, and he resolved to remain awake, to keep watch over her.

She burrowed into him, soft and warm and vulnerable, and the wetness of her tears soaking into his t-shirt, her sweet scent all around him, the trust she had given up to him, all made him feel more like a man than he ever had.

He remained awake, caressing her with unbearable tenderness, until he couldn't anymore.

When he awoke, ninety minutes into the final conference session, he was alone.

She awoke in darkness, aching with fatigue, exhaustion almost like wine in her veins and muscles … it took a moment for her to remember where she was, to pick up the scent and warmth of a man, to realize it was him … *not her husband* … and remember what had happened.

She remembered … the sharp pain … the sudden blood …

The anguish …

Her eyes welled up, and she fought with everything she had to stop the surge of sadness, despair … struggling not to feel the sudden emptiness of her womb, this latest loss … she focused on her husband, on how she would tell him, on how they would absorb this new disappointment together …

… and she suddenly felt warmth on her neck, the man who now enfolded her, this dear friend whom she knew to be smitten but who had been so good to her, so respectful, so supportive … this man whom she had turned to in this horrible moment, who had given exactly what she needed, with no thought for himself … and she gently eased into his arms one last time, reveling in the safety and sacrifice and pure love. She kissed him on the lips with impossible gentleness, letting a final tear spill, and carefully eased out of the bed, out of the room, and back into the world…

91

Nothing was said.

Their interaction was mercifully cheerful and warm and ignorant of all that had happened as they laughed off their absence from the final conference session. It was pretense, and he knew it, but he set that aside as they had one last coffee at the airport, parting swiftly when their flight landed. He watched from a distance with inexplicable emotion as she ran into her husband's arms.

It had been the most intimate night of his life. He didn't understand.

She was absent from work for several days.

But on the day she returned, he found a rectangular mint chocolate on his computer keyboard.

S3

He'd been at the computer for over five hours, since just before 6 a.m., cranking out a technical article and feeling his neck grow sore. The refrigerator beckoned.

"Alexa, play the Beatles," he said, as he always did when he stopped for lunch. As *Abbey Road* crept out, he opened the fridge and sought out the leftover chicken from the previous evening.

As he was closing the door, he noticed a bottle at the very bottom. He bent down and took it out.

Riesling
Chateau Ste Michelle
2016

Her favorite.

He held the corked, half-empty bottle for a moment, realizing that it had been in there since the holidays – over eight months. *Geezus. By now it's turned to battery acid...*

His nickname for the Riesling was "S3" - mastering the name "Chateau Ste Michelle" was beyond him, and he repeatedly fumbled it, defaulting to "St. Something Something", which in turn became S3, just to conserve syllables. When he'd learned it was her favorite, he immediately made it a point to always have some on hand.

Emotions suddenly welled up. Not because he was here and she was there, though those emotions visited almost hourly, but a surge of gratitude for her presence, through this fortuitous artifact. He was actually holding it lovingly, he realized, and he gave his feelings some room.

Three years had passed since their Tuesdays and Thursdays.

It had been early in their knowing one another. He had the freedom to work from home, several days a week; she had just finished another master's degree, and hadn't yet gone back to work. She came here to his home, then, on Tuesdays and Thursdays.

It was winter and the skies weren't bright, and she would arrive in the morning. He would be waiting, and would get up from the couch to kiss her when she arrived. They would sit on the couch and listen to music or talk or watch television, and their standard lunch was a shared plate of salami and cheese and crackers, there on the couch – and wine, S3 for her and pinot noir for him.

And then they spent the afternoon making love.

When the moment came, she would lead him by the hand and they would go to his room, dark even in daylight because of the black Dark Side of the Moon beach towel over the window.

They made love, and in no particular hurry. They made love and joked and giggled. They made love and spoke of the future. They made love and dozed. And on the occasions when she dozed and he didn't, he held her tightly, and breathed her in, and felt like the luckiest man alive.

She would stay for hours, until she had to pick her son up from school. It was never long enough for him, and he always lingered on the porch, watching as she drove away.

He blinked away a tear as he held the bottle, not because he was here and she was there, but – well – yes. Because that.

He seriously considered drinking a glass of the S3, but didn't.

Instead, he put the leftover chicken back in the fridge, fixed a plate of crackers and cheese, and ate lunch on the couch, listening to music, the bottle sitting on the coffee table.

Making Out

What happens in Vegas...

The annual conference, four days of dull presentations and evening fun, four blessed days away from home. Dancing and drinking and oh, what a surprise he was, and she didn't regret anything they'd done.

Shouldn't there be guilt?

It had been wild and unfettered and in some ways over-the-top, more than she really wanted or even liked, usually, but part of it was anger working itself out and she was self-aware enough to realize it. It had been defiant, delicious, and over too soon.

Today had been too long, this first day back... he was only 24 hours behind her, and nowhere up ahead. They'd never meet again and they both knew it and that was fine. But today had been too long. She'd come home and realized how tired she was and taken a long, hot shower. The bed she shared was empty when she climbed into it.

Tell him about Vegas? No, then it becomes about that, and it's not, and I won't give him the satisfaction...

Tell him I'm leaving?

Am I leaving?

She took a book off her nightstand, opened it, closed it, put it back. She was glad he wasn't home yet. She'd stayed in the clouds on the plane, and today had been a long day, and she hadn't thought through any of the weekend yet.

The rest of it she'd thought about for months, many months. At the conference, she'd just snapped. When she tried to put reason to it, she came up short: they didn't hate each other, they still loved each other - as far as she could tell - and whatever was missing was just, well, missing. Not my fault, not his fault.

Why am I angry?

Did it matter now?

Whatever had once been there between them, binding them, allowing their lives to flow into each other, was long since gone. The kids were gone. Their dreams were half-realized, half-abandoned. They accommodated each other, polite, benevolent...

Loveless?

At the conference, in the bar, on the dance floor, in the room after, she'd felt alive. So alive, more than she'd felt in recent memory. He'd made her laugh. And the sex had been, well, amazing. She loved feeling that way. She deserved to feel that way.

Here, at home, in this bed, she didn't feel that way.

She would tell him. They could begin the process of unraveling this, and pursuing what they'd both lost. Vegas had shown her that it was out there, just a matter of finding the courage to pursue it.

She turned out the lamp on her nightstand and turned the pillow to the cool side.

Remembering the hotel bed, the sense of not being alone, the warmth of another person, made her feel suddenly vulnerable. She drew the blanket around her neck and curled up, missing the hotel room, resenting being home.

Yes. They needed to talk. Leave Vegas out of it, but they needed to talk.

They would talk tomorrow.

She heard his muffled presence downstairs and waited without enthusiasm for the bedroom door to open. The doorknob turned. He was thoughtfully quiet as he undressed in the dark and slid into the bed. She played possum, realizing this was just stupid - he could always tell. Like it mattered.

There was a long, awkward moment of quiet nothingness.

Then, out of nowhere - strong, warm hands found her in the darkness...

No... oh, not tonight.

In a fleeting moment of stupidity, she actually did play possum, as his arms enfolded her gently but firmly, bundling her up against him. She prepared to utter a half-asleep objection. And then ---

None of the usual moves.

Not that usual kiss, not the usual hands. None of it - he just held her tight, and her mind raced, trying to understand.

A memory embarrassingly distant came to her.

This is how he used to hold me, after...

She was so astonished, so confused, that she gave no resistance as he gently turned her toward him and pulled her close again. She realized immediately that he was naked.

I knew it...

And she felt a twinge of disgust. Still... the way he'd held her...

With the same gentleness, he gathered her into his arms, without agenda, driven not by passion but by something else, and his hands began caressing her, lovingly, without lust. Her mind whirled, unable to fit this into any framework she could understand. He did not press in any way; whatever was passing from him to her, whatever she was able to receive, was enough.

She let herself relax into his embrace, tentatively, without promise. His response was uniformly tender, not a seeking-of-cues, but a reassurance. Reassurance of what?

What is he trying to say?

Why now?

Strong fingers began to stroke her hair, and more memories from long ago began to flood into the present. She realized with surprise that she had allowed their legs to tangle, and was suddenly self-conscious that she hadn't shaved them when she had taken her shower.

His other hand crawled to her lower back, to that one place he used to know so well, and his fingers did what they used to do, and the years began to fall away. She did not fully understand what was happening, but something within him was determined to connect with her, in the ways he once did so well. Part of her could not help but wonder... part of her had needed this for so long... she suddenly found herself fighting down both tears and anger.

And his lips found hers.

She felt as if she was dissolving.

She could not even say what year it had been, when he last kissed her like this. Conflicting emotions screamed within her, and she just let them fight it out. She did not fully respond to his kiss, but neither did she fight it. His hands, his legs, the surface of his skin, every part of him communicated - and she was at least willing to listen.

She was not clear at what point her nightshirt disappeared. But it was not long after that when she found herself fully returning his communication.

Naked in each other's arms, their embrace became increasingly heated, their kiss increasingly enflamed, and yet he did not press; the only contact with her breasts was the firm pressure of his chest, and his hands confined their exploration to her back. The familiar tingle within had surpassed a stirring and become a roaring fire, and he would do nothing more than he was doing now to address it.

What is going on here???

Why now?

And it came to her in a sudden, chilling realization: He knows...

He must... this can't be a coincidence...

It wasn't being apart for four days. They were often both home for weeks and weeks, never touching each other.

But how?

And she knew, it was simple, he's not stupid. Three phone calls during her trip, and he's a smart, perceptive man, and he knows me well, and it must have been in my voice. I'm bitter. I've been arrogant. I'm sure I wasn't trying very hard to hide it.

Oh god, I feel seventeen...

The more they went at it, the hotter she became, and still no move beyond... what did we used to say? 'Making out'...

Why this? Why isn't he furious?

And the answer to that hit her even harder.

A surge of rage rose up, and she began to wonder who it had been, and even as she began to detach from the moment, he turned up the heat, and found herself in the vast shadow of her own hypocrisy. All the answers were there, in his kiss. Everything she needed to know, she was learning in his arms.

A wave of shame rippled through her, and she realized it had passed through him, as well. And they were moving beyond it, together...

Oh, god this is hot!!!

On and on they went, rolling around the bed, skin on fire, both aching for release, and his arms and legs forbade anything beyond the embrace and the kiss. Her nipples dug into his flesh like gravel, her fingernails etching violent desire into his back. She was ready to scream, to claw him red, anything! and he would have none of it. They were going to make out - and that was how it was.

And it dawned on her. He had reignited it all, in one bright burst.

He had shown her how much he wanted her, how much he wanted them back, in an apology and an earnest offering like nothing they had ever shared. The flame between them, stone-cold for longer than she could remember, was bonfire-strong. More than passion, more than night heat - heart-fire, beyond sex, something stirring in his soul, which he lay before her with persistent tenderness.

He wound it down slowly, letting the fire dissipate into both of them as a soul-healing warmth, knowing they would take it up again before they slept tonight. The tension and desire spread through them like butter through a Thanksgiving turkey, and she felt a peace and safety with him that she couldn't remember feeling before.

Something within him had changed, and he was willing to give whatever it took, to preserve what they had.

She lay in his arms, taking it all in, and began to feel a trickle of real joy.

She forgave him. She forgave herself.

She began to plan what she was going to do to him, as the night lay before them.

Yes... they would talk tomorrow.

Second Trimester

It was, hands-down, the best lay she'd ever had.

Her eyes were drowsy-open as she inhaled sharply, which brought her fully awake, and she realized she was soaked. She had sweated all through her long t-shirt, which was bunched up around her waist, below which she was even more soaked.

She was still trembling as she absorbed the fact that it had been a dream.

Well, dream or no, it felt like she'd come, and more than a little bit. In the three weeks she'd been having these smoking-hot dreams, she described them to several friends, who either rolled their eyes and patronizingly told her the orgasms were imagined, or nodded vigorously that the same thing had happened to them, around the time they'd started to show.

Oh, that was *good!*

The after-tingle was that familiar healthy *omigod* that called for an instant replay, and she shed the t-shirt and rolled through the damp sheet toward the night table drawer for her favorite toy, and –

Oops! You're home, dear!

There he was, between her and a battery-powered encore, completely exhausted, snoring lightly. She'd forgotten this was one of his half-shift nights. He was working so much lately with his regular day job and the part-time second job, the poor dear, that she was losing track.

Hmmm...

Who needs toys, when...

She didn't bother being gentle.

She had him naked in thirty seconds, and her hands were warm and wet, working him up to full strength before he was really fully aware of what was happening. Fortunately, it had been awhile, so he had enough of a charge stored up to overcome his exhaustion. She was so wired already that she could, at least, spare him the effort of foreplay.

Wrapping a slick, sweaty arm around him, she pulled him onto her and into her with one Herculean motion and he, confused, did her bidding, but with a lumbering, half-asleep rhythm.

Oh, this won't work …

Realizing he needed a little encouragement, she grabbed his ass with both hands and dug in with her not-inconsiderable fingernails. He woke up fast, and sped up accordingly – slightly frightened - and she was sliding home in less than two minutes – and loudly enough that he was certainly wide awake now.

More …

She rolled out from under him and was on all fours, demanding his attention with familiar utterances, and he took her from behind, wobbling a bit, but responsive to her uncharacteristic commands!

Harder! Don't hold back, baby!

She thought, with amusement, of the baby, right at this moment. *I hope this little peanut doesn't mind a bumpy ride! But … what kid doesn't love a roller coaster?*

Where he found the energy, she couldn't say, but it was there. She knew how much he loved this position, with its great view and her scent and its slam-dunk finish, but for the first time she found herself finishing before he could. And she was even louder this time.

How is he not falling over?

More!

More, yes, but now compassion took over, and she pulled away and pulled him down on his back, mounting him and taking over the moving parts. It wasn't all altruism – she was masterful at hitting all of her own perfect spots this way, and hit them she did, with a slow grind that paid off faster than usual all the same. This time she sighed, a long, slow sigh with a slight moan, and as her spasmic muscles pulled at him, she knew he was almost there.

Let's give him a treat – he's earned it!

She eased off, and he made a sound of protest, before realizing she wasn't done. She turned and mounted him again, facing the other way, leaning forward – and then worked it with fire and purpose. He lasted all of thirty seconds.

Tingling, she spread her slick, warm body over his, panting onto his neck, nipping at him, licking him, happier than she could remember being. Her fingernails rode over his tired skin, and she just soaked up his warmth, letting it feed her own sated coals, appreciating him, so grateful for him, so giddy and drunk with this new-found lust. Her understanding friends had told her this would last for weeks - weeks and weeks!

Would he survive it?

He was rapidly slipping away, and she quickly spooned back into him, feeling a sleepy arm slip around her, his hand coming to rest above that occupied place within. She loved him for all his hard work, to bring in extra money ... for his patience with her moods ... his willingness to give ...

Most of all, she loved the way he was holding her.

Like he was holding a family.

Fetishes

He'd needed to hear it, couldn't get there without it. Never.
Say it! Come on, say it!
And she said it. Over and over again, from tenth grade to senior prom. Every time. She'd been shocked out of her mind the first time, which had been her first time - and, even worse, she had never used that word in her life - but two of her best friends confirmed that it was pretty common, nothing to get excited about. Preferred terminology varied; syntax was more or less invariable.

The thing was... saying it removed her completely from the moment, and though she had loved him, she'd never been able to express it that way.

She had been genuinely surprised, her freshman year in college, when the next guy hadn't needed to hear it. It was a huge relief, until... they'd gotten busy, and he hadn't gotten, well, functional. She assumed his massive overdose of beer to be the culprit, until he reached under his dorm room bed, and pulled out The Collection.

A few minutes of browsing was all it took. He became suitably inspired, and from that point forward, wasn't bad at all; without having to say anything, she was able to focus, and generally had a good time with him. She learned to occupy herself during his magazine time, and did not mind terribly when he urged her to read the letters out loud. She actually found them amusing, and bought an issue or two for herself from time to time.

Her first fiancé had ramped it up, preferring animate stimulation, and in the days of videotape, this amounted to quite a bit of shelf space. There was foreplay in his car, in her apartment, and occasionally some really fun and racy canoodling under staircases and in elevators (and once late at night on a golf course!), but the main event was always at his place, and always after a screening. She rapidly learned which were his favorites, and could pick out the more frequently-employed performers. She learned, less rapidly, to tune out his enthusiastic observations about the women - words that never seemed to come her way - and never quite learned to stop comparing herself to them.

His successor had needed pot, which seemed counter-intuitive; and the guy after that had needed alcohol and a new variation of saying-it, in combination.

And then came the real challenge... the third party, which had seemed adventurous at the time, and even benevolent when the poor dear just couldn't get into it (and oh, how she'd wanted him to!) when it was just the two of them. There had been a rush of excitement at first, until she noticed how quickly he sprang to attention for their playmate, and how he'd give her some attention for awhile, but then finish with their guest. She'd never made it to a third round.

Then came Fiancé Two, about the time the Blue Pill hit the market.

First dates were always events, with a shopping spree, new hair, the works. It distracted her from the inevitable discovery. It hadn't been an issue; that first night, he had kissed her good night (and what a kiss!!!) but hadn't made a move.

Or the second night, or the third.

She was torn between a sense of dread and a growing joy, as their time together became increasingly fun, adventurous, and close, and she began looking forward to every moment with an enthusiasm she'd never felt before. But he never pounced, and that meant... whatever he needed, it had to be worse than all the others.

She smelled wonderful kitchen smells as she entered his house, and he looked a mess - what man doesn't, when he tries to cook? Yet he made up in culinary skill what he seemed to lack in neatness, and the meal was wonderful. She knew wine well enough to know that this had cost him something, and as messy as the kitchen was, his living room was immaculate. Her favorite music was on, and there had been hand-dipped chocolate strawberries for dessert.

He's up to something... here comes his fetish... oh, god, let it not be midgets filming us, or animal sacrifice...

They watched a DVD, a romantic comedy she'd regretted missing during its theater run, and then took her by the hand...

She'd been in his bedroom before, but they'd never lingered there, and she'd never been clear just why. He kept it reasonably clean - man-clean, anyway - and tonight it was perfect. But there was more, and it took her breath away.

All around the room, on every piece of furniture, there were burning candles.

No lights on. Just candles. Dozens of them. The beauty of the moment only slowly gave way to confusion.

He needs... candles???

Her mouth was open as she surveyed the room while he softly closed the door behind her. When she felt his arms encircling her from behind, she shivered, completely taken by surprise, completely uncertain of what was next.

Without a word, he undressed her slowly, in glorious flickering light, and took her into his bed.

No saying-it, no pictures, nothing more than good food and wine... no guests...

And his eyes, eyes like she had never seen in a man before, lost in her, as candlelight bathed her naked body, eyes that shone like no man's ever had, drinking in every detail, appreciating her, glowing with longing... lingering on every part of her, every curve, every mole, every extra pound, seeing into her in a way that made her feel more beautiful than she ever had.

And then came his hands...

They were well on their way when it dawned on her that there would be no surprise... the biggest surprise of all...

As she surrendered to the first of many waves of ecstasy, moments later, she had a stray thought...*we're going to have to blow out every single one of those candles...*

And they did, exhausted, more than two hours later.

In the darkness, in his arms, there was one unthrilling surprise. He snored, just a little.

But the arms around her said something far louder, far more thrilling...

I only need you...

Left Behind

The house was disturbingly quiet.

In a bedroom upstairs, his seven-year-old daughter slept.

Here in the family room, in the midnight dark, a clock ticked. The house phone sat at his elbow. His cell phone was in his vest pocket.

Far away, in another state, he was certain that his wife's hotel room phone would not be answered. Her cell phone, he knew, would be powered off. *It was charging*, she would say.

A tumbler of half-melted ice and Maker's Mark chilled his hand as he sat in the darkness, as he numbly followed the *tick ... tick ... tick* of the clock behind him.

He swallowed another stinging burst of bourbon, grateful for the fog that was descending over his feelings. He knew where she was right now, at the "conference." He knew who she was with. He knew, and it heaped shame on top of shame, and he remembered simultaneously the bottle sitting an arm's length away, and the daughter innocently slumbering upstairs.

He idly scratched at his unshaven chin, overly aware of the gray that had crept into it ... gray she artfully removed from her own glorious hair, gray that he hoped looked "distinguished." He worked out – a lot – and jogged, and was far healthier than he should be. It was how a man with too little to do spends his free time.

Since his software royalties had dried up, and he'd only had internet articles to keep money coming in, he'd fought his feelings of inadequacy with all his might, buying used books online to keep up on the technology, and scrambling to keep enough technical articles in the pipeline to make her aware that he was trying, doing his very best, in a market where his skills were too common.

The days were so long and empty.

When she was here, they didn't talk, they didn't do anything together. She would be with their daughter, or huddled over the computer. Her vast network of friends kept her occupied, building her up, supporting her, saying God-knows-what about him. Their counselor outlined shared activities, scheduled talks, quality time opportunities, which they always pledged to pursue and never did.

He swirled the remaining ice around, idly wishing he could have another, knowing he couldn't … wanting to be numb. He knew what was happening at this very moment, and wanted to erase the awareness.

"Distant." She'd said he was "distant." That he had become cold to her, unreceptive. Well, that was probably true. He'd had no idea how to respond. *Women are so quick with words like that … it's such an easy accusation, a fast win, when men cannot explain themselves – and doesn't that just prove her point? But it isn't something men even fully understand, and if they did, the words spoken out loud would make them small and weak. Life just doesn't prepare a man for this.*

… tick … tick … tick …

Does she think I want it this way?

How could anybody want *it this way?*

What is "distant?" Having nothing to talk about? Or being uncertain of how to endure the discomfort of discussing what amount to daily humiliations? How does a man discuss his perception of himself as failure, with the one in whose eyes his failure is most devastating?

Was it "distance" when it was the other way around, and they didn't talk or share or spend time together for years because she was getting her law degree and he was looking after a toddler?

He knew it was coming.

"We need to talk."

There would be suitcases packed, and documents signed, and a cold hug goodbye, and he wouldn't just lose her, he would lose his daughter, the daughter he'd been there for, every day for seven years …

He knew, and there was nothing he could do about it, just as he couldn't magically restore his career, or conjure up the words that used to flow so easily between them.

Is there a way to explain to a woman what it is to be a man?

Is there a way to make her understand how it feels inside, to need that center, that sense of self-possession and control that empowers a man to face the world? Do men really understand it themselves, or is it just the fact of the matter? Do words that can fully capture it even exist?

Is there a way to explain to a woman how it feels to know just how much women need to see that self-possession and control in a man, to know that it's essential to their idea of manhood, part of love, part of sex, part of what makes women feel like women, and to know what a man becomes in a woman's eyes when those things have slipped away?

How do you look into the eyes of the woman you adore, and allow yourself to see that those things which used to shine in her eyes are no longer there? How can you see that, and then be expected to "talk about it?"

I need you ... more than ever ...

Where were those words?

I need for you to need me ... I need to give you those things I have always given ...

But she needed someone else now.

She had talked about "working on it," "getting it back," and he believed she had been sincere. He knew that she really did love him. But her sense of order, her idea of progression, always began with her agenda. She'd fill her life with this goal, that goal, burn endless energy chasing them, and then feel unfulfilled, all the same. And he was never made part of those things.

Maybe she was right. Maybe he needed to lead, to take the initiative, to take these challenges in hand and go down swinging. Women need to see strength in a man, it's how things work. But, for men ... strength is an idea as much as a state of being, an idea that can slip away before he knows what's happened.

... tick ... tick ... tick ...

The Maker's tasted so good ... the haze, light though it might be, was so welcome. It was a shield between him and the knowledge of where she was and who she was with and what they were doing.

It was safety. No tears would come.

Across the room, in the dark, a logo silently bounced from side to side on the computer monitor. It reminded him of Pong.

I'm old enough to remember Pong ...

... and with a sharp, familiar twinge, he suddenly stared at his own internet indiscretion, very young and very beautiful and very full of life and unaware of the gaping holes within him that weakened him like bleeding bullet wounds. Weeks of emails and chats, which became phone calls, and then that day when she traveled across three states to meet ...

He had dressed perfectly, business-casual and well-fitting enough to show off the fact that he was in far better shape than men half his age. She was almost twenty years younger, with long, dark hair, intelligent eyes, a soft smile and a body that would inspire songs. They'd met in a restaurant, and she was there waiting, watching for him, bursting into a grin when she recognized him from his pictures. He had insisted on a "chemistry test," to give her an out if they didn't click in person, but she was in his arms in the first ten seconds …

… and they were in bed within an hour, after a drink on a couch in the apartment of a friend. The preliminaries had been brief, talking and laughter and her great delight in her slow reveal, wrapping those long legs in an uncharacteristic long skirt and allowing him to discover them, wide-eyed …

They had wasted no time. They were like teenagers, heated, eager, tearing at each other's clothes.

Her body was lean and toned, powerful, radiating youth and energy, and when he gathered her up in his arms, he glowed along with her, radiating strength and resolve. His hands roamed her hungrily, with authority, with confidence he hadn't felt in years. In a few heartbeats, he was himself again, filled with power and life. She responded to his every touch with one of her own, echoing his desire with the reckless lust of youth, teasing him, drawing him in, opening herself without hesitation.

She was taller, leaner, with different eyes, different skin, different scent … smaller breasts … a lower voice … and an innocence that precluded the agonies of a shattered marriage, a failed career. All of life lay before her, unspoiled, rich with untapped energy, energy that her sweet body radiated for him with desire surpassing his own.

Her fingers danced, and youth aside, she knew what she was doing. She encouraged the animal in him, teasing him to greater aggression, making him wild. Their bodies fit well, both athletic, both lean, and they rolled as they explored one another, and it was electric.

Muscles surged beneath his skin as she awakened all that had fallen away within him, and he was a man again, strong and filled with fire, and he didn't wait for cues. She gasped when he took her, hard, and their tangle intensified. When he was close, she rolled them, putting herself on top, and took control, but in a way that proclaimed her extended need of him, a way that made him her source, her strength … and he allowed it, reveling in having enough to give that he seemed generous. Her long hair swayed above him as the waves crashed higher and higher, and he let her go all the way to the edge …

… and he took charge again, rolling them over and locking their bodies together, every muscle tensing, pouring all that remained into a forceful rhythm of his choosing… sending her over the brink, with gasping cries, and burying all of his grief, all of his torment, in the blue-hot glow. It was bright enough to allow him to see himself again, and big enough that he could wish these things for his marriage without losing the moment.

He had pulled a muscle, badly, but he managed to keep it to himself. She saw no weakness in him. No failing. She saw only the man.

How he had needed that! And yet …

Not his wife.

When he'd told her, she had of course been stunned, eviscerated … *a younger woman?* Was there a greater insult, a more callous indignity? They hadn't spoken for days.

A single chunk of ice remained. With a sigh, he let his hand fall away from the glass.

… tick … tick … tick …

There was no point in addressing the double standard. There was no point in calling her out on the stacking of the deck here, the way she had cultivated the sympathies of friends, created a circle of voices that echoed back what she wanted to hear, validating the viewpoint she had so carefully crafted. She lived in a world that told her only what she wanted to hear, dispensing permissions for all the things she wanted.

But not every set of eyes would see it her way.

There was one pair of eyes, and one pair of ears, that would know.

There was one who looked at him and didn't care how much he earned, or what his standing among his peers might be. There was one who looked at him and saw the strength that no employer, no woman, no crisis could ever take away. One who needed him, and always would.

She would never tire of his embrace, and would always seek his eyes when she needed love or comfort.

She would grow to womanhood, and she would learn the ways of her gender, through experience and observation, and she would know.

Nothing that happened, none of the trauma and ordeal to come, could change it. Not the internet or the circle of voices or the man in the hotel room tonight.

His eyes grew damp.

It would be many years from now. But there was a spark, a light, a confirmation that he had done something right, that for all his stumbling and all his mistakes, he truly was a man, and could stand tall – a spark that cut through this night, this long, terrible night that was only now beginning.

Someday, his little girl would know.

End of the Month

He sat with his face in his hands, paper piles spread before him on the dining room table. The light hanging from the ceiling above, which seemed so warm when the family was eating, somehow made him look tired.

The piles were segregated: open paid bills on one side, open unpaid bills on the other, and unopened bills behind the calculator.

Everything was in its usual place. Checkbook to the right; stamps and blank envelopes next to the calculator. Bank statement next to the open-unpaid pile. It was a monthly ritual, always this precise, right down to the bourbon with the melting ice.

The ritual would end in dejection, with slumped shoulders, with a vague air of defeat. He would not be smiling. The piles of paper always balanced out in the end, but sometimes it was close. And on those nights, it was written in his eyes.

But she had rituals of her own.

The kids had gone down early, as they always did on this night, and a single candle burned in the room beyond. A fresh drink was ready in the kitchen.

She waited patiently as the tap-tap-tap of calculator keys continued, followed by the scratch of the pen and the tearing of another check from the checkbook. Again ... and again, until she heard a final assault of numbers upon the keypad, followed by his signature sigh.

And she was silently there behind him, her fingers beginning to work his knotted neck and shoulders, digging out the tension and depression with firm and loving intensity. He slowly relaxed into it, saying nothing.

Eventually he rose from the table, as if he didn't know what was coming next, reaching to put away his work, feeling her hand grasp his upper arm and squeeze, telling him to leave it. He turned, and the new drink appeared, and he followed her into the bedroom, where she vanished into the bathroom on the other side, to change into something, but also to give him time to finish the drink.

And she came back out, and undressed him slowly, and pulled him down …

You mean so much to us …

The shoulder rub continued now as a full backrub, and she had gone to considerable effort to learn how to do it right, even buying a book and a video last year. She straddled him, her motions unhurried, deep and slow and ungentle. An occasional moan escaped him, letting her know she was getting to it, and as always she kept at it until she sensed he was truly relaxed.

She bent down, kissing the back of his neck slowly, kissing his shoulders, leaning up again and running her fingernails down his back. She briefly appreciated his still-muscular form, once athletic, as taut as three trips a month to the gym could keep it, trips squeezed in between overtime at the office and yard work and T-ball coaching.

You work so hard …

She rolled him over slowly, still straddling his naked form, met his eyes. This part she loved, and candlelight just made it work. She gave him a slow smile, a simmering smile, her eyes bright with lust and candlefire as she slid a hand under one strap, then the other, shedding the bra … her breasts were baby-chewed, in her opinion not quite as spectacular as they'd been five years ago, but candlelight flattered them and his eyes were fixed as she felt her nipples swell … and another swelling began.

Oh, this part she *really* loved … She was proud of her body, and even with the kids being as young as they were, her part-time job gave her twice as many trips to the gym each month as he got. And moments like this were the pay-off.

She closed her eyes, tossed back her hair and began to sway, her panties grinding against his increasing firmness. Now she gave him a visual feast, running the backs of her fingernails across his stomach and up hers, till her fingertips found her breasts, and she began caressing herself in front of him …

This was practically hypnosis, and his eyes locked in a daze on the display as she kneaded herself as sensuously as she did in more private moments, moaning freely, releasing all inhibition.

At his best, he was virile and aggressive, and many nights he would leap on her like a tiger that hadn't been fed in a week. Tonight, he was tired and half-drunk, and if it were left to him to perform, it would probably be a modest performance at best. The show she gave him set that worry aside. The performance tonight would be hers, the very best she could offer.

Our home is wonderful …

Now she bent down over him, her body covering him like a blanket, her hair falling around their two faces like a tent. His hands came to her hips as she kissed him deeply, continuously, deliberately. In this space she sheltered him, creating a quiet pocket of passionate comfort and seclusion. Nothing could intrude; even the candlelight was obscured as the kiss deepened.

She covered him with all her warmth … with all her need … with the comfort and promise of the trust she placed in him, the admiration she felt for him … and in this way she told him he was her home, her refuge, and she wanted to be his …

The kids adore you …

Now she leaned back again, this time to receive, not for herself but for him … his hands drifted from her hips, encompassing her stomach, making that swirling motion she knew so well. She always felt a trace of reverence from him when he touched her like this, his fingertips expressing something close to awe as he caressed that place where their babies had grown. A forefinger traced the stretch marks that no longer embarrassed her, and after a lingering moment his hands found her breasts. He fondled them with a touch so different from her own, his eyes closed, his breathing quickened …

But even that can't compare to what you mean to me …

Her dampness was now outright wetness, and she felt herself surrendering to his hands, and had to pull free, remembering her task.

Backing away, she eased off of him, crawling downward, kissing his stomach as she went, downward farther still ... to give him the treat he loved so much.

She'd gone slowly all evening, as if determined to outlast the candle – but now she took it to a whole new level, a lazy, tantalizing tease. She worked him artfully, sensuously, in agonizing rhythm, weaving a spell that had his pulse and breathing almost suspended, as if he might shatter the sensation with one false move. She sped up; she slowed down; she took it to the point of torture.

She took him right to the edge. God, he'd earned it. But there needed to be more.

You're a man and a half, and I'm proud to walk through life beside you ...

They needed to join ...

She finished her delicious tease, drawing a short burst of protest, and slid off her panties. She straddled him once again, this time taking the object of her attention in hand and guiding it into her, easing down with almost cruel slowness, squeezing him rhythmically, until he was as deep as he'd ever been.

And now she leaned back, steadying herself with her hands on his legs, and began to move up and down ... not easy, but she knew she would not tire, no matter how long they took ...

Each surrendered to this excruciating joy, to oneness that was strong in a moment that was fragile and unbearably tender, letting the fierce tension mount within a connection that drew each of them from very different places into a perfect unity.

She gave herself in earnest, but the truth she didn't speak to herself was that this position could easily be considered selfish, as it just thumped away on all her sweetest spots - and as she felt him peaking, spasms began to thunder through her. She cried out, more than once, and he followed her with a release that threatened to wake the children.

Before he finished she threw herself forward, still gasping from her own tremors, and clenched her body hard to his as he erupted into fierce thrusts. His arms wrapped around her like steel cables, holding her tight, as their panting subsided, as the heat persisted, as all of the unspoken things settled like dew upon them both.

Long moments passed.

She didn't move for a long time, remaining draped over him like a blanket until his breathing settled into deep slumber. Then she leaned over and blew out the candle, pulling a blanket over them both and nestling into him.

Thank you ...

The Scarf

The air around her felt cold – maybe it was the darkness – and she pulled the comforter more tightly around her, bunching it up at her neck.

A full moon was easing into the bedroom window frame, throwing dark-blue shadow across the bed. It filled her with dread; and she idly wondered, suddenly, if moonlight had ever made her feel differently.

She heard the sigh of warm air stirring in a vent and realized that the chill she felt wasn't really in the air. Her tendency to feel cold had been life-long – she couldn't remember a time when it had been otherwise. She rearranged her legs, unconsciously seeking a comfortable position for motionlessness. He would be home soon.

She was well-insulated, pajamas over a t-shirt, making her chill all the more surreal. When he came home drunk and she was asleep, or pretending to be, the number of layers she was wearing often ran up against the limits of his persistence. It had worked many times. But not all the time.

Her arm ached.

Three glasses of Riesling and she was wandering back, and the conscious thought took hold that she hadn't invented this routine for him, or for the man she'd been with before, or the one before that. She'd been bundling up like this, avoiding, almost since she'd been a girl.

Since the Incident at the Family Reunion?

He would be home soon, drunk, and what happened next would depend on how much money he'd lost. She prayed for sleep, but it never came. She would, as always, pretend, and hope to wait him out.

As the moon came fully into view, lighting up the room, she felt exposed and vulnerable, but not enough to get up and close the curtains. If he came in while she was out of bed …

Her thoughts drifted back to her college days, and how her dorm room window had caught the moon in just this way. And it was autumn again, that day at the commons, that terrible scene with her boyfriend …

He'd been worse than the others, verbal as well as physical, demeaning and harsh, and not particularly concerned about who saw what, when they were in public. She had learned to cover up, to keep her head down. She remembered the commons, the next day … cold wind, leaves fluttering like angels' wings … bunching her jacket around her neck, as she was doing with the comforter right now …

Head down, she'd almost run smack into the boy in the gray wool coat, and her muttered apology brought the first smile she could remember receiving all semester.

Aren't you freezing?

What's your name?

Here, take my coat, I'll walk you to your next class …

… and he'd launched into the reasons why he wore such a totally geeky coat, it had been his grandfather's, his grandfather had written for a newspaper, he wanted to be a journalist, and he talked and talked, and she walked in terror that her boyfriend would see them together, wishing he would go away.

She had returned the coat with a half-smile and a minimally-polite Thank You and vanished into class.

And there he was, the next day. And the day after that. And the day after that.

He was just slightly taller than she was, not as muscular as the men she'd been with … very gentle features, not a particularly deep voice. Incredibly polite and friendly … nothing like the men she usually wound up with. He laughed easily, smiled easily, and there came a day when she began to venture a smile herself. Lord knows he knocked himself out trying to draw it out of her, with horrible jokes and clever observations.

Every day he walked with her. He never asked for more.

Early December, and he was carrying a bag. Very theatrically he pulled out a very beautiful, very expensive lavender scarf and wrapped it around her, standing closer to her than he'd ever been. For the first time, she really saw his eyes … for the first time, he really saw hers, and what he saw there caused him to frown slightly.

Finals Week, and her roommate met her in the lobby of their dorm.

He's up in the room and he's really really pissed ... you can't go up there now!

Her boyfriend had found the scarf. He knew how much money she didn't have, and had assumed it was a gift. He'd torn it to pieces.

Again, the plea for her to go to the police. Again, the reminder of the shelter for women, here on campus. Again, she didn't hear.

She hugged her roommate, assured her she'd be fine, and walked out of the dorm. Then she ran, hoping, praying ...

He wasn't there. But she waited, and waited, and finally saw the familiar gray wool coat, and ran to him.

I've never seen where you live, she had babbled, and she swept him off whatever course he'd been on. It turned out he lived in a third-floor walk-up, decades old, shared with three roommates who were finished with finals and already headed home for the holidays. He'd put on music, and she had finally let herself laugh at his jokes, and she had suddenly broken ...

Hold me ...

It was a very different full moon, a bright moon, a once-in-a-lifetime moon, shining into the warmth of his too-small bed. He was different, not muscle-bound and twice her size, and gentle, and slow, and in his arms, she felt ... beautiful, for the first time.

His lips and fingertips explored her with wonder, taking time, awaiting her responses, even needing them, before proceeding, filling her with unfamiliar feelings. He demanded nothing, took nothing, shared everything, and she could not connect this moment to any other she had lived. That was okay; she wanted it to last and last.

And he had kissed her with a tenderness that made the moment feel desperately delicate, as though the slightest tremor would shatter it.

And yet ... there was a tremor, later, a deep and happy tremor, and it was new to her.

Her tears spilled onto his shoulder. He asked. She couldn't answer.

When he finally fell asleep, she slipped away. She never walked through the commons again.

Tears began to spill onto her pillow. She reached into the pillowcase.

She wondered, as the moon began to slip away, where he might be tonight, all these years later. There was no question in her mind that wherever he was, he was happy. And the piece of him she carried was her one reminder that such a thing was out there, possible, somewhere ...

A distant rattle and thud told her the bedroom door would open soon.

Slowly, quietly exhaling, she wiped her eyes a final time, and tucked the surviving patch of scarf back into her pillowcase.

Not That Into You

There he sat, alone in the booth, without a care in the world. Black leather jacket, hair mussed, long-neck beer bottle. If he'd noticed her, he gave no sign.

He looked much the same as he had when she'd seen him last, at her brother's Super Bowl party. He'd told her about this place. He'd talked about the kind of woman he was into, although she couldn't quite tell if he had been serious. As she approached him, she concluded that he couldn't have been. He gave a half-nod and a half-smile when he saw her, did not budge from his comfortable sprawl in the corner of the booth as she sat down across from him.

You're doing it all wrong!

Amused, he submitted to her energetic lecture as she pointed out his various mistakes. He was just sending all the wrong signals. Hadn't he seen "He's Just Not That Into You?" Didn't he understand that how a man presents himself makes all the difference? The woman he wanted wouldn't get anywhere near him if he kept sending out this vibe.

When a man's not interested, he's not interested, and women today TOTALLY get that, she informed him. If you don't show that you're interested, she'll completely miss you!

Are you listening to me?

He killed off the beer with a ghost of a smile, waving the bottle at a server - not offering her anything - and she held up two fingers at the server as she returned to her lecture. Women let the disinterested male drift by today, she insisted. You've got to put yourself out there! Show some interest!

The beers arrived and she took a breath.

No, he hadn't seen *He's Just Not That Into You*, first, he wasn't a woman, and second, everything she was saying was wrong.

She sighed, and prepared to start over.

Let me see if I've got this straight...

He stood slowly and pulled off his jacket, handing it to her. He tucked in his shirt, pulled a comb out of his back pocket and straightened out his hair.

Watch closely...

He left the booth and headed for the bar, his expression eager, his motions rapid. He sought out the first attractive woman who seemed unattached and approached her in the friendliest, most polite way, sitting on the bar stool next to her, leaning toward her, maintaining eye contact. They were too far away for her to hear what was being said, but he was clearly driving the conversation. He seemed to offer to buy her a drink, and she seemed to decline. In less than two minutes, he smiled politely and shrugged, and moved on. This time he approached a pair of women, leaning in, smiling, obviously interested - and lasted a few minutes longer.

He turned her direction and shrugged again.

Now watch this...

He un-tucked his shirt and put the jacket back on, then mussed his hair again. Beer in hand, he walked slowly, deliberately, to another corner of the club, found an empty booth, and adopted exactly the posture he'd had when she'd first spotted him: leaning back, taking up twice as much space as he needed, disengaged, like he had all the time in the world and nothing to do. When an attractive woman passed, he would survey her openly, without apology, and look away.

In less than five minutes, a woman he didn't know was sitting with him. He remained in his laid-back posture. She leaned his direction as they began to chat. His smoky stare and easy smile projected no interest, only amusement. It was clear that the woman offered to buy him another beer, and he shrugged a negative.

When he returned to his original booth, he had her phone number in his hand.

Do you want to see that again?

She was just blown away. *That was amazing!*

He didn't seem very interested in explaining it. She persisted, however, fascinated, and he dispensed tiny morsels of male reasoning, there in the booth, until the crowd and the music were too loud to talk over. She insisted he come back to her apartment to continue the conversation, and he shrugged and went along. She didn't notice that he left the phone number in his beer bottle.

When she'd gotten everything out of him that he was going to let loose of, she offered music, food, DVDs - and he asked if she had any coloring books. She set aside her astonishment and dug out some crayons and an activity book she kept around for her niece, and they sprawled out on the living room floor, coloring, wine glasses on the coffee table. And then on to her stuffed animal collection, in her bedroom, with which he demonstrated his idea of childrearing techniques.

It wasn't until she was pulling his shorts away and kissing her way back up his left leg that it dawned on her.

It wasn't until he was body-painting her naked form with cream cheese and strawberry jam, giving meticulous concentration to the bumpy flesh around her nipples, and flourishes along her inner thighs, that she realized how completely un-random the evening had actually been.

It was during their steaming-hot shower, bathroom light out and single candle burning on the sink, when she was dying for him to take her there, leaning against the towel bar, that she realized how undercover the other gender really was, and how much the movie had left unsaid...

It was in her bed, in the dark, where he tended all the usual spots but found others no man had ever probed - the tip of his tongue finding that place just below her vulva... his teeth artfully tugging her nipples without actually biting (how did he *do* that?)... the heel of his hand pressing into the small of her back as she rode him, throwing hot sparks into her slow grind - that she realized he'd been right about everything, all of it to the last detail.

And it was much later, when she felt his light breathing on the back of her neck, felt his oh-so-warm body spooned to hers, and his arm around the front of her, holding her tightly - that she realized how premeditated it had all been, and who had really been into whom.

And she had never in her life been so happy to be wrong...

Shower

She awoke earlier than usual, for no particular reason.

He was not lying next to her, and glancing at the clock, she realized that he was already up and moving, as usual. It was still dark, before sunrise.

She eased out of bed, stretched, and noticed the light coming from the bathroom door, which hadn't closed all the way. Beyond, she could hear the shower running.

A thought occurred. *I'll surprise him …*

As she approached the bathroom, however, she caught his image in the mirror above the sink, which hadn't fogged up, because the door was open and the heat of the shower was escaping.

The view of the walk-in shower was … quite a view.

Omigod, is he … ?

He was.

Fascinated, she crept as close to the door as she dared. She could see everything, not quite perfectly, but well enough. There he stood, naked, wet, muscular, and highly stimulated, and deeply caught up in continuing the stimulation.

They had, a number of times, had such experiences, together, lying side by side (which she considered pretty progressive) but at such times, she'd never had a view approaching this one. She could see exactly what his hands were doing, the expression on his face …

This was more than just fascinating. This was seriously turning her on.

His face, eyes closed, mouth slightly open, almost grimacing, looked similar to how it did when he was above her (or, for that matter, below her) but somehow more intense. Enthralled, she realized that it probably was more intense … faster, more focused … and she found herself studying his face, studying his hands, soaking up the details. She found herself comparing the way he touched himself to the way she touched him. She wondered what the differences were.

A slight sigh escaped him. He was, of course, trying not to wake her, but she recognized the sound, the expression, the tension –

He erupted, at great length and with considerable force, and she thought, almost involuntarily, *what a waste!*

She was completely revved up, but appreciative of the education she had just received. And it suddenly occurred to her that she was in a unique position to give just such an education.

Tip-toeing, she turned back to the bed, removing her t-shirt in the process, and spread herself out on the bed.

Morning light was just starting to trickle in, and she was careful to choose a position that would give him a good view through the half-open bathroom door.

She heard the shower turn off, and busied herself, already pretty far into it from the show she'd just been given.

If I'm going to show him, no point in going halfway, she thought, double-teaming herself as she often did in private moments, one hand working her breasts, the other farther down. Determined to make this little show educational, she was equally fixed on giving herself as big a treat as he'd gotten in the shower.

She was, well, rough. She loved having her breasts handled, and loved handling them herself, and when her nipples were hard, she loved handling them even harder. The poor dear, he sort of got this – he would nip at them lightly – but he was still a little too gentle for her.

Maybe seeing this would inspire him!

She could hear water running in the sink, but it was never interrupted, so she knew he was just creating noise – he must be watching!

If she was rough up top, she was even rougher down in the Netherlands, where her fingers flew, making circles (*take note! Circles!*) hard and fast, keeping her fingers wet, and finally, as she felt the explosion closing in, went inside with her other hand, stimulating herself from both directions as her body clenched and prepared for ecstasy.

She hovered, briefly, suddenly a bit self-conscious, but the energy she'd built up was overwhelming. As the spasms began, and a sudden surge of wetness surged over her aching fingers, she breathed in sharply, almost biting her tongue to keep from crying out. Her back arched sharply, and she drank in that delicious tensed-muscle pleasure that made coming so much better. Hard to do with him on top, always a treat when she was.

She stopped at just the right moment, about two-thirds of the way through the spasms, that push that kept them rolling without sending that too-sensitive after-jolt through her. *Another lesson for him,* she thought: he didn't quite have the hang of knowing when to back off, and sometimes squelched an otherwise successful orgasm by pushing into that overly-sensitive moment.

In just a few minutes, she'd managed to make a huge wet spot all by herself, hopefully given him as good a show as he'd given her, and even more hopefully had inspired him back to full attention – right now, she wanted nothing more than for him to lose it, to burst into the room and take her hard, really *really* hard …

As her breathing began to slow back down and her heart began to calm, it dawned on her that he wasn't coming out, and she was suddenly baffled. She was sure he'd been watching! If he'd actually been shaving, or whatever, the sound of the water wouldn't have been so steady …

She rolled off the bed, naked, and tip-toed to the bathroom.

He was, of course, back in the shower …

The Kiss

It felt like a death.

If felt like that space, days after a funeral, after the tears have been cried, when a deeper sorrow comes, an ache so vast that tears will no longer come, when you realize that someone you love with all your being is beyond your reach forever. And that, indeed, was what she now faced.

The man she'd walked with, laughed with, raised a daughter with, fought with... held and loved and laid down beside, all these years... was cold and beyond reach, not in the ground, but in the past... forever untouchable, forever lost. For weeks, she had cried, and now her sorrow was ocean-vast, and she just floated, chilled, exhausted.

Standing in the darkness of the hotel room, she was momentarily very self-aware, feeling a slight chill. She realized, as a brief embarrassment accused her, that she had over-dressed for the cocktail she'd just shared downstairs in the hotel lounge. Her hair, outfit, perfume --- all calculated to seem indifferent while still being fabulous. She was so skilled at this, after so many years of being the woman who gets not two looks but three, that she could dismiss it as reflex --- but in her heart of hearts, she knew the truth, and she felt sixteen again.

He was an old friend, nothing more, but one who cut through all those layers of propriety that she navigated so expertly. Even as kids, he'd had those eyes that looked right into her, beyond the exterior that every other boy found so delightfully disturbing, and a mind that leapt to understanding at the slightest cue. And a voice without guile, the teasing, laughing, affectionate voice of a brother who would solder all her bra clasps together, but would suffer black eye and cracked rib without a second thought, defending her. When they'd met tonight, she'd been unable to remember how long it had been since she'd seen him.

Eyes and a voice she could completely trust, and did, tonight, all these years later.

He'd let her talk about her failed marriage, and said a few words about his... he'd let her drink just a little too much but not way too much, and he'd looked at her with those eyes, and spoken in that voice, to reassure her and comfort her and give to her, without condition, without any trace of the usual despicable male agenda. In the darkness, she idly touched her hand, remembering the kind warmth of his. They'd lingered, but it had ended too soon. She had felt so unburdened, being able to tell him the things she hadn't told her family, or even her therapist. Even the most embarrassing things. She knew it was okay, and she had needed to say them.

Without turning on the light, she stepped out of her jeans and unbuttoned her blouse, feeling her way to the bathroom, where she splashed warm water on her cheeks. Bending over the sink, she realized her muscles ached, and felt a surge of mixed gratitude and regret that she would now lie down, alone, and release it all.

Turning out the bathroom light and moving toward the bed, she was startled by a knock on the door...

She jumped at the sound, and her heart raced. It was, what, one o'clock in the morning??? Involuntarily, she surged toward the door, and her response was so wearily impulsive that she didn't even flinch at the realization that the conflict between the men she wished to see in that moment was already settled. And the alcohol was probably to blame for the fact that she had already turned the doorknob and half-opened the door before she realized she was standing there in panties and undone blouse.

And, of course, he seemed not to notice at all.

For the first time in a lifetime of knowing one another, he didn't wait for a cue. He stepped into the darkness, closing the door behind him, and she felt his fingers on her shoulder. Without a beat, she leaned into his arms, which enfolded her with a warmth and completeness she hadn't felt in many years. Tears welled, and in two heartbeats, she was sobbing.

Strong arms tightened around her, as if never to let her go, and she wept and wept, weeks of torment and disappointment and loss soaking into his shirt, her sobs loud against his chest, and his fingertips crept into her hair and massaged her neck, and his lips brushed her forehead, promising comfort. He stood unwavering as she leaned into him, letting it out, for a full ten minutes.

He could have carried her to the bed and she wouldn't have cared. As it was, she was not fully aware of how they got there, but the sheets were cool and she felt so safe and she was so deeply grateful not to be alone that she didn't question it. A trickle of moonlight outlined his form next to her, and there was a brief pause as she wiped her face and took a deep breath. She knew, as surely as she knew her name, that there was no chance in the universe that he would ever, ever exploit this moment, and yet it occurred to her that it would be just fine with her if he did. His pause was for her, and it empowered her, and she loved him all the more for that.

She cast aside her blouse, but more for its inconvenience than anything else. She sank into the bed, and he did the same. Calmly, deliberately, and with slowly returning strength, she nestled into him. He received her gently but firmly, enfolding her body in arms and legs - where had his trousers gone? - without eroticism, but with an intimacy that was opening her more fully than passion ever had.

Breathing deeply, her sobs and tears receding, she became aware of her own skin, of his, of the incredible warmth he gave off. She pulled back a bit, seeking his eyes in the darkness, then began to unbutton his shirt - not as prelude, but simply to experience his warmth. She lay again in his arms, her cheek against his bare chest, reveling in the safety of the moment, in their shared strength, in his understanding, in a love so pure it stirred a new hope within her, like the seed of an unborn child burrowing into womb.

Suddenly he breathed deeply, and she wondered for an instant what this moment was costing him. She was grateful for her bra, which would hopefully hide any sign of arousal, knowing that it would remain as firmly in place as if he had soldered the clasp (and she smiled, remembering how he'd bragged in the past that he could open them with one hand). And she realized that his own signpost was carefully kept from contact with her, so that she wouldn't know one way or the other. How was he doing that? He must be pulling a muscle somewhere, the poor dear. God bless him... !

This was a comfort unique in her lifetime. A perfect moment, exactly what she needed, from the one man willing to give it.

She relaxed more fully, and his arms tightened. She was suddenly aware of his scent, calming and welcome and masculine, and suddenly wondered about her own - now that would be a dead giveaway - but he seemed as relaxed as she. Her arms slid around his back, and she lay with her face to the side, finding and listening to his heartbeat. It was like a song, and it draw her in, filling her with peace. One of his hands slid between them, to her chest, softly pressing, finding her own heartbeat... and a wave of almost unbearable tenderness swept over her, bringing her almost to tears again, stirring her, lifting her.

When had she felt this loved?

She pulled back, again seeking his face, and his hand found her cheek and eased her head to the pillow. He shifted, slightly above her now, and as he gazed down on her, she could make out the gleam of his eyes, in moonlight.

And she suddenly knew that, while the perfection of the moment would be unspoiled by the dance of genes, there would be an event.

There would be no sex at all between them tonight. But there would be lovemaking.

She could feel his face only inches away, and felt that point-of-no-return closeness between lips approaching, that fleeting space when a woman decides...

There are kisses and there are kisses, and she knew them all. There was a kiss that always happens in this particular configuration of man-with-woman, the ancient, familiar Fuck Me Kiss. She fully expected it, was ready for it, was surprised to find herself accepting it, even eager for it.

There are kisses and there are kisses, and she *thought* she knew them all.

It began with a tenderness usually reserved for one's children, the loving reassurance after a scraped knee or a broken heart, the deep and unconditional love and affection that the kiss states clearly will always be there... her heart responded as his lips softly touched hers, and there was a surge she didn't fight, and they entwined in that melting way that is always prelude to the deepest entwining - but not tonight. His lips pressed deeper, but not in pursuit, and strength flowed through his arms as he took control of the dialog, confident of her attention and acquiescence.

Where tenderness usually dissolves into lust, he held back heat and maintained warmth, allowing their entangled limbs to move, but only with slowness and calm. She felt him mustering strength, and realized he was refusing to let this tenderness dissipate. How is it possible to do that? How can we be here, where we are, and not move forward??? The tension held them back, but also drove her nuts! How can he keep control?

The kiss was becoming something else, hovering on one side of passion, unbridled in affection and depth, but steering around lust... the faint taste of alcohol, a warmth of primeval familiarity, the taste of

130

need, the taste of complete acceptance... inevitable stirrings surged, and she knew he could not possible be immune, but his attention was so deeply within the kiss that she could not help but be amazed: men are always on to other things, in their minds, during this kiss! Yet he could not let it go. He wanted this kiss. The kiss itself is what's important to him. He needs to give me this! She melted more deeply into him, following him with uncompromising trust.

You are special... you are precious to me...

Their mouths were open, but unexplored... that kind of kiss, yet not that kind of kiss... arms and legs freely flowing now, immersed in the melting, tantalizing but not... becoming one being, but without the genetic violence...

I believe in you... I will always be here, always...

All attempts to obfuscate desire were gone --- if his nipples are hard, then it's okay if mine are, goddammit! --- but it simply didn't matter. They would not go there. It was okay to want, and even to need... but desire would be soothed in another way, this night.

I am not yours, you are not mine... but I do love you, so much, in ways I've never loved before...

She was completely aroused, and no longer cared what either of them thought about it, and any outcome was bliss to her. Where was this coming from??? And he suddenly tensed, and grabbed her without boundaries, taking complete control. And the kiss became something else again.

And she realized, breathless, that they were not hovering on the near side of passion... they were beyond passion, far to the other side, in that place where most people can never go without sex. He held her as if she was part of him, permanent, till death tore him away, and his kiss became hot and purposeful. Tension flowed between their bodies as their embrace tightened almost beyond bearing, and something happened within her, dizzying and electrifying, and realization rippled through her in waves...

He has given me something he has never given before...

Strength flooded into her, and she pulled him to her, matching him, surpassing him, taking the control he had just unleashed, and gathering it into herself... Strength she hadn't felt in years, affirmation, authority, celebration... and suddenly he was so vulnerable, she knew that a lesser woman could destroy him with a word. And she then knew, with stunned realization, what this night had cost him.

In the moonlight, she saw the boy... sixteen, so long ago... the brother, the prankster... who teased and defended her, and in some quiet chamber of his heart, adored her... and she found a new store of love within herself that she'd never known was there, like that trunk-in-the-attic archive of love we unpack for a newborn child... and the kiss was now hers, tender again, adoring in return, strong and equally purposeful... and a trembling crept through her as she realized what had happened, to bring them to this place.

His body had given hers all that it had to give... he had offered all of his strength, all of his trust, all of his hope, all of his love, to her, in his most vulnerable way... he had held absolutely nothing back from her... something permanent, something unique had passed between them, born in this moment... and she would never, ever be the same...

Thank you...

She realized she had rolled them over, and she lay on top of him, his arms holding her firmly, her breasts warm against him, their legs entangled, their passion obvious and strong but almost trivial... and she knew that the moment was hers to end, and that he was offering that... but she needed to give to him in return, and signaled it by lifting slightly, and shifting one of his hands to her breast...

Full circle, she gave him adolescent permission, and they were sixteen again... And he rolled them to their sides, equal, neither in control, and the kiss became something completely new... the tentative, awkward fumbling of the young, brought to life again. And his mouth changed, and sought her anew as ancient echoes from his young soul crept out across the decades. It was now the kiss of youth, of wonder, of promise in the stars on summer nights, promise that neither of them had found, for all their searching, in their years of wandering... but she returned the kiss, with a girl's eagerness, with fire and light and joy, with the safe and fragile passions of the young, with tongues and happy mistakes, and they both found that childlike light renewed... sweet geezus, what a gift!!!

The promise is still out there, waiting for us... we've failed, both of us, but we have a second chance...

And as I search, I will always have this night to guide me...

She left it to him to end the kiss. Time had dissolved. It had been the longest kiss either had ever shared.

And it was her turn to be the one to hold on as if she'd never let go.

132

He would stay the night... by God, he'd better!!!... but he'd slip out before morning light, to spare her any awkwardness. She knew she would awake alone.

And she knew, as she felt his breathing fade into slumber, and a final, joyous tear spilled from her, that she would never, ever be alone again...

Trio

She searched herself again for desire, and finding only the barest trickle, simply hoped it would come.

Again, his favorite game. Again, she, the facilitator, he, the recipient.

It had not been this way in the beginning. In the early weeks of their relationship, he had been so attentive, so accommodating, so available... and she had treasured that, after so many years of feeling invisible.

He let out a moan, and it occurred to her that the sound no longer thrilled her. She didn't stop, but there was a change within her in that moment, and her thoughts began to drift...

I am going to leave her... it's just going to take some time...

How many times had he told her that?

She looked down at his body, and what a work of art it was - she still felt that, as strongly as ever. But even now, really working it, she found herself almost unable to really respond. Something was changing.

How did I get here?

He had spotted her a mile off, she had realized... lonely, hurting, empty, needing to be filled up with someone - and he was just so unhappy, so unfulfilled... so neglected by that selfish, demanding wife of his. It had been easy to believe, early on. She had needed so badly to be needed.

And then these fantasies and games had begun, and been so much fun! She had felt wicked, desired... and the little voice in the back of her mind had been easy to ignore.

When she was with him, she felt something different. She saw something different in the mirror. She had begun to see what he saw. When she was with him, that's who she became.

He moaned again, more loudly this time, and her attention snapped back to the moment. Nope. Still nothing.

A thought occurred.

I'm me again.

I'm with him, but I'm me again!

She glanced at the clock. Less than forty-five minutes... he had said they would have to hurry, she couldn't stay. No worries about the little woman, she was visiting relatives. His friends were coming over to watch some ball game. The thought passed quickly, as she returned to her realization.

Always what he *wants... always what* he *needs...*

Would it ever be her turn again?

Deep in her heart, she'd already realized that he wasn't going to leave his wife. Deep in her heart, she knew what this really was, and her true role.

And now, in this erotic heat, this endlessly repeated moment of service, she felt it like a chainsaw ripping through her soul. She had been split in two. He had taken the woman that she had been, broken, still searching, unsure, and rebuilt her into someone else - twisted into a shape that pleased him, patched with promises and gifts. As long as she provided what he wanted, as long as she was willing to do this, to be here, to cater...

An electric jolt ran through her, and it wasn't the usual one. It was... rage, so fierce that a tear threatened to fly out of her as she worked it, worked it, and his moan this time sounded grotesque...

Suddenly she was looking at her other self, the woman he had created, the woman she had been these past few months, and she felt ashamed. Who had she become? How had he done this? Why had he done this?

Worse - *how could I have allowed him to do it?*

This isn't who I am!!!

He let out a cry...*oooo, he's so close. And, of course, company is about to arrive...*

Well, you're with me now, boy, not your little fantasy girlie...

It wasn't just conscience. It was resolve.

Right is right, and wrong is wrong, and this is wrong!

This isn't who I am.

She decided, with the force of a bank vault slamming shut.

Now you've had your fantasy of being with two women at the same time...

He was right on the edge...

She rolled off the bed, scooped up her clothes and her self-respect, throwing on her coat without even bothering to dress. Behind her, he cried out, frustrated and completely confused.

You're a grown man... figure it out!!!

As the front door closed behind her, she heard him cry out again, pleading.

Oh, he's not worth the trouble.

Let his beer buddies untie him...

Pillow

Even in the dead of winter, they always slept naked.

Her strategy was to have a space heater cranking on her side of the bed. His strategy was to have an extra comforter on top of the first comforter, on his side of the bed.

They both liked having the other naked at all times, and they both liked unfettered access.

Except for …

That damned pillow.

He was tall and broad-shouldered, which was delicious in many ways. But these yummy traits also triggered most of the downside of mammalian bipedalism, including backaches. When sleeping on his side, he needed a pillow between his knees to prevent the onset of a backache.

And the pillow just annoyed the daylights out of her.

It was always, *always,* in her way. It had reached the point of drawing muttered curses and an exaggerated fling across the room whenever she had to get it out of her determined path. What made it worse was that this always amused him.

On this particular night, she got to him just as he was rolling over, pillow in hand, and before he could imprison it between his knees. It was a splendid move: as he rolled toward her and lifted one knee, pulling the pillow over from behind him, her thigh slid firmly and warmly over his, and presto! She became his knee pillow.

He pulled her in close, and they kissed a kiss that provoked choruses of angels. She needed this, lots of skin on skin, cuddling, near-constant contact. She'd always had trouble getting to the mountain peak, not just with him but with anyone, and it usually took an exceptionally long session with her on top, completely in control, to get her there. Most of the time, he couldn't take it for as long as she needed it, and that would be that. And it never happened with him on top. As it was, every little bit helped, to get her there at all.

She let them simmer, crock-pot slow, letting him wrap himself around her, fingernails teasing hot skin, legs intertwined like pipe cleaners in an arts and crafts class. Taking her cue, he worked the kiss, prolonging, exploring, even experimenting a little. *Oh, this one is going to be good …*

He was making noises, which was always promising, animal noises that usually accompanied an aggressive enthusiasm that always made her feel unbearably feminine. And oh, he smelled *so* good!

She loosened herself slightly from her nestled position, making space for a southward hand – not that she wasn't already fully aware of his status – and started doing that thing she did, to bring him completely to the level of rigidity that their approaching posture would require. He soaked up the sensation, moaning appropriately, and rolled onto his back to give her room to work.

She really needed the fireworks this time around, so the more prep, the better, and she abandoned fingers for her more effective instrument, kissing her way down his chest as she went. As good as he smelled, he always tasted even better, and she loved this part. But this required an even more delicate balance: her oral attention could turn him into carbon steel, but it could sometimes set him off, and tonight of all nights she needed him to hang in there! She decided to go slowly, keep things simmering but not rushed.

She had mastered a trick that she was pretty sure he'd never caught. When she was going down on him, using one hand in the process, she usually positioned herself so that she could use her other hand to bring herself up to speed. Flat on his back, with no view but the ceiling, he couldn't see. This time, more than ever, she needed that boost, which had the added benefit of truly signaling her own readiness for the main event.

She mounted him quickly, impatiently, but almost with a sense of tremendous relief, as if she was sinking into a hot tub after a long workout. A sound escaped her, and she felt herself squeezing him hard as she lowered herself all the way. Oh, he was huge! She had done well.

Leaning back, she went into the familiar rhythm, seeking out *that spot* and working it, slowly at first. She knew what worked, and while it required a real effort to make it happen, she would get there in the end, if nothing went wrong.

He moaned with her, more loudly than usual, and in the back of her mind she remained aware that timing was everything here. He had to last for as long as it took.

Almost there ... almost there ... and ...

Now!

She leaned forward, into the final impassioned stage, from the sweet scratch of *that spot* inside her to the rigorous, relentless bump and grind of her enflamed button against his pubic bone, the bump and grind that would bring her home in mind-numbing ecstasy. Just a few minutes ... just a few ...

He had gone from sporadic moans to one ongoing, rising sound, forming a cry. He was no longer passive, but was moving to meet her, adding pressure to their contact, his hands digging into her hips as she rode him harder and faster. The cry burst out of him, and in a dream-shattering instant, he pulled her down and rolled.

No! No!

She had been so close!

She wanted to scream. And to make matters worse, he had rolled her onto -

That damned pillow!

It was right under her butt, completely uncomfortable, lifting her up, and –

Oh.

Oh!

Oh!!!

Now the angels sang.

As he unleashed a torrent of raw animal energy, digging for China with purpose, she felt him as she had never, ever felt him – or any man – before, sweet heat on *that spot* while he just thumped her button again and again. It had never been like this, never this intense, never this complete –

A pillow? After all these years – that's all it took?

Go with it, girl!

Another half-minute and she was screaming, and he was right there with her. In their long time together, they'd never crossed the line at the same moment, until tonight.

It took her ten minutes to calm down, and when she finally opened her eyes, she looked up into eyes taking in her face, as he stroked her hair. She muttered something, she wasn't quite sure what – but otherwise there were no words.

Within minutes, he was drifting off. And as he rolled her way, she slipped the pillow between his knees herself.

One Hundred Twenty

Oh, yum...

She hadn't been this naked in almost a year. And he was delightfully naked, *sooooooooooo* hot... well, not *hot* hot, by firemen's calendar standards, but plenty hot for her, and... *yum...*

God, he can kiss!!! Oh, he tasted so good, and he was one of those men who totally knows how, offering up that kind of kiss that curls your toes and makes things all crinkly. And a face, well, not a George Clooney face, but a face, and a smile, that a woman could definitely wake up to for the next fifty years or so... not gorgeous-handsome, but definitely handsome, and -

Stay in the moment, girl...

He hadn't shaved in a week or so, probably by design, and he was a little bit scratchy as he nuzzled into her neck, and it tickled her in that makes-me-shiver way, and she leaned her head back, urging him on...

Southward he roamed, and having felt those lips, that tongue, on her own, and on her neck, she was literally aching for them to arrive over her thundering heart, and quickened lungs, and he did not disappoint. He had that subtle, tantalizing combination of force and finesse that men find so difficult to master, when it came to a woman's breasts. Men spend so much time there, how is it they are so slow to learn? But this one had learned... oh god, had he learned!

She totally immersed herself in the moment, both fixing beneath his skilled oral attention and squirming in her skin, soaking up his magic hungrily, even greedily, oh it's been so long... !

It is NEVER this good the first time!!!

?

As the thought crept in, he released a nipple from a not-quite-gentle tug that she felt both northward and southward, and proceeded with feather-light kisses, across her stomach, pausing at her navel to do a thing with his tongue that she had never ever felt before. Oh, that's a keeper...

She took pride in her inventive and immaculate southern grooming, with intent to entice all the more, with an irresistible visual. A man's oral attention was very, very high on her list, and she went all-out to get him there, including giving her very best effort to reciprocation.

But... oh!!!

Without hesitation, he just swept her out of herself, and into herself, hovering over her well-kept secrets, the warm air of his breathing thrilling her, stirring her perfectly-trimmed patch, his lips purposefully setting to work, the tip of his tongue as expert as she could imagine any man being, and her ecstasy was driven as much by the fact that she had herself a man who really knew what he was doing down there, as by what he was actually doing, and in less than ten minutes, he took her from *mmmmmmmmmmm* to *oooooooooooooooooooo* to *ahhhhhhhhhhhhhhh* to the edge of *uuuunnnnnnnnhhhhhhhhhhhhhh...*

And a thought crept in...

He went straight to it...

Again --- ???

And her mind just would not stop.

It is NEVER this good the first time...

His tongue worked magic, relentlessly, purposefully, and she knew without a doubt that her bell would ring once, twice, maybe even three times, before they even got to the main event, and ohgod, and --
-

It is NEVER this good the first time...

And she couldn't help but think...

He just got down to it... he hasn't --- explored me...

What is going on here???

There had been first times. Not, well, not many, but more than a few... and...

It is NEVER this good the first time... we need to explore, to learn each other...

As his tongue drove her to ecstasy she'd never experienced from a man's tongue before, her mind continued to intrude.

Something is terribly wrong here...

She did the math. She was on the edge of the best fuck she'd ever, ever had, under the tongue of the most skilled lover she'd ever been with, and...

Something is terribly wrong here...

He didn't explore me at all. And he gave me no cue, no opening at all, to explore him...

Isn't that what the First Time is? Exploration? Learning each other? Touching, hesitating, reaching... ?

Stop thinking!!! her body roared. *Enjoy it!!!*

Oooooo, tough to do... but...

She remembered a football player she'd dated. He loved to talk about the game, about the strategy, about the playbook...*and that's what was happening here... he's running a play!*

Her mind went to work. What kind of man runs a play from a playbook at a time like this? *How does he know? He just doesn't... he's running on autopilot...*

Oh, it's working... but that's just dumb luck...

Look at him! Knocking himself out to knock me out... giving giving giving... asking for nothing...

And it hit her like a rock...

The bitch... that bitch!!!

She was feeling the touch, taking the love of a man who had been with one of *those* women... one of those please-me-or-else bitches who take the quiescent, loving man, and wring him out till he screams for mercy, taking taking taking and dominating, exploiting his sweet nature, berating him when he falters... manipulating his self-esteem...

He thinks I won't love him if he doesn't completely deliver... he's spent years becoming convinced that his worth as a man is all about my orgasm...

She lost focus.

Stop thinking!!! her body screamed... *We're SO close...*

Her fingers were all tangled up in his beautiful hair, pressing into him as his tongue artfully teased her closer and closer to heaven... and she softly lifted his head from her very aroused, very damp hot zone, and pulled him up to her face.

He was confused, and he even trembled a bit.

He's afraid he isn't making me happy, she realized, and resolved to make herself very, very clear...

A man who gives one hundred and ten percent, in the clutches of one of those selfish bitches who takes one hundred and twenty... well, he's in the right bed tonight...

She guided him into position above her, reached down and guided him in, gently, lovingly... let him settle into her, and wrapped herself around him, legs and arms, completely enfolding him... and guided his face to hers, and pulled him into a deep, long kiss...

You don't have to cater to me... You don't have to fulfill any expectation of mine, other than being as close as we can possibly be... !!!

Her body screamed frustration, but her heart took charge, knowing that a deeper satisfaction lay only moments away.

Her kiss was deep and full and loving. Tasting herself, she set aside eroticism and poured all her passion into a single message...*I want to be with you because of who you are... not because of what you can do for me...*

Her legs, wrapped firmly around him, tightened, and her arms clutched at him with all the strength she had. *Oh, you beautiful man,* she struggled to say with her kiss, her touch, her embrace, you've been too long in the grip of a woman who just takes... and all you want in the world is to give...

Her body focused all the pent-up, unspent desire into a single surge, a melting-together that wasn't about getting off, or power, or any of those games the bitch had used to mold him into her fantasy machine, afraid to express himself, afraid to truly speak to her, from his heart, with his body...

You're home, her body sighed to him, as she held him tight with her entire being, not letting him move. *I want all of these things you have to give,* she said with her fingertips and her tongue and her scent and the longing in her embrace, *and I want to give every one of them back to you... over and over again...*

It took a little while, but he began to relax, to flow with her, to begin to understand what she was offering... they began to move together, in perfect rhythm, in the deepest ancient duet, and she felt a freedom in his touch, his motion, his heat, that she could easily imagine was new to him...

... and next time around, she thought with deep joy, *we'll go exploring...*

Three Sets

It starts with deep fatigue... you did three sets for a packed house and you're drenched in sweat and exhausted... you are too tired to even take a shower... you fall across the hotel bed in a dirty t-shirt and panties, in the cool dark... fingertips sliding onto your back, beginning to rub the tension from your aching shoulders, and it hurts, even pretty bad at first, but the pain gives way to relief and relaxation... and his warm skin touches your sweaty wet thigh as he eases down your body, to your lower back, where the soreness has taken root, and his strong thumbs dig into the hard knot there, causing you to wince, but then sigh as the soreness begins to fade... then he kneads your calves, which you burned down to hard coal with your strutting and pose, and he prods them with hard fingertips until they are once again soft and relaxed... and his hard fingertips also turn soft as he flips you over and hovers over you in the dark, not nearly as sweaty and smelly as you, quiet and strong, bending down to nip at your neck, and your nipples are hard as diamond as he refuses to give you any but the most fleeting body contact, and he breathes gently as his mouth finds the place below your ear, and the warm air teases and makes you tingle and you rake at his back, pulling him down to you...

He resists, refusing to be pulled in, his hard, tired muscles rippling as he continues to hover above you in the dark... you try to force the issue, reaching down to that place where your fingertips and lips and tongue usually rule, and a firm grip clamps around your hand, and then the other one, and he covers you like a quilt, pinning you with arms above your head, and his mouth finds yours, and you know in an instant that this is one of those nights when you aren't going to have any say in anything... he is in control...

He tastes sweet and sharp, with a little bourbon and coke, and he is devouring your mouth, indifferent to your fatigue, intent on taking you to the place you thought you were too tired to reach. His chest is both soft and hard as the pressure of his body lightly crushes into your own hard/soft breasts, and his legs are pillars falling across yours... he settles against your stomach and OMIGOD... that part of him you know so well, with its many moods and textures, is harder and hotter than it's ever been, and you curse your fatigue, wishing you were totally energized for what is about to come --- but knowing that somehow he has sensed that your deep emotional state and physical darkness are simply a medium in which his fingertips, and other member, will spin flaming art... your body begins to scream at you, hot blood flooding into the cold, tired vessels, and you know he has you, completely, and you can do nothing but let him take you where he wills...

His lips are agonizingly soft and burning hot as they graze your lips, departing from your mouth, which he has violated more intimately than those other more southward lips, and he bites hard into your neck, and WHOA you're a little more awake now, and he is no more gentle with the first nipple he finds, biting and pulling and teasing the tip with his tongue, as he moans aggressive desire in no particular direction... you are absolutely drenched already, and so relaxed from his violent massage that you can do nothing but lay there for him and drink in every sharp, flashing sensation... a cry escapes you as he finds the other nipple and pulls even harder, and you can feel an electric shock below as he pulls it into his mouth for even rougher treatment... one of your hands digs into his lower back as the other gropes for him in a vain hope that your grip will give you some control - and still he eludes you, and pulls away, shifting down your body and wrapping steel arms around your thighs as he turns the attention of his tongue to your deepest vulnerability, with even more heat and hunger...

His arms are steel cords wrapped around your thighs as he sinks his hard/soft tongue into you, and you are more or less his prisoner, with nothing to say about it... a burst of concern that you are too sweaty to be sweet to him is swept aside by his obvious lust for this, and you are so hot/wet right now that it is quickly clear that your scent and wetness are driving him even wilder... and his hard tongue, driving you into a frenzy, gives way to a harsher intimacy as he takes your pearl into his mouth and pulls it in and out, and you become dizzy, moaning unashamedly, crashing toward a hard, violent orgasm, and he will not stop, and your calves once again ache as you strain against him arms...

When you finally explode, you almost scream, and he does not relent, and the pressure of his arms cause the tension of your orgasm to slam thru your thighs and legs almost painfully, and only with reluctance does he release you, as another flood surges out of you, to his waiting tongue... He is ready to take you, and there are no more rules...

You have already had one nerve-shattering orgasm, and now he is not at all subtle, not even polite, as he plunges into you hard and almost violently, his arms sliding up under you, across the wet, warm flesh of your back, and his legs entangle yours --- you are so completely embraced that no movement is your own, and he thunders into you with a passion so hot and raw and deep that you can scarcely breathe --- and you completely surrender, beyond fatigue, beyond electricity, knowing only the rhythm of his desire, his deep need...

... and in that thunderous pulse, you hear his deepest song, the echo of his ache for you, and only you, a passion that is so enslaved to you that he can think of nothing else... his love for you writhes and pulses in this happy violence, this deeply loving lust that screams your name, your taste, your scent, your wetness, your hot skin, your weary heart, your needy soul... A hot tear spills down your cheek as he breathes heat into your mouth, sweeping you into a second hard climax as his own passion comes close to erupting... you cry out, shouting your orgasm into his mouth as your heart swells... You are so in love, and so completely ready to receive his love...

So many times, you've sung this ancient rhythm with him, molding your body to his as he molds to yours, surrendering to the perfection of skin against skin, muscle on muscle, taste and scent and sigh, but tonite is different, and his release is more, the unleashing of an ache and hunger so deep that you have no way to respond other than to simply receive him, limp and willing and warm, and offer a loving moan, to say to him how deeply you need him, how willing you are to receive his need, how much you treasure him, and your passion is the merest shadow of the depth and fire and need that ripples thru you for this man, your love, your friend, your soul mate...

So exhausted you can hardly think, you dig fingernails into his back as he sinks into you, completely spent, and it is a full 10 minutes before either of you are breathing normally... and you are half-asleep as you pull his mouth to yours and taste him and melt into him... strong arms enfold you and you are asleep in seconds, feeling his heartbeat merging with yours...

... and you know you are home...

Internet Sex

MaterialGrrl85: Sorry I missd u! I wuz out w/ my BFFs and cell fone was in my purse. Talkd about u all nite 2 them! They cant wait 2 meet u! btw I cant wait 2 meet u either

NightInWhiteSatin: Glad you had a good time! If we met in the real world I'm not sure I'd know you – your profile pic is cute but the lighting is strange.

MaterialGrrl85: LOL! That pic is not the best. I will snd u sum privately.

NightInWhiteSatin: Private pics?

MaterialGrrl85: Ooo now thatz a great idea! We can snd each other private pix b4 the bg mtng

NightInWhiteSatin: You mean

MaterialGrrl85: O this is so romantic! Lets send each othr 3 pix ea

NightInWhiteSatin: By pix you mean romantic pix?

MaterialGrrl85: Sexy romantic ;)

NightInWhiteSatin: I don't usually do things like this.

MaterialGrrl85: LOL! Me ether! But u r special

NightInWhiteSatin: It has been awhile since anyone thought so.

MaterialGrrl85: ROTFLMAO! Frm ur profile pic I cant believe u r very lonely

NightInWhiteSatin: You'd be surprised.

MaterialGrrl85: I luv r talks. U dont talk down 2 me and u make me feel good always

NightInWhiteSatin: You've made me feel good, too.

MaterialGrrl85: Now u r making me feel sexy! Wait 15 and I will snd u pix. U have 2 promise 2 snd me sum!

NightInWhiteSatin: Romantic pix?

MaterialGrrl85: Yes really sexy 1s! ;)

NightInWhiteSatin: Okay

MaterialGrrl85: ☺

She'd never done this before. Well, once she had, but in the end she hadn't sent the pictures she'd taken of herself, and she hadn't saved them, either. No cell-phone cam for these, she decided: she dug out her digital camera, undressed and partially redressed, made up her bed for a decent backdrop, and spent a good twenty minutes getting three shots she was pleased with.

She transferred the pictures to her computer and emailed them to Night, with the note, "Thinking of u ..." The pictures he'd sent were already waiting in her email In-box.

Before she even opened them, she realized how aroused she was. She'd started getting that way while taking the pictures of herself, getting just naked enough to be seriously hot-looking but not enough to spoil the treat for the eventual live show.

She was still nearly naked and, at this point, eager. She set the laptop on her bed and lit candles, then turned out her bedroom lights. She grabbed her favorite toy from the nightstand drawer and opened the first picture, expecting to see a serious piece of steak.

It was a station wagon.

An old, beat-up station wagon. It was shiny and clean, at least as shiny and clean as a twenty-five-year-old car could possibly be. Lovingly cared for, anyway. But an old, beat-up station wagon, all the same.

She was confused. Was this a joke? And then it dawned on her …

He's sending me pix of places he's done it!

Ooo, this really was sexy! She looked at the picture, soaking up all the details, then leaned back into the pillows and turned on her toy.

She was sixteen again, and imagined herself in the back of the station wagon with him … parked in the high school parking lot, late on a Saturday night after seeing a movie together … the windows open, cool air … slightly afraid that a random cop would happen by …

She imagined breathless kisses, frantic undressing … pictured herself naked, her body displayed for him in moonlight, his hands and light kisses roaming over her, her nipples hard – and not from the cool air – his lips drawing them in, the tip of his tongue …

She imagined him above her, ready, pressing into her … felt him thrusting hard and fast, with the unrestrained energy of youth …

In only a few seconds, she experienced a crashing orgasm, dropped the toy onto the comforter, still humming.

Oh wow …

That had worked out so well, she couldn't wait to open the next picture.

Giving herself a few minutes to settle down, she reflected on the brilliance of sending that picture. What an interesting guy Night must be! Most guys wouldn't have thought of that. They'd have sent some studly pec shot, or even a pic of the Little General saluting. But Night …

She'd hooked herself a true romantic! And he actually had an imagination.

She opened the next picture.

At first it wasn't clear what she was seeing. Lots of trees, shadowed, deep in a forest … ?

It was a cabin.

It was so deep in the trees, so nestled away in the forest's heart that she could hardly make it out. And not just a cabin, but a log cabin.

Who is this guy???

She began to revise her earlier estimates of him. She'd figured him to be at least five years older than her, maybe more, by the maturity of his responses – way beyond what guys her own age were capable of. Now, with these pictures, she was seeing that he was not only more mature but more experienced. Deliciously more experienced …

The fire roared in its stone chamber as he poured the wine and handed her the glass, the two of them skin-comfortable on the warm floor, bearskin beneath them, light evening rain outside. There was music playing softly somewhere.

They sipped their wine and laughed, and he kissed her, lightly at first – then more deeply – and the wine glasses were barely set aside without spilling. He gathered her up in his arms, strong arms, and they rolled together in the fire's heat.

There was no real foreplay, only this heat which wrapped them completely, and he entered her, and they both surrendered to the ancient rhythms … alone together, safe, withdrawn from the world in an isolated moment, a universe all to themselves … here beneath a wet twilight sky, surrounded by the peace and silence of the woods, lost in an eternal primeval reverie …

She felt a sense of belonging, stronger than anything she'd experienced before. She cast aside the toy and let her fingers continue, some outside, some inside, striving not for an ecstatic thrill but for the sense of connection and natural energy she was experiencing within.

She immersed herself in the heat as it melted them down, turning warmth into life, her deep sparks bursting to flame in a series of passionate expressions, each sweeter than the last, until she felt totally spent.

She continued to caress her own skin, now as damp as it was warm, imagining his arms bundling her up lovingly and possessively in afterglow, and wondered what it took to arrive in such a place with such a man.

She almost drifted off.

But … *there's one more picture …*

Long minutes passed before she could bring herself to open it. What she was experiencing was so different from what she had expected. All of this was new to her, opening her up in such strange and wonderful ways. She found herself apprehensive, a bit unsettled.

She opened the final picture.

It was a mountaintop.

It was a mountaintop like none she had ever seen, so high, so far above the endless, untouched expanse below that she wondered how he had gotten there. The horizon beyond was another world, an untouched place where souls were unbound, where every moment burst with life. It was so beautiful, so clear, so endless that it took her breath away.

And the *sky* ...

If the horizon below was wondrous, it still had nothing on the sky. An evening sun was sinking into time, saving its best for last, casting careless splendor in orange and red and violet, seizing the remaining clouds and adorning them in a beauty so random and inspiring that she longed to be a part of it ... fingers of radiant longing, lacing heaven and earth together in brilliant purpose. Twilight teased the edges of the sky, starfire biding its time before unleashing its own passions in the sun's lazy wake. It was the most beautiful evening sky she'd ever seen.

Or was it morning? Had they climbed this mountain by day, and loved there in the sunset? Or had they loved through the night, camping under the stars, and awakened to this beautiful dawn?

Who is this guy???

How did he get to that mountaintop?

She closed her eyes, and the dampness of her skin became the sweat of a day's climb ... she was staring into the evening sun, and she felt his arms ease around her from behind. He was sweatier than she was, and it was a thrill to feel the cool evening air hitting her skin as he unbuttoned her shirt ...

She didn't bother with the toy at all as she let her fingers explore her own moist surface, her muscles aching slightly with the evening's exertion, now an imagining of the happy fatigue of the mountain climb.

This was their shared reward, their prize for an incredible feat, a long and difficult journey – not without its dangers – a journey of thrill and challenge and unfaltering mutual reliance. And here she was, at the end of that incredible journey, savoring this sweet reward ... in his arms, safe, and offering safety in return ... a sacred celebration.

This loving was different, quieter, deeper, still passionate but somehow a perpetual thing, not just a moment ... and the ecstacies were perhaps less electric, but carried a deeper energy, something eternal. They cast themselves through her body like this blazing nebula before them, opening her soul to the starlight to come …

She realized she was crying.

Who is this guy???

Only after lying there for a long time, reflecting on the powerful experience Night had just created for her, did she begin to wonder just what kind of woman would have shared those three incredible places with him. For the first time, she began to wonder what her own role was, in all of this. It was more than just a flirt, more than internet fun: she had learned more about loving, more about what she herself really wanted, in this past hour than she had ever known before.

He had shown her what oneness was.

A knock on the door brought him back to the moment, and his son stuck his head into the room. He noticed that the boy's sideburns were beginning to gray, as his had done at that age.

"Dad?" he said, and his eyes added an unspoken *You okay?*

He smiled back, glad that he'd minimized the photos that had been on the desktop monitor moments earlier.

"You buried in the internet again? Come downstairs. There'll be highlights from the game on ESPN."

He smiled again. "Kinda tired, buddy. I think I'll turn in."

"You've been awfully quiet today."

And he felt both happy and sad inside …

He felt slightly embarrassed, under his own scrutiny, for chatting on the internet at all. But he'd been so lonely these past few months, and he needed company, an undefined something that neither his friends nor his son's family could provide.

When he'd seen her pictures – R-rated at the very least, one of them borderline X … do they still have an X rating, he wondered? – he'd realized that '85' was her birth year, rather than the year Madonna, the Material Girl, had appeared. He'd assumed her to be well into her thirties, from her profile picture – a trick of the light. Well, his own profile picture hadn't exactly been accurate: when that picture had been taken, his son had been in grade school.

And the pictures he'd sent her – wow, what a ridiculous thing to do! They had such special meaning to him, such powerful memories … she must have thought he was some really strange guy, sending those pictures. She'd surely been fishing for something R-rated from his side.

It had probably been quite a disappointment. She clearly had something very different in mind.

   "Dad?"

Again, he was taken out of the moment.

"I'm sorry," he said, trying to sound casual. He sat on the edge of his bed. "Today is an anniversary ... "

His son frowned, stepped into the room.

"No, Dad," he said gently. "It's tomorrow. Mom died a year ago tomorrow."

He saw concern in his son's eyes.

"Not that anniversary," he said. "I was thinking of something else."

His son smiled a bit, his eyebrows still furled quizzically.

"You're sure you're all right?"

He nodded.

"You sure you won't come down and have a drink with us?"

He shook his head. "I'm fine."

"Okay," his son said, turning. "Well ... good night. Love you."

"You too, buddy."

A year ago tonight ... he felt his eyes burning as he remembered the last night he had been with her, the last private moment they had shared, the last time he had been one with his lifelong love, going to sleep together in each other arm's ...

He logged onto the internet one last time, and deleted the account.

Squeeze

He was already sound asleep. In the darkness, she could feel his warmth, hear his almost-silent breathing, smell his tired skin... she nestled herself against his chest, and his heartbeat crept into her ear...

An almost unbearable wave of tenderness swept through her, but she couldn't bring herself to wake him in the way she usually did when her need burned in her... she kissed his chest so softly he couldn't feel it, and ever-so-gently slid out from under his arm and slowly lowered herself onto him, without waking him...

His body responded despite his sleep, and without benefit of her hand or lips, he began to swell, and she waited, patiently, as she felt herself beginning to grow damp... she gave herself plenty of time to grow very wet, sensing that this exquisite moment could only work if she could leave him in slumber, and finally she eased herself down onto him...

Her body melded to his in the sweetest union the two had ever had --- not passion, not lust, but tenderness and sweet spiritual oneness so powerful that tears began to well up in her eyes... this time it was a holy bond, and she shuddered, surrendering to the perfection of the moment... she rested her weight on her elbows, desperate not to disturb his sleep, and the warmth of his chest and the gentle up-and-down of his breathing overwhelmed her...

She felt herself tightening around him, grasping him with her lower muscles, and with each constriction she felt closer to him... not the same as his motions in loving, but powerful, somehow even more powerful, and she began to rhythmically caress him within herself, causing him to pulsate, responding to her caress, and her tears flowed freely, spilling onto his chest... she surrendered to this new rhythm, this strange new loving embrace, and felt ecstasy flooding over her like a tide... she trembled as it surged through her, and she bit her tongue to keep from crying out... a deep, humbling peace descended, and the wave continued to ripple, and suddenly she felt his pulses within her, filling her with warm, loving moisture... a soft sound escaped him, and he was half-awake, half-drowsy, uncertain of the moment - and as one of his hands slipped around her back, her body clenched him, attempting to completely cover him... she tasted his skin, and her own tears, and caressed him back into slumber - and within seconds, she joined him there.

Friends with Benefits

They were just friends.

Very good friends, for sure, the kind of friend you call two or three times a day, have standing lunch days and video game nights with. The kind of friend you can text in a meeting, or abruptly abandon in a phone call with no repercussions, the kind of friend whose favorite drinks and TV shows and pizza you know as well as your own.

But just friends, all the same. Neither was particularly attracted to the other. He didn't "smell" right to her, didn't make her weak in the knees; and he never undressed her in his mind. They were both healthy, fit, and reasonably attractive; there was just no "spark," as women often say.

They were highly available to each other, as friends tend to be, for TV during the week and mall-wandering and hanging out at the park on weekends. They were each other's go-to for movies they wanted to see that no one else could be dragged to, and they were constantly adding to each other's iTunes libraries.

And so it was that on the weekend they started having sex, she carefully characterized their negotiation as "friends with benefits," a new phrase she'd heard, meaning that they would be sexually available to each other, but without being in a "relationship." Their friendship would proceed as it had been, only with sex added, and any time either of them began an actual relationship with someone else, the deal was off, and they'd simply continue the friendship.

It had been her idea, and he had been surprised. They were at her place when it came up, and they'd only been through one glass of wine, so it wasn't one of *those* decisions. He ended up staying all weekend, and by Monday morning, he'd long since lost count. She was counting – for herself, anyway – and her tally was nine.

They didn't really discuss it. They simply began picking up signs, as friends do when they want another beer from the fridge or there are too many onions on the pizza. They'd be watching a movie, he'd start to bulge, she would notice and take care of it; she'd get squirmy, he'd reach into her sweat pants.

Just friends!

In bed, it was so much easier than a relationship. For one thing, there was no performance anxiety; it was okay if he needed a break, or if she was starting to get sore. There were no feelings to hurt. On the contrary, because of this casualness, there was far more mutual accommodation, more backrubs, more foot rubs, more warm-down.

Because it wasn't a relationship, neither worried at all about how the other saw them. She didn't think twice about her fifteen extra pounds, and he didn't worry that his arms weren't that impressive. On stay-over weekends – which every weekend rapidly became – they washed each other's underwear without a second thought.

Because they were friends, there was no "sequence" to their sex life. There was no dance, no ritual that had to be executed step-by-step with military precision, lest one reject the other; no worries about a too-soon use of the "L" word, no faux pas in timing or magnitude of gift-giving. No too-serious too-fast mistakes. There was no "next step" to take, and so no anxiety about next steps at all.

There was just the friendship, which had been strong to begin with, and the sex, which had none of the usual complications. Because the whole idea was mutual satisfaction and accommodation, rather than "couplehood," it never occurred to either of them to be shy in the least about asking for whatever they wanted, or telling each other how they liked things done. As friends, they were already good at listening to one another, and sex was no exception. Each got what they needed from the other – all the time. And it was, ironically, almost effortless.

Because it was not a relationship, there were no jealousy issues or territorial behaviors. Rather than being threatened by the other's attraction to someone else, they were accommodating, as friends will be. When one would mention an attraction to a co-worker, the other was not only unhurt, but would sometimes go so far as to help role-play the seduction, an exercise that was always incredibly gratifying – the end result of which was that neither ever felt the need to pursue such a seduction in the real world.

Just friends.

Because it wasn't a relationship, there were no power issues. When things were rough at work, he shared his concerns with her, not worried in the least that it would make him seem weak. She, in turn, was unconcerned with seeming needy, having turned to him for support long before the FWB.

The sex didn't hinder the friendship in the least. When she got sick, he was there for her as always. He never left her side, burning through all of his vacation time and personal days without a second thought. When his father died, and he broke down, she held him all night. As friends will do.

Because they were unconcerned with appearances, they became comfortable in skin around each other on their shared weekends. This led to common spontaneous tacklings, on the couch, the dining room table, the kitchen floor.

And the lack of self-consciousness went to the limit, as when he walked in on her watching porn (which she'd stolen from him), and he simply sat and watched it with her. This in turn led to self-servicing while watching, which in turn led quickly to the abandonment of the porn – they decided they would rather watch each other, and often did so.

Just friends!

They could ask one another for things they couldn't have, in a relationship. "Could you help me wash my hair?" was the most casual of requests, yet an intimacy she would never have dared impose upon a boyfriend.

Hugs were constant – but then, they always had been. Kissing was now constant, as well, but given the very oral nature of their mutual accommodation, it made practical sense.

The sex itself was even less inhibited than their friendly lifestyle. Their names for each other's body parts were funny, rather than flattering; their fantasies were shared as easily as video game scenarios and movie plot summaries. They didn't think twice about their "O" faces or voices.

Just friends.

And they never talked about it.

And when they had long since passed the point where no other love could ever come close to matching what they had accidentally created together, it was never discussed. Whether or not either of them ever realized it was never revealed. If either was aware that their bond far exceeded what most married couples manage in a lifetime, it went unspoken.

Instead, they simply bought a small farm beyond the edge of town, and raised four gorgeous children together, through many, many happy years.

Good friends!

White Roses

Dressed in clean slacks, his nice dress shoes and one of his best shirts, he rang the doorbell.

A long moment later, the door crept open hesitantly and she peered around it. She burst into a big smile and leaped into his arms, completely forgetting that she was in her best dress.

Her mother – his ex – had taken the trouble to do her hair, a not-insignificant gesture, given her shallow understanding of this whole exercise. She lost a shoe mid-leap, and after a big hug, he sat her carefully back down on the front steps and slipped it back on for her.

He retrieved the white rose he'd been hiding behind his back and then dropped when he caught her, presenting it to her with silly formality. She giggled, delighted, and held his hand as he escorted her to the car and strapped her into the safety seat.

Before pulling out of the driveway, he asked her where she would like to have dinner, presenting her with options. Her choice was immediate.

Pizza!!!

Walking hand-in-hand with him through the restaurant, she beamed with pride as other parents noticed her outfit and complimented her. She felt so grown up that she pretended to read the menu, which she couldn't, as he offered her options for pizza she hadn't known existed. In the end, she went with something new: the extra cheese she was used to, plus pepperoni, which she knew Daddy liked. He quietly arranged with the server to have it half-and-half, in case the pepperoni wasn't a hit with her.

Then it was off to the arcade until the pizza was done. She completely forgot she was in her best dress, and he completely failed to notice. Or care.

Over the pizza, he asked her about what she was doing in pre-school. She told him all about the new games, which ones she and her best friends preferred, and how the mean boys sometimes hogged them. He shared her disapproval. He then asked about her upcoming birthday, wondering what she would like for a present. She meandered through the possibilities, and he took careful note.

Movie! The new Pixar. Popcorn only. She crawled onto his lap halfway through, and almost fell asleep.

Ice cream?

Yesyesyes!

Single scoops, to minimize the sugar and Mom's irritation if she didn't go to sleep promptly. Great care was taken to protect the dress. Then, a final happy hand-in-hand stroll through the mall, singing some song from one of her TV shows, with Daddy getting most of the words wrong, even with her patient correction. As the moment ended, he squeezed her hand.

Sleep, in the SUV.

He intended to carry her, undisturbed, into her mother's house, but she stirred as he unbuckled her, and insisted on walking to the door, hand-in-hand, carrying her white rose. As the moment ended, he squeezed her hand.

More than 200 white roses followed, as she grew.

Daddy, I know you can't hear me ... and if you could, I think you already know what I would say ...

Any time now, the doctor had said.

She slipped her fingers into his, squeezed gently, knowing he could not respond.

The man standing behind me now ... the father of my babies, my husband, my best friend ... I have that because of you ... because of all of our times together, as far back as I can remember ... you taught me to look for him, to find the man who would treat me the way you did ... always respecting me, treating me with kindness, adoring me as you did ...

Quiet tears spilled.

You taught me never to settle for anything less. And I never did, Daddy ... I waited for the right man, and all of our happiness, I owe to you ...

She felt her husband's strong, gentle hand on her shoulder.

I know I'll be okay ... we all will ...

But how can I tell you goodbye?

And as the moment ended, he squeezed her hand.

Big Rock

It was called Big Rock for exactly that: the creek - a beautiful, meandering stream that wound through the city's east end – had a massive rock smack in the middle of a broad expanse below a cliff, to which the rock had once belonged. Kids could, and constantly did, wade out into the creek and climb on the rock, which had a large, flat surface atop that could fit a child's birthday party.

It was a little Garden of Eden hidden in a bustling part of town, and wildly popular – from April through October, it was always filled with playing children, picnicking families, and couples like the two of them.

She had always loved Big Rock, and in the early days of their dating had suggested it as a fun place to meet. They would sit by the creek's edge and watch the kids at play, the cyclists whizzing by up near the road, the dog lovers playing frisbee with their pets. Other couples would walk the perimeter of the playground near the shelter, hand in hand; on the far side, where it was more private, a couple would sometimes string up one of those hammocks that zipped up, and climb in (they would then joke about what was going on in there).

Most days, they would chat and hold hands, occasionally taking off their shoes and wading, and from time to time they'd bring a picnic lunch, spread out on an old blanket under a tree.

He had taken to it immediately, and constantly looked forward to their next Big Rock afternoon.

Today, she had teased in an earlier text, she was bringing a surprise.

He wondered what it could be. She had just bought a condo, and he would be moving in soon; maybe something to do with that? Or maybe a picnic basket with something new? Nope, it was mid-afternoon. A bottle of wine they'd never tried?

He parked his truck and wandered over to their usual spot by the creek. Moments later, her car pulled into the lot.

Instead of heading his direction, she crossed the playground, a large package in hand. Spotting him, she waved, firing off a quick text:

Come see the surprise!

Curious, he hopped up and followed. By the time he caught up with her, she'd opened the package.

It was a hammock. The kind that zipped shut.

He laughed, and the two of them set the hammock up between the two sturdy trees they'd seen other couples use.

Setting it up had been easy; getting inside the damn thing was another matter. They slipped off their shoes and gave it a shot.

Twice, she'd gotten in first, and he'd almost flipped her out onto the ground trying to get in with her. Her practicality rose to the surface: *You get in first, since you weigh more.* That worked much better – he nestled in, and over the side she came, not upsetting things nearly as much as he had. She laid down on top of him, then they scooted around a bit until they were side-by-side.

We need to zip it up, don't you think?

Well, duh, and so he half-sat up and reached for the zipper, creating a playful solitude that immediately put them in a fun frame of mind.

Okay, now what? he said.

Do you need instructions?

This thing came with instructions? They must have fallen out of the package, I'll hop out and -

She poked him hard and giggled, and he kissed her.

And kissed her. She felt so warm, she smelled so good!

This moment always surged between them like an ocean tide, and desire welled up rapidly. He knew how to hold her and where to touch her, and -

Damn, there's no room to move in here!

This was going to be a challenge.

He began fumbling, proceeding not very creatively, but even such a simple thing like touching her breast was nearly impossible in such close quarters. As usual, she set him straight: she'd conveniently worn a light skirt, which she reached down and lifted.

She unbelted and unzipped his shorts, giving his proud flesh some much-needed breathing room. It was clearly impossible for him to lose the shorts and drawers altogether; his legs were simply too long, and the hammock was too short. So she just started stroking him as he was.

He immediately realized that was a dead end. He was wildly excited, but what exactly happened next? If they proceeded like this, there would be an unfortunate result. He put his hand on hers, to stop her. She immediately saw the problem.

He then kissed her again, reaching down between her legs. The adventure of doing this just 20 yards or so from the frolicking public made it all the more exciting.

She sighed as his fingertips explored her – slowly, they had all day! - and after a lazy tour of her labia, he slipped two fingers inside her, finding that one spot...

She gasped softly, and it occurred to him he was in a bind: his left arm was wrapped around her – trapped – and so he couldn't touch her with both hands. He couldn't do anything about that, so he just went with it. She'd let him know what it was time to proceed.

He took his time.

When her breathing had quickened and she made the little sound that signaled the next step, he eased his fingers out, and let his forefinger travel upward.

This, too, would be a challenge: she was a technology enthusiast, a vibe grrl, and she needed speed. He'd never brought her home by such simple means. But here they were, and she was so close...

He was, as it happened, a rock musician: fast fingers came with the turf. This was a situation they'd never before experienced.

He was enjoying this so much. It thrilled him to be making her feel this good. Usually they were done in ten minutes, and he realized in this moment that ten minutes just wasn't enough to fully experience and appreciate her passion and pleasure.

He intensified his touch, and her body tensed. She gasped again, trying to stay quiet, not forgetting their audience, and quivered. Suddenly it happened, and her rigid muscles made it all the more intense.

She gasped for breath and trembled, and after giving her a minute to settle down, his fingertip proceeded.

The next time was faster.

The next time, faster still. This was a first.

As for his proud flesh, it would have to wait.

As he cuddled her, smiling, and the two of them reveled in the joy of the moment, he reflected on the ways in which their lives and love were about to change – living together, waking up every morning together, fixing coffee and breakfast, taking turns cooking dinner – and days at Big Rock would be fewer, if not over altogether. But moments like this one – they could make as many as they wished.

And as her breath slowed and softened on his neck, and she half-dozed, he was struck by the message in the moment, the directive that the universe had embedded for him in the substance of what they had just shared:

Put her first...

The Wallet Card

Strong arms, gentle breathing against her neck, hairy legs against her own still-shaved-every-other-day pair ... as familiar and timeless as the morning sun.

All these years later, and he still always Held Her After. And the way he looked at her in these moments -

They'd started this drowsy morning sex – when was it? – after their youngest had headed off to college, and it had become an unexpected favorite among their rituals. Today it was more unexpected still, in her sister's otherwise-unoccupied New England home, where they were staying during unfolding wedding festivities.

It was equally unexpected that the weather would be so perfect – the forecast had said otherwise – and both had forgotten the beauty of New England in autumn. So it was, that when he suggested they get out and sight-see, she was unprepared, and shrugged that she had nothing to wear: she had packed only what was needed for the wedding, and some clothes for pre-wedding chores.

She resigned herself to reading in her sister's garden, since the next round of preparations didn't include her until evening. She didn't notice when he slipped out.

Two hours later he reappeared, motioning her into the house. Seating her on the couch, he presented her with the first of several shopping bags.

There was a gorgeous light sweater ... a cheerful, slightly bold blouse that matched the sweater and her eyes ...

He watched, eager, as she looked them over, astonished.

Do you like them? his eyes asked. She was speechless.

Provocative yet reasonable slacks, still matching, and a pair of sassy but ergonomic shoes.

Her eyes were as wide as saucers. He'd spent a bundle!

Tentative, he handed her the final bag.

Lingerie, the sexiest she'd seen (let alone worn) since before their last baby. She laughed in amazement, and his face was pure joy.

He'd spent a bundle, and the colors were all exactly right, the style was spot-on (did he really pay that much attention?), and everything looked both sexy and comfortable. Everything was perfect …

… except the sizes. But for the shoes, nothing was even close.

Oh, how do I tell him?

There was just no getting out of it.

"Oh, they're just beautiful! But – "

His face froze.

"Sweetheart," she said, with all the gentleness she could muster, "None of these things are going to fit me!"

Distressed and confused, he protested, "No, no, I was sure I got them all right! I have them right here …"

He pulled out his wallet and removed an old piece of 3x5 card. He held it out for her.

Reading the card, she felt her astonishment surge to a whole new level.

Oh, you dear, sweet, wonderful man …

And she could not stop the tears.

On the card, he had carefully recorded all of her sizes. And every one of them was correct …

… in the year that they had married - when she had been nineteen.

Pillow Talk

I saw that friend of yours from school today,

the one that wears those horrible wigs.

Where?

At the store.

What does she have to say?

She's getting divorced again.

Again? What is that, four?

Three, but lots of smaller breakups in between. She did mention
something that kinda floored me. She says you used to give her
relationship advice.

Hm. I guess.

You guess?

Well, yes. Long story.

Your advice must be golden!

Hey! It doesn't come with a warranty.

You gave somebody relationship advice? You?

I'm surprised that you're surprised.

Look how long it took you to get to me! Stop, that tickles!

169

I give *great* relationship advice! I could write books. Doesn't mean I'm actually better at relationships than anybody else. It's a forest-for-the-trees thing.

My thing is, why are you doing it at all?

Well?

You won't like it.

Probably not.

Try me!

I tried you half an hour ago. You were –

Stop it! I want to know.

Okay.

You know how it is when a guy hits on you …

If memory serves.

Ow! Stop!

What you women do when a guy is coming on to you and you want him to get lost, you send the message 'I'm not interested,' and you try to do it without being awkward, so you don't have to come right out and say 'I'm not interested.'

Hm. True.

If a woman is even halfway hot, and you're at least three-quarters*OWWW!*

…TOTALLY HOT, she's been doing that most of her life …

Also true.

That really bums us out. We don't much like it.

170

I imagine not.

So, us guys, some of us have a better way.

Really? By all means, enlighten us awkward bummer females.

Okay, this is just my own personal way. Can't speak for-

Yeah, yeah.what?

Well?

Well?

I want a free pass out of this if-

Dammit! Ooo! *Stop!*

Oops

DON'T TICKLE!

Free pass?

OKAY!!!

All right.

Where to start ...

In my younger days, when a woman would approach-

This happened a lot, did it?

More than you would believe, wench. It was the guitar.

Mmm. Okay, yes, it was the guitar. Hmp! *OUCH!*

You love it

Mm, you smell good

So do you.

You *really-*

That is so damn important to you guys

Focus!

I'm not the one-

FOCUS!

Okay. I had a way to deflect women that didn't say 'I'm not interested in you.'

Do tell.

If a man has a woman hitting on him, and he wants to divert her without hurting her feelings, there's a simple one-step go-to.

?

Just get her talking about an ex, any ex, and most women have plenty to say …

Seriously?

Seriously. And once they're talking about their ex, I would jump in with advice.

You have got to be kidding me.

See, this is why I didn't want to-

Go on. Go on. Sorry.

Once I'm giving her advice, a switch flips in her head, and she doesn't even know it.

A switch …

By opening up, and by responding to my council, she has become vulnerable.

Vulnerable...

Seriously. Am I right about this or not?

Hm.

Hm. Depends on the woman.

Yes it does, exactly! Some women, and some men, for that matter, believe relationships are about balance of power. Don't you know women who feel that way?

Okay, yes. Yes, I do. Quite a few, actually.

When a woman believes relationships are about power, she subconsciously realizes that I now have the power, and we're only five minutes in. Without even thinking about it, she takes me off the table, and I don't have to do anything else to get out of contention.

The power thing is bullshit, you realize that, right?

The power thing is bullshit for men and women who really get it. That's a vanishing minority.

Also true. Okay.

So that's how I ended up being a relationship guru. Fighting off unwanted women.

So, you were that much in demand, were you?

Again, the guitar. And my sizeable-

That's a secret we'll keep, I think!*OUCH!!!*

Well, you know, they were almost always drunk.

They would had to've been, to-

Hey, you started this!

Sorry!

There's something I don't get.

What?

This explains the drunk bimbos at your shows,

but it doesn't explain-

Ah, girls I went to school with. Yes. That deserves some explanation. Well, they get drunk, too.

So why-

It was my only go-to. I was even more reluctant to hurt the feelings of girls I knew than drunk bimbos I didn't. The problem was, once you give relationship advice to a friend, they keep coming back for more.

Ah. Well, that must have been rough, Dr. Phil!

Oh, you have no idea! I can't tell you how many nights I was on the phone at two in the morning ...

I get it.

Except I don't.

What don't you get?

Nine years ago. The club, after your show.

Your hair smells nice.

Nice try. The night you first-

Wanna go again?

Focus! That night … I had broken up with

I remember.

And I told you *everything*, and you started going on about

I remember!

I remember, Dr. Phil! Word for word!

"Your head is always somewhere else," you said.

"You need the guy that focuses totally on you, and enables you to totally focus on him. You need the guy who listens and pays attention, so you'll start listening and paying attention!"

And I said, "How do you know so much about me?"

And you said, "Because I listen, and pay attention."

So …

So what?

So what's your problem?

If you weren't trying to deflect me, why were you giving me relationship advice?

Force of habit, at that point.But why would you think I was deflecting you? If I was deflecting you, why did I proceed to ask you out that night? See, I'm not the mystery here, you are! How is it you didn't feel vulnerable? You told me in excruciating detail what had happened with-

I felt *totally* vulnerable. The things I told you-

Okay.

Okay, you've got me there. Why did you respond at all, if you felt so totally vulnerable?

Because, that night, I knew for certain...with you, I could be.

The Peach Basket

Her scent greeted him before she did, a welcoming, sensual citrus in salt breeze. He smiled, waiting for her to speak as he always did, and held out the peach basket. As he always did.

Smiling softly into the sightless, leathered face, she reached into the back of the basket - *the best stuff is always in the back of the basket!* he had always said - and chose a peach. As she always did.

Today was different. Even so, this was their ritual, reaching all the way back to her earliest memories, and though her thoughts were heavy with the question before her, there would always be time for this.

He was dear to her.

How was your day? he would always ask, though a decade ago it had been *How was school?* or some variation. And the candidness and completeness of her replies had not waned as she had come to womanhood. He was dear to her... and, she had eventually realized, her best friend.

She would sit with him at his stand, sometimes tending customers for him, after eating her peach - for which he had never charged her. Her daily reports had changed over the years, but the comfort of the ritual had only grown deeper.

But not today.

Juice ran down her chin, and she impatiently wiped it away and discarded the fruit. She hadn't come here to chat.

Reaching into her pocket, she pulled out a tiny black-and-white picture, torn from one of those strip-of-four pictures the old photo booths used to produce for a quarter. Weathered with time, it showed a giggly young couple and a wide-eyed infant, a random signal from some other world.

She placed it in his hand. Of course he couldn't see it, but he would know what it was.

I found this in a box at my parents' house, she started, and her cell phone bleated.

She knows!!!

Damn... it's my office, I have to go. She wrestled with herself, trying to justify remaining and seeing this through. But her courage was fading, and the phone call was an escape hatch.

Tomorrow.

I'll see you tomorrow, she said, leaning over and kissing his cheek.

Smiling, he kept his reply to himself.

Lazy smoke hung in acrid layers, pulsing with a dim red-orange demon's glow from rooms beyond, and panic rose hot into his throat as he stumbled and coughed.

Get her out!!!

Dizzy and confused... scooping up the quiet bundle... shouts, so far away... a loud cracking sound... a figure in a dirty, thick coat, grabbing the bundle...

Silence behind him.The floor giving way.

He cried out, soaked in sweat, gasping himself awake. It was a nightmare from another eon, a random signal from another world - but no, not random.

She knows!

He lay awake for long moments, letting the nightmare play. The shape of the fireman holding her close - the last thing he had ever seen - the black terror of the hospital. The new and endless darkness. The voice of the pastor...*I must tell you about your wife...* And the permanence of his prognosis.

Then, arranging the adoption, and the determined resolve to be nearby, anonymous, sharing some small part of her life.

Twenty-five years. And worth every minute.

But...

She knows!

Now, all he could do was embarrass her.

He rose slowly, and began packing a duffle bag.

She thought she had arrived early, but he had already been here.

Sounds of birds and gentle surf and children's voices. Golden whispers of sun. Timeless blue above, clear and beautiful, a doorway into thousands of mornings when she had stopped here at the fruit stand, on the way to school, to a playmate's house, or just to see him. Her best friend.

The stand was empty. Except for the peach basket.

Fresh peaches!

Nothing else. The tables and the shelf - and his chair - were all empty.

A sense of dread rose in her like a sudden fever, and she clutched the old strip-photo with a sweating hand.

I'll wait.

And she waited, into the afternoon, sitting in his chair. Knowing he would never come.

As the finality began to sink in, the crushing weight of unbearable loss pressing so deep that she could hardly breathe, tears began to leak out, and a selfish thought intruded.

Now I will never know for sure...

The peach basket sat before her. And suddenly her heart raced.

The best stuff is always in the back of the basket!

... and in the back of the basket, she found a strip of three photos.

The Talk They Never Had

He woke at 5 a.m., as he'd been doing for years now. It was when she rose to get ready for work.

At first, when he'd been living at his house and she'd been living at hers, he had set his alarm to wake when she did, and would communicate with her by text while she started her day. It was a connection, and he came to treasure it (though his beer buddy, whose wife also rose early, thought it was insane). Later, in the year they'd lived together, the 5 a.m. alarm would ring and he would fix her coffee while she got in the shower.

Now 5 a.m. was written into him, as he rose alone each morning automatically, back at his house.

It's what old people do, he thought resentfully as he fixed a pot of coffee. He was pushing 60, but he refused to feel old.

Coffee in hand, he walked out onto his porch into that cool darkness before dawn that had come to define him. He loved the porch, a place where morning coffee and evening wine and endless relaxation and contemplation had been happening for many years now. In their early days, they had spent hours there, talking about their day, their kids, their plans. It had made the porch, which he had always loved, a new place altogether.

And it was something else again, now, without her.

The old man who lived up the street shuffled down through the dark, leash in hand. In daylight, they'd have waved at one another. In the shadows, the old man was a ghost.

There I go, he thought to himself.

They'd been sitting on the couch, Netflix-binging, as they'd done hundreds of evenings before. Wine and chocolate and walnuts and pecans had become their happy ritual, and it had become his favorite part of the day.

He had no idea how it had started.

They'd been watching TV, and something was said, and it escalated, and within minutes he was in his car, headed back to his house, completely confused. He'd said some things. She'd said some things. The following morning, he couldn't remember any of it.

Several angry days followed. He ached to talk to her, to understand, to piece together what had happened, so that he could see how it had gone wrong.

They still saw each other. He had returned to her place several times and cooked meals for her, and they'd even repeated their TV ritual. They'd met for dinner and made fumbling attempts to talk about it, attempts that paused. There had been both warm and cold text exchanges.

There had been no heart-to-heart.

Looking back, he had realized that in all their time together, there had *never* been a heart-to-heart.

Dawn came, and he fetched a second cup of coffee. The neighborhood was stirring; one car, then another, then another set out into the world. School-bound children began to gather at the corner. Soon, he would put on tennis shoes and go running, before it got too warm.

It wasn't that they never talked. They did nothing *but* talk! His life was more deeply intertwined with hers than it had ever been with anyone else's, even the mother of his children. They did everything together, shared everything, and the future was a calendar filled with plans of things they would do – together. He had become part of her social world, and all of his friends were friends of hers, friends they saw frequently.

"How's your world?" "Oh, she's fine," goes the meme – but it was very true for him.

They did nothing *but* talk. But somehow, they couldn't talk about this. They couldn't push past the hurt and help each other heal. Thinking back, they never had.

It hadn't been that important. They argued and fought far less than most couples he knew of, and certainly far less than in any relationship he'd had. Since he'd moved in with her a year ago, almost all of it had been conflict-free; only two or three times had there been words over the past summer, and in fact their 10-day vacation out west had been the happiest trip they'd ever had.

Moreover, they'd managed twice to de-escalate their argument rather than ramp it up, and he'd been very encouraged by that.

And now this.

They were broken, and he didn't know why, and they needed to talk.

He'd spent the first couple of weeks since leaving thinking about what he would say when they did talk. This had led him to ponder many things: his long history of saying the wrong thing at the wrong time; his belief, four years deep now, that the two of them made a perfect couple, happy and compatible and mutually supportive; his boundless naïve optimism, which he oozed over every quadrant in life, lighting both his professional path and the shadows of his somewhat helpless fatherhood.

But mostly he had pondered the changes in his life that were becoming very apparent, now that he was back on this porch – changes that had occurred in his life because of her.

When they'd met, he'd been adrift – successful enough professionally that no one would notice his lack of motivation, but not truly engaged. What happiness he derived from his day-to-day existence back then had centered mostly on the daughter he doted on, a joyful child whose endless energy and enthusiasm gave him reason enough to get up in the morning.

Four years later, he had become a very different man. He was focused, motivated, succeeding far beyond any measure he'd ever set for himself. He'd always taken pride in his accomplishments, but knew inwardly that when he'd been pursuing this or that achievement, it was a way of hiding from something else. Now, he was running toward his visions, rather than away from them.

And he was realizing that he owed that to her. Whatever industry or motivation he now embraced was a result of living alongside her own, as well as her constant support and encouragement and interest in his ambitions. She had inspired him as he'd never been inspired before. And that inspiration persisted even now, on the porch, in her absence. She had, through her love, remade him. The changes that had come to him in their life together were a part of him now. He would never stop being grateful for that.

Pulling on his tennis shoes, he picked up his Bluetooth headset, then set it down again; no podcast on this run, he decided, his thoughts would keep him company. He walked out the front door, not bothering to lock it – he never locked it, his neighborhood was pretty much Mayberry – and jogged down the driveway and onto the street.

This was another change brought on by recent events. His running had grown sporadic at best, but now he ran almost every day. The endorphins pushed back the clouds of depression. He reflected, with irony, on the walks they had begun taking around her own neighborhood this past summer, and how much he had enjoyed them. That had been a step in the right direction, so to speak, a habit that would made a very healthy addition to their evolving life together, had that life continued.

He picked up speed as he turned out of the neighborhood onto the main road. He was up to 45 minutes at a stretch now, and would be doing an hour a day before cold weather arrived. The light of early dawn was energizing, a metaphor to which his soul responded, and his thoughts briefly slipped into the day ahead: he had more work in queue than he'd ever had before, and had been accomplishing more, day in and day out, than he'd have thought he was capable of. He had a new business going in addition to his regular work, and that new business was ground-breaking, perhaps the greatest achievement of his professional life. And he was enjoying it all more than ever. Again, all because of her.

His thoughts returned to the dinner they'd had, their fumbled attempt to talk through it.

She had brought up his past comments about how he felt they were perfect for each other.

I've had a sense that you have this idea of 'perfect' in your mind, this idea of how we should be, she had said to him. That had surprised him; he would not have expected her to say anything like that.

It seems to me that 'perfect' isn't a pre-conceived thing, she had continued; *It's something we should work out together, day by day...*

Wow.

That had been a very wise observation, and he had taken it in and worked with it. There was a sense in which it had helped clarify his focus and productivity in this new season, what was pretty much the worst month of his life. That idea of letting life happen, rather than gaming it all out in his head beforehand – she'd certainly been right in implying that 'letting life happen' wasn't his style. Not before, anyway. Now, he realized he'd been giving it a try, and it was working for him.

With a trace of resentment, he reflected once again on how unfair it seemed to him that these things he'd needed to do, these changes he'd needed to make, were now happening beyond the haven of their love. He turned back onto his street, headed for the house, and pushed that thought away.

They were broken, and he didn't know why, and they needed to talk.

A week ago, they'd tried again.

He had found a new recipe, bought some groceries, and gone to her place to cook dinner. It had worked out well, and afterward they'd done their TV thing – but they had also tried to talk again.

He'd made a lot of progress in his thinking. He had set aside the misguided notion that there were some words that would fix whatever was wrong, and he had realized that he wasn't going to get her to open up. Both his hurt and his ego needed to be in remission. He had tried to focus on what she needed, and in the absence of clues from her about what that might be, the answer became simple.

I'm not going to say much, he told her; *I am realizing that you don't need to hear me say things, you need to see me do things.* Actions, not words.

And in response, she'd offered up at least a few hints about what had been said that night. He didn't remember them, but wasn't about to admit it; that would bring the too-much-wine elephant into the room, and he was eager to hear more from her.

She said little else, though she later confessed she had more to say. He never heard what it was.

But he had something he could work with. He had spent the next two days thinking through why he had said the things she'd mentioned, and the answers were obvious. Those answers were missing pieces, part of the talk they needed to have. They cut to the core of his mistake, illuminating that part of him that he needed to set right, if he wanted to be the man she could feel safe with and count on.

He took a quick shower, pulled on jeans and a t-shirt. Walking through the house, he smiled absently at the disarray of the upstairs bedrooms and the mountain of furniture currently cluttering the dining room. This, too, was the product of her presence: he's always been an absent-minded packrat, with his guitars and keyboards and CDs and DVDs and a library that could service a small town. But she had now instilled a sense of environment in him, as she had patiently set about painting and decorating her own home, and he had now committed to setting his house in order. He was redoing two upstairs bedrooms, one for his daughter – now college-age – and his grandson, now in high school. He was giving more attention to creating a comfortable, inviting living space than he ever had before.

Because of her.

Sipping his coffee, he felt the post-run rush invigorating him, even as he slipped back into reflection. The sheer scope of their life together loomed over him, and he once again questioned whether his surge of interest in his work was authentic, or just another effort to hide. It wasn't just their day-to-day living, their routines, their comfortability; there was her son, whom he'd come to care for very much, a young man whose humor and interests and loneliness reflected his own faraway youth; there were the visits to her brother's family, whom he deeply enjoyed, visits that had increased in frequency this year.

And there was their social world, which was really *her* social world, where he'd dwelled four years now.

Early in their conflict, he'd told her that he'd need to leave it behind, if they could not reconcile.

You can't leave, she'd implored him, *We're your tribe!*

That was absolutely true. There were more than a few of their shared friends that he could truly say he loved, and the joy and energy of their activities – the wine club, the monthly dinners, the outings – represented the most social era of his entire life.

But there was no help for it. She was sometimes too loose with her anger and criticism, and one of her friends had already been subtly rebuking him online. There was humiliation ahead, and that would be a serious impediment to the work he was determined to continue within himself. He did not doubt that he deserved her anger; but no one deserves humiliation.

And he had long since realized that the anger in her had been there a very long time, that there was some part of her that hadn't been at peace in years, and he'd seen it leak out many times, in many directions. She could be harsh, and he had reflexively resolved to stay out of her anger's path. That had led him to make terrible mistakes as a partner, and regret welled up in him. She had come by the anger honestly.

It also brought to light his endless quest for resolution, and the realization that it was a quest ill-applied in their efforts to reconcile. She had walls up inside her – not because of him, but all the same, walls that might not ever come down, and certainly would not at his convenience. Being with her might mean accepting those walls permanently.

And in a flash of insight, he realized that the talk they hadn't had wasn't about his shutting up and listening – well, it was, but it went deeper – it was that what was missing here wasn't what passed between them; it was their failure to create and paint and decorate an emotional space to share, an inner room they could both inhabit with the same ease they had physically lived together.

It wasn't just the need between them to learn to communicate in new ways; it was even more the need to create a place to do it. Had they built and decorated that emotional room, their life together could have been long and happy. But neither of them knew how.

There was anguish in the insight. Warm tears welled up and spilled down his cheeks. He let them fall, having been reminded of their importance. It's said that the ending of love can be as bad or worse than death, and he knew that to be true. He needed to grieve, and grieve deeply; and not just for the loss of his love, but for the loss of his tribe.

He had the tools to rebuild his life, and he looked forward to that. He did not resent the need for it; he only resented the circumstances. He had the strength to embrace and fulfill his dreams, and they excited him.

And he would continue grieving, until the need for grieving passed. And he would long to tell her things, knowing she would no longer listen. She needed space, and now she would not lack for it. He would ache for her, and that ache would continue much, much longer.

They were broken, and he didn't know why, and he had begun to realize that he never would.

Breakup Sex

Physically and emotionally exhausted, she waited in the darkness of the bedroom they had shared, with the door slightly open so she could hear him leave.

He was gathering the last of his things, after a half an hour of packing and loading his car. They'd agreed she'd keep the apartment; he would take the house he'd bought recently, the one they were to move into after the wedding. He'd been living there these past few weeks, during which they'd hardly spoken.

She hadn't known what to think of him when he'd knocked on the door earlier. It had been his apartment, too, for almost three years. He still had his key. He hadn't been back to get his things, because ... well, for the same reason she'd stayed clear of the house. They didn't know what to say to each other anymore.

She thought she'd already cried the last of her tears.

Seeing him again was terrible. He'd been cordial but distant, not wanting to start anything, not wanting to trouble either of them. The awkwardness was like a heavy fog. She had said a few polite words, then retreated to the bedroom while he packed his CD collection in a box and sorted out the things in the kitchen that were his.

Her hands clenched into the blanket she was sitting on - the blanket on his side of the bed, the one he kept for himself so he wouldn't pull hers away. She'd washed it since he'd first gone, but it somehow still smelled like him.

Her eyes damp, she reached inside for some sign, some echo of how she used to feel. She wanted to love him. She wanted them to work. And she found nothing.

After the breakup, he'd tried for weeks to talk to her, to restart their communication, to hold onto what they'd had. Many lunches, several dinners, and he became a broken record, endlessly recalling their good old days, their successes, we can have that again!

And she knew that what they'd had couldn't have worked. The misunderstandings that became meltdowns, the harsh words that slipped out unintended - it was all too familiar, and it happened too often. She couldn't go back to that.

Suddenly he'd gone silent. No more messages, no more emails, no more requests for lunch. She knew through mutual friends that he had seen other women.

She was the one who wouldn't budge. Yet she was the one having the hardest time moving, now.

Out in the living room, he was boxing up some books. The living room door was half-open; their neighbors stepped into the hall and saw him, smiling awkwardly. As they left the building, he pushed the door shut. It slammed a little harder than he'd intended.

In the bedroom, she took the sound of the door to be his departure. She fell back onto the bed and wept.

Are you okay?

He was at the bedroom door.

Both startled and embarrassed, she sat up, composing herself immediately. She smiled in the darkness, pointlessly.

I'm fine.

He sat in the darkness next to her. Placing a hand on the bed, he inadvertently covered hers.

This is it. *This is goodbye ...*

He squeezed her hand. He didn't speak. A wave of sadness swept over her, but no more tears were coming, and she felt a terrible resignation. She did love him, there were no hard feelings ... she just couldn't go back. They both needed to move forward now.

He lifted his hand and touched her face in the darkness. He cupped her cheek, and she was comforted.

She suddenly felt his lips, and pulled back a bit, but his gentleness was so obvious, his tender intent so clear, that she paused and allowed the kiss.

It wasn't a Goodbye kiss; it wasn't a Fuck Me kiss; and it certainly wasn't a Friend kiss.

It was warm and unbearably gentle and loving and unassuming, not a kiss preceding something else.

This is how I feel ...

She's grown colder and more resolved over the previous months, as his attempts to break through her reserve had only made things worse. She had stopped listening long ago, not out of malice or disdain, but out of futility.

But this, this was something different ...

He's trying to communicate with me!

It was he, not her, that leaned them back onto their bed. He didn't do it forcefully, and he did it in such a way as to offer her an easy deflection. She felt very safe, despite her resolve about the state of things, and leaned into his arms.

Is this breakup sex?

She'd never done breakup sex. A few of her friends had, and they'd sung its praises; it was the perfect way to part, they had argued, ending things warmly if sadly, but without hostility. A gentle goodbye.

Okay... I can do that...

It was him, but it wasn't.

Continuing to hold her face in one hand as he cuddled her body against the mattress, he kissed the corners of her mouth gently, tenderly, without the usual mad rush to passion that both of them frequently undertook. His thumb stroked her cheek; his other arm slid under her neck.

He kissed her lips softly, without aggression, taking them into his own and savoring their warmth, and she felt ... different. He felt the same, he smelled the same, their bed was the same, but the feelings she was having were something new.

He's trying to tell me something...

She felt a flash of suspicion - that whatever new stuff he was about to lay on her was something he'd learned from someone else - but the way he was holding her brushed that thought away instantly. This was something just for her.

It was she, not he, who grew impatient, and she slid her free arm around her neck, pulling into his kiss. Her tongue crept in toward his, and she trusted herself to release some of her feelings into him.

This is just for tonight... it doesn't mean anything...

They were both wearing jeans, and their legs slid uncomfortably together into their familiar positions. He stopped abruptly and sat up in the shadows, pulling back a bit, and eased her up in front of him. He pulled her close, and she realized he had shed his shirt.

He cradled her head in one hand, pulling her close to him with his other arm, leaning her cheek against his naked chest.

What the hell???
Then she realized she could hear his heartbeat.
He's taking in my heartbeat!
She realized that she had begun slowly rocking them.

After what seemed forever, he eased her back onto the bed, then delicately removed her jeans. She made no countermove, entranced by whatever ritual he was developing, and was surprised that he made no follow-up. He slid alongside her, returning to their kiss, and his fingers on the buttons of her blouse were so subtle that it was almost open when she realized what he was doing.

He didn't dive for her boobs, as he usually did. Instead, he laid his head against them gently ... taking in *her* heartbeat.

Her hand cradled his head as the other pulled him closer, and she felt her eyes watering.

He kissed one of her still-covered breasts, then lifted himself on one arm, sliding the other arm under her and lifting her a bit. She took the hint and eased her blouse off, and with his usual deftness, he undid her bra with a quick flick of his fingers, and took her in his arms for real.

His own jeans were gone - when had he done that? - and their bodies tangled, but more slowly than usual. Their routine scramble for friction was absent, and she found herself easily surrendering to whatever he was trying to present.

It won't be like it was before ...

Without losing their rhythm, without compromising the welcome pleasure he was providing, she began to pay attention to everything he was doing, realizing that there was something there for her in every touch, every move.

As their kiss slowly deepened, his hands explored her slowly and warmly, without his usual intent to tease - but she found herself teased all the same, wanting more. She was surprised to realize that her own hands had taken on a life of their own; she usually stroked and grabbed in places that made him moan, but she found herself simply indulging herself, taking polite advantage of this odd moment, pressing fingertips into muscle - and grabbing his ass more forcefully than she had ever done in the past.

This isn't like it was before...

This was something new.

It was something new, and she felt emboldened, intent on understanding what he was doing, but giving herself permission to explore and communicate as he was. If she got it wrong, or he didn't get it, what did it matter? It was over anyway.

She took his head in his hands and returned it to her breasts, and he laid his cheek on one of them again, not for her heartbeat but for her softness, and her nipple couldn't have been comfortable. He had always given her breasts plenty of appreciation and attention, and he'd never been too rough (as some of his predecessors had been), but neither was he particularly nuanced ...

... until now. With a few light kisses on each breast, he let the tip of his tongue trace its way to the edge of one of her nipples, not quite getting there. She found herself shifting, unconsciously trying to get under his tongue, but he withdrew, repeating the gesture ...

He's being patient ...

And that, too, was new.

His tongue teased at her nipple, then pressed against it, warm, wet, unmoving. She found herself surprised, then squirming, trying to make her nipple move. He responded, firmly taking it into his mouth. Usually he sucked them - too hard, sometimes - but this time he simply stroked it with the tip of his tongue, as his lips covered it.

She was breathless.

On and on he went, repeating the ritual on the other side, and he just kept at it. He had never lingered on any part of her like this before.

Why isn't he spreading my legs by now?

Then it dawned on her. *He's waiting until I let him know I've had what I need.*

So she let him go a little longer.

Normally she would give him a gentle push, to propel his tongue further south. Instead she took his head in her hands as she'd done before, but lifted him to her face. She kissed him deeply, with purpose...

I understand what you're doing right now. I'm hearing you...

Then she pushed him south.

He'd learned early on that she liked oral sex - a lot! - and she had trained him well. He'd been clumsy but willing, early on, but it had rapidly become part of their routine and he'd dutifully done a good job on her, most of the time. She came easily that way, and it took pressure off him later - though she was much more likely, he knew, to come when he was inside her if he went down on her first.

He was usually opening her legs and spreading her lips five seconds after her push, but this time he just wandered down her stomach, breathing on her warm skin, kissing her lightly ... and when he arrived, her legs spread wide, she realized she was still wearing her panties.

He didn't remove them. He breathed in her scent, wrapping his arms around her thighs, and pressed his face into the soaked cotton, a pressured kiss that was maddeningly distant through the fabric.

His fingers stroked around her edges through the panties, and he began kissing her as if they weren't there. The kisses were firm, lingering, his mouth partly open, the tip of his tongue between his lips. If not for the panties, they would have been mind-blowing. Why was he doing this to her?

Your barriers are holding us back ...

She got it.

Pushing his head back, she pulled her legs up and shed the panties herself. She understood that he was telling her that she needed to be the one to pull down her barriers.

He kissed his way up her thighs and took up his old rhythms, doing the things she loved most - the difference being that he went much more slowly than usual, giving her plenty of time to get lost in the building ecstasy. What he'd done to her breasts he now repeated, resting his wet tongue, unmoving, until she squirmed for the sweet friction.

She had always appreciated his willingness to please her this way, and he'd never seemed to mind, but this time he was really into it - she knew he'd be happy to keep his tongue on duty as long as she wanted. And he played it, stopping at maddening moments, kissing her, drawing a wet finger around her contours, pinching her lightly at the bottom. When his fingers slid inside, she sensed her own overwhelming wetness, and she knew it was going to be good.

It was. Normally her climax was like ascending a steep hill, and it was a relief when she got over the top without collapsing. This time --- *ooh* ... this time she found herself holding back, fighting to stay there on the tantalizing edge, pushing it away until it overwhelmed her like a tidal wave.

She cried out.

It lasted and lasted and lasted, and when her ecstasy began to recede, she realized she was holding his head with her thighs in an almost vice-like grip, her hands clinging to bunched-up bedsheets. She panted, lost in the echoes of her spasms, and he eased alongside her, kissing her neck ...

I was wrong to force things ...

This was where he'd usually get on top of her, and that would usually be fine.

Instead, he was waiting for her.

She smiled in the darkness, meeting his lips, and turned him on his back. She breathed him in, moving from his mouth to his neck to his chest, tracing little trails with her tongue, and found that he was still wearing his boxers. She felt his swollen cock through the fabric, playing as he had played with her, and he moaned a little as she half-grasped him, appreciating his arousal as always, but feeling oddly liberated by his earlier attentiveness.

No "duty" here.

That being the case, she pulled his boxers away with something more than excitement. This was lust, more honest than she'd felt in a very long time.

After long moments of deftly fondling him, not neglecting the stepchildren, she herself headed south, only to feel his hand on her head, stopping her-

What? But he loves this!

He guided her head into a different position, and she instantly understood.

I don't want what I used to want ... I want something new ...

She took him in one hand, then began running her tongue slowly from bottom to top in long, lazy strokes, lingering teasingly at the top. He moaned, and with some delight she indulged in the torture, doing for him what he had done for her, with no sense of duty at all, just sheer enjoyment of their shared pleasure. She gave him more than she thought he could take, then finally took him in, firmly and with purpose. He didn't last long.

It took him almost as long to recover as she had taken, and as she crawled back up into his arms, knowing that they must finish this the right way, she prepared to wait him out, only to find him returning to her breasts, starting over ...

He was going to do it all again!

She almost always wanted that, but only a handful of times ... special occasions, trips out of town ... had he gone down on her more than once in a single night. If she had her way, she'd keep him down there till she'd come three or four times, every single night.

193

And now, in a flash of insight, she realized that he knew that. And he was telling her ...

I understand that I let your needs go unmet ...

She came even harder this time, and he lingered, keeping his fingers inside her, and continued working her G-spot, pressing with his other palm from above, increasing the pressure. She relaxed into it, ignoring the screams of her clit, and it took awhile - but she came yet again, this time spraying his hands with wet warmth, her muscles screaming with joy ...

... and while she was crying out, he merged with her, easing into a powerful rhythm, hovering above her, pulling her legs against his chest, thrusting to please himself. He took his time, absorbing the last echoes of her climax, burying himself in her ... his fingernails raked against her legs, giving her chills, and she reached above to grip the headboard, to steady herself and give him something to push against.

As his release approached, he backed off, pulling out and rolling her over. He lifted her up and took her from behind as she laid her head down, not propping up on all fours, and as he began to move within her she steadied herself with one hand and found her outer spot with the other.

She had never touched herself while he was inside her before. Now, it seemed as natural as breathing. She was really wet, and had no trouble building to another orgasm.

Then he rolled her over yet again, while she was still trembling, and took her the old-fashioned way. He pressed hard into her, and in moments they convulsed together, releasing months of stress and pain and hurt and confusion in a moment that purged and purified them both - mutual surrender, mutual desire, mutual respect ... mutual joy.

They held each other for long moments, their damp bodies clinging, and he remained inside her for a very long time, a tender intimacy ... and his hand cupped her cheek, as when they'd begun, and he kissed her as he had before ...

I'm listening more carefully now ...

He wasn't asking for anything. This was just a moment.

But she realized that something had changed, in those weeks they'd been out of touch. Something had happened to him. She didn't know what. He had tried to tell her, and she hadn't heard him. She hadn't given him a chance.

He couldn't tell her with his voice. So he'd told her with his body, with his fingertips, with his kiss.

There was no going back. But he didn't want to, any more than she did. There was only moving forward. Their old relationship was dead, and would remain dead.

But there could be something new. It would have to be a start-from-scratch effort, taking nothing for granted, with all that it implied. But it *would* be new. He had changed. And she wanted change for herself. Neither changing the other, but both growing, with the other's love and encouragement and support.

She nestled into his arms, sleep not far away, and with her embrace, she sent a message of her own:

Stay ...

Golden

Her hand trembled a bit as he eased onto the bed, his naked form so enticing in candlelight, and a trickle of wine spilled onto the sheets.

Glasses touched, sips were exchanged and her lips were wine-sweet to him, but they were anyway, and the glasses were ungracefully set aside.

If she admired his body in candlelight, with the ripple of delivery-truck muscles and the limber of the biking he did to save them money, he admired hers all the more, with its deceptively fragile curves and an equally deceptive, almost unbearable softness, covering a firm strength that no carriage of children could ever bend, and a sweetness that made him burn. They were a couple made for candlelight - and tonight they would burn the candle down to nothing...

Their loving was a dance, subtle and powerful and expressive, and they preferred a clean dance floor. Their bed was characteristically blanket- and pillow-free, nothing but sheets, and they worked their art with focus and passion and intensity. Fingers intertwined as he raised her arms above her head, kissing his way down them to her shoulder and neck, lingering there in that place beneath her ear, and she sighed, her fingers spreading across his chest and pressing into him... she nipped at him in the way that told him she wanted to be kissed, and the taste of wine lingered as she did her familiar fingertip tease of his offering, now pulsing and strong...

And he countered, prolonging, drifting to her white bosom, the raspberry buds far sweeter than any wine, teasing them, tasting them, nipping at them, till they were rubies, and her fingers stepped up their insistence...

He rolled her on her back, covering her body with his, immersed in the tingle of skin, his firmness gracing her with clear intent... fingertips worked their way across her back, starting in that sensitive place on her neck, working all the way down to her most sensitive places...

Her scent provoked him, sweet and feminine and hot and randy, and he responded in masculine kind, turning her again, covering her again, his arms extending over her, his body finally taking hers...

Their melting together was crock-pot slow, with a controlled ferocity, tremors that rose within them both and synchronized, and they took their lazy, lustful time. They kept eyes open, as always, and he stared into her as their thrusts quickened, as tension mounted and ecstasy beckoned, adoring her, wanting her, needing her, worshipping her, receiving all her secrets and hiding them away...

Afterwards, their fingers intertwined again, two golden bands catching candleflame, precious circles pursuing infinity, eternity, and on this special night, truly golden... passing fifty years together...

A final kiss, and he nestled against her, spooning...

It was well past midnight when his son's phone rang, dragging him to coherence over his wife's hostile grumbles. It had not been a happy evening. He quickly slipped out of the bedroom, not anxious to irritate her further, and into the hall.

He saw by the number that it was the cell phone he'd given his father before his mother had died, when she'd been so ill. As far as he knew, his father had never used it.

Dad...?

Cold November wind and bottomless dark encased them, the moonless sky adding a harsh foreboding to the shadows cast by the SUV's headlights. The engine was off; there was no sound but the rustle of leaves, and his father's breathing.

Dad, we really shouldn't be out here...

His father could not hear him, did not seem to remember he was even there. He'd worried more and more about him, these past few months, but there had seemed to be nothing he could do. This bizarre late-night request had been a relief - *at least he needs something -* and anything that got him out of the house wasn't a bad thing.

But now he worried even more, as he watched his father kneeling... his face was in shadow, obscured by stone, and he knelt for a better view.

There was something new in the sounds from his father's chest, more than just labored breath, and in the shadow he saw the old man's face... his own breath stuck in his chest at the sight.

There was a grief so deep, a pain so vast, a longing so unending in the old man's wet eyes that he had the impulse to reach out and hold him. His father stared straight ahead, as if to hold the emerging tear back by sheer willpower... he failed, and it spilled onto his cheek.

His son saw the tremors, the shaking hands clinging to the tombstone as it were the side of a lifeboat, and he was shivering in cold waters...

...and isn't he?

Watching closely, he understood his father for perhaps the first time ever, and saw in the haunted face a truth he'd never given proper notice, when his mother had been alive.

I'm glad she went first, his father had said, and this had puzzled him. Why? To be left like this, too lonely to live, to face days like this, to ---

Of course.

Of course each had wanted the other to go first... each of them had wanted the other to be spared this, the endless grief, the vast loneliness, the balance of a life without what they had shared. A bond so incredibly deep, so infinitely special, that the idea of "moving on" or "starting over" was just absurd.

Dear god...

He had never known, he had never realized... He looked at his father as if for the first time. The trembling... not the wind, the old man was wearing a coat made of fleece half-an-inch thick... the trembling was pure grief, grief which had been killing him slowly,a day at a time, grief he had desperately needed to come to this place to release.

The enormity of the moment chilled him more deeply than the wind, as a lifetime of memories of his mother and father swept through him in a moment.

Will I ever know this, myself?

Moments later, the old man seemed to sag, and he held out a steadying arm.

Let's get you home...

The son slipped back into the bedroom as quietly as he'd slipped out, undressing in the dark, and eased back into bed. All that he had seen played again and again in his thoughts, and he knew he would be a long time understanding it fully. But he had seen in his father something... something that lay beyond him for now, something of immeasurable worth, a path his parents had walked, in their intimate universe, a path...

As gently as he could, he nestled against her, spooning...

Harvest House

A Coming-of-Age Story

I

The bright blue of sky and white blaze of sun made it seem like a summer morning, but the chilled visibility of breath beneath wool caps and earmuffs told the real story. The new year was still new and the layers of frost endless renewing, morning after morning, declared the winter that defined this Saturday morning.

Gary Riddel held his unbuttoned overcoat closed with one hand as he crossed the street and waved to Richard and Wayne, whose moms didn't make them wear overcoats but who also seemed untroubled by the cold that was seeping thru their jackets. The rest of the group was not so patient.

"Gary! Hurry up, we're freezing!"

Kim. With her girlfriends Stacy and Elizabeth and another girl Gary didn't know.

Along with a couple of kids from another church, whom Gary didn't know, it was more or less the usual Saturday morning group assembled on the porch of Harvest House. A couple of the regulars were missing, probably having to work at the grocery store or the bowling alley or Burger Chef. Gary, usually the first to arrive, was last today – and, because he was the pastor's son, had the key.

He bound up the stairs to the porch of the old two-story house, past thick wood columns and old sitting chairs. The crowd parted to give him access to the weighty old door with its rattling black-iron handle and lock, which yielded under a half a minute of fumbling from Gary. Everyone poured into the house, the girls chattering as they proceeded to the kitchen to un-bag and distribute donuts and orange juice.

Richard and Wayne stayed in the living room with Gary as he pulled off his coat and gloves and cap and kicked the heat up a bit. Gary surveyed the room, with its many recently-deposited boxes of clothes and canned goods, not really listening to Richard and Wayne arguing the subtleties of how the Cowboys were going to pulverize the Dolphins in the upcoming Super Bowl.

As Richard re-deified Tom Landry as a god among football coaches and the boys began toting boxes into the Game Room for sorting, Gary found his thoughts drifting. Harvest House had only been operating for a couple of months, since before the holidays, but it seemed that they'd been doing this forever, pulling in donated food and clothes from the community, putting together care packages for local families in need.

Gary wasn't sure whose idea Harvest House had been. But it had begun that night back in November, the night of the pile-up out on I-74 near the exit, when seven vehicles had been involved in a terrible collision. Four people had died; another nine had been injured, some very seriously. An eighteen-wheeler, a station wagon, a Chevy van, a pick-up truck, and three smaller cars had all been demolished when the truck jack-knifed. Three of those killed were local people: a man and his infant child, whom Gary didn't know, and the aunt of one of Gary's classmates. Four of the nine injured were also local, two of them cousins of the classmate, a man from Gary's church, and someone else Gary didn't know.

Harvest House had begun as the church's way of responding to the tragedy, calling for meals and visitation and comfort to the families involved. The response had been so strong that the church had rented this old brick house in town as a base of operations to continue the work.

Gary's father had volunteered him to lead an effort among the young people in the community, in connection with Harvest House. On Thursday nights they would walk around the community in groups, requesting donations and distributing leaflets, then meet back at the house for pizza and a Bible study. Saturday mornings they would sort donations and make up care-package boxes, as they were doing this morning, which other volunteers would later distribute to families the church had identified as needy.

"I'm glad you got here when you did," came a voice. Gary turned and faced Kim, who presented him with a donut and a Styrofoam cup filled with orange juice. "We were half frozen!"

It always took him a moment to think of something to say to her. Kim was his age, seventeen, with bright green eyes and curly blond hair. She was always smiling.

"I had to take Joanie to her dance class," he explained, sipping the orange juice so he wouldn't have to keep talking.

"We knocked and knocked. That woman is supposed to be living upstairs now, we thought she'd let us in. But no one answered."

A protest from Richard caused them both to turn. His pool game with Wayne was ended when Stacy and Elizabeth began emptying cardboard boxes filled with old clothes onto the pool and ping-pong tables. Rather than immediately starting back to work, they allowed themselves to be displaced, grabbed donuts and juice and joined Gary in the next room.

"Kim said somebody lives here now," Gary said.

Richard looked at him. "You didn't know that? There's a fox living upstairs." He took a bite of donut. "And when I say 'fox,' I mean... *total* fox."

"Complete fox," Wayne nodded. "How come you didn't know? I thought it was your dad's idea."

It was all news to Gary.

"My mom said the church wanted someone to be here all the time, you know, so the place wouldn't get robbed. Lots of food and stuff lying around most of the time."

Gary nodded. It made sense.

Kim called from the game room. "You guys want to do some actual work?"

Richard and Wayne wandered back in. Mercifully, someone had turned on the radio. Pop radio was forbidden in Reverend Riddel's strict, conservative home.

Bye, bye, Miss American Pie!

WLS-Chicago. Gary's leading guilty pleasure. When he was alone in the family car, he always turned it on, careful to change it back to the gospel station before he parked in the driveway. But right now he wasn't listening; he found himself looking back across the living room, to the staircase on the far side.

On the second floor was a living area, two rooms, a bathroom and a small kitchenette. He remembered helping his father with repairs to the kitchenette and bathroom when the church had first rented the house, back in the late fall. His father had said something about subletting the room at the time, but had said nothing to him since.

As he took a bite of donut, the front door suddenly opened, and a young woman slipped in with a single bag of groceries. She wore a thin tan coat, a multi-colored scarf and dark blue earmuffs. Long brown hair flowed down her back, and her cheeks were cold-red beneath her large, chocolate brown eyes.

She tried to close the door behind her but almost lost the bag of groceries in the process.

"Let me get that," Gary suddenly blurted, and he dropped his donut on the floor to free up a hand. Instead of taking the groceries, which would have made a lot more sense, he closed the door for her. And felt stupid.

They were inches apart. She smelled like flowers.

She smiled at the gesture. Shorter than he was, she was also older, college-age or more.

"You're Gary, aren't you?" she asked, and he was completely taken aback that she knew his name.

"Thank you," she said, before he could answer, and disappeared up the stairs. He didn't see Kim watching from the other room.

Sunday dinner was always meticulously timed, rigorously ritualized. Since the entire family was engaged in many church activities on Sunday mornings, and Reverend Riddel insisted on very traditional family routines, the after-church dinner was always a precarious undertaking, subject to any one of a number of interruptions that might upset the schedule, delay or ruin the meal, and leave Dad in a foul mood that might result in the younger children being banished to their rooms for the afternoon.

To accomplish the meal, Gary's mother typically spent Saturday evening preparing whatever could be safely done in advance of actual stove or oven time, and popped long-term things for baking into the oven before leaving for church Sunday morning, getting up before 6 a.m. when the cooking time factor demanded it. Joanie had been assisting in the after-church meal preparation for several years now, and in general they could have dinner on the table in 30 minutes or less, much to Dad's satisfaction.

The meal was on time and well underway when his mother, who rarely actually sat down, leaned over and refilled his tea and asked, "How did things go at Harvest yesterday?"

Her face was suddenly in front of him, and he was reliving the door-closing incident, when his father turned to look at him as well.

"Ah... Fine."

"How many did you have?" his father asked.

"Eight."

His father always frowned, no matter what the number.

"We should do better."

"It's such a good work, the house," his mother said as she took her seat. "It was terrible how it came to be, but look at all the good that's come of it since."

The reverend looked at Joanie, who sat across the table from Gary. "You and your friends at church will be starting high school later this year," he said. "With Gary and some of the others graduating, it's time you started pitching in."

"Yessir," said Joanie, keeping her face carefully neutral. Gary was well aware that Joanie wasn't the least bit interested.

"And on the subject of your graduation," his father continued, facing Gary, "it's time we scheduled a sit-down with Mr. Price from Trinity, and started your paperwork."

There was no answer acceptable at the dinner table other than "Yessir." Gary had tried to argue with his father several times over the past few weeks, but not at dinner. It had always been assumed that Gary, Joanie and their younger brother would follow in their parents' footsteps, attending the bible college where they had met, and where their father now served on the Board of Trustees. Gary himself had never questioned this plan. Until lately.

He stabbed a piece of ham and realized his father was still watching him, beyond his "yessir." He gave a weak smile and drank his tea.

But the coming argument with his father over his college plans wasn't on his mind. He realized he was thinking about long brown hair and cold-red cheeks under large, chocolate brown eyes...

Locker doors rattled open and banged shut all around him as Gary sat down on a bench and began pulling on his socks. Wayne plopped down beside him, still sweaty.

"Valentines Dance coming up, Brother Gee," he panted. "You gonna get off your can once and for all and ask Kimberly?"

That had actually been Gary's plan. Until...

Richard suddenly appeared on the other side of him, trapping him there on the bench.

"Yeah, what about it, Riddel? What do you need, an engraved invitation?"

No escape. "We'll see."

"If you don't ask her," Wayne persisted. "We can always ask her for you."

"We'll write a note for you," Richard said. "'O Kimberly, thou who doth make me ever horny, who doth wiggle her tits and get my wang up–'"

"What makes you think she'd go with me?" Gary interrupted, just to shut him up.

Wayne snickered. "Are you kidding?"

"How obvious does she have to be?"

Richard looked at him. "You're in, man. How can you not know that?"

"You are *so* in. Oh, man, she'd do anything you wanted her to do."

Wayne wasn't just talking dirty. Gary could tell by his expression that he was completely serious. He turned to Richard, who nodded.

"Anything."

Gary wished they would both just go away. He knew, on some subconscious level, that they were probably right. And he had avoided getting too close to Kim for exactly that reason. Things probably would happen. And he didn't know how to feel about that.

But now there was something more. He thought about Kim, a lot, at night. Or he did until this week. Now, he thought about...

Sliding on his loafers, he stood and walked out of the locker room. His friends looked at each other and shook their heads.

The sky was twilight-blue as coats and gloves and caps and earmuffs came off and piled up on the game room floor of Harvest House. Pizza was on the way, but several of the girls headed straight into the kitchen, putting on water for hot chocolate.

Gary dutifully pulled out his guitar, and in the momentary absence of girls, launched into the opening of "Roundabout."

Richard loved that riff. He motioned to Mark, who along with Richard was in marching band, and who showed up at Harvest with him from time to time. "Check this out."

Gary played it again.

"Isn't that cool?" Richard nudged Mark. He turned back to Gary. "Wouldn't your dad be ticked off if he heard you playing stuff like that?"

Gary half-smiled. "I practice it when I hang out at Wayne's."

On cue, Wayne plopped down on a bean-bag chair, a stale donut from the previous Saturday morning in his hand. "He does. He's played that record so much it's all scratchy now. I think you need to buy me a new one, man."

Kim and her friend Elizabeth approached, Kim with two cups of hot chocolate. Gary began playing the chords of a praise chorus.

Kim set the hot chocolate down next to him as he played. Wayne and Richard both gave him a look.

A dozen choruses and four boxes of pizza later, Brother Mike, the youth sponsor, pulled out a contemporary translation of the bible and read a passage about caring for the poor, a theme which seemed to permeate the entire New Testament. As he was talking about the verses, Gary became aware of a pulse, a faraway sound.

"It's Cream!" Wayne whispered. "Man... I love that song!"

I've been waiting so long... to be where I'm going... Eric Clapton's voice, muffled, in the distance.

Richard pointed upward. It was a stereo, in the apartment above them.

Brother Mike rose with a trace of impatience, crossed into the living room, and rapped his knuckles loudly on the heavy wooden banister. He paused a moment, then repeated the gesture. The volume of the music dropped sharply, but it did not go away completely.

Wayne and Richard and Mark thought this was funny. Wayne continued to mouth the lyrics, faint as they were, as Brother Mike resumed his lesson.

Twenty minutes later, Gary was helping with clean-up, folding up pizza boxes and stuffing them into the trash can in the kitchen.

"Young lady," came Brother Mike's voice from the doorway. Gary looked up.

She was standing at the refrigerator, taking an ice cube tray out of the freezer. Barefoot, dressed in patched blue jeans and a t-shirt, the long brown hair in a pony tail. Gary felt his pulse thundering in his ears.

"On Thursday nights we have our bible study with our youth volunteers," Brother Mike said to her. "I would appreciate it if you would save your music for another time." There was just enough disapproval in the way he said your music to make it clear that Eric Clapton was not an ideal choice.

She smiled back. "Of course," she said. "I'm sorry, I didn't mean to disturb anyone. I can play music tomorrow night."

Brother Mike nodded and smiled thinly. "Thank you." He disappeared into the game room, where Wayne was fiddling amateurishly with Gary's guitar, the other boys were playing ping-pong, and the girls were gathering up the hot chocolate mugs.

"You like Cream?"

She was standing right in front of him. He caught himself staring at her boobs. He looked up suddenly, embarrassed, and nodded.

She smiled and looked right into his eyes.

"Tomorrow night," she said quietly, and she headed back upstairs with her ice cubes.

Her meaning had been unmistakable.

He stood on the porch, in the dark, in the cold. For the third time, he lifted the key to unlock the door, wondering if this was appropriate, if he should knock or something. And he again wondered if he had completely misunderstood the exchange in the kitchen the previous evening. The porch light had not been on. Yet as he had approached the house, he'd seen the lights on upstairs.

He was grateful for the darkness, afraid that someone might see him here, otherwise. He had no reasonable excuse for being here.

And he had *lied* to his parents! "I'll be at Richard's. We're having kind of a pre-Super Bowl party." It had sounded good as he was saying it. He felt a deep twinge of guilt over the lie, and was uneasy that his mother would have some reason to call Richard's house.

Then he heard music, faintly. "Roundabout." Yes. The song he'd been playing on his guitar.

He unlocked the door and stepped into the dark living room of Harvest House. Light poured down the stairwell, and the music was louder. The door to the apartment, at the top of the stairs, was open. He looked up.

"Hello?" he called.

She appeared at the top of the stairs, once again in blue jeans and bare feet, her hair once again pony-tailed. But tonight she wore a bright blue blouse, and held a wine glass in her hand.

"Hi!" she called out brightly, and bounced down the stairs with a smile, managing to keep the wine glass perfectly steady. She stood before him, uncomfortably close, looking right into him.

He had no idea what to say.

"I'm listening to Yes," she said, "Didn't you play this last night?" He nodded. "Come on up!" She turned to go back up the stairs.

He didn't budge.

"Come on," she said, reaching out and taking his hand with another smile, "It's okay. Let's listen to some music."

Alarms went off inside him, one after another. There were so many things wrong with this, he could hardly list them. At the same time, he couldn't think of any place he'd rather be.

Every step he took up the stairs felt incredibly ominous.

The apartment looked nothing like it had looked weeks ago, when he and his father had done the repairs. The outer room contained a weary couch and chair of indeterminate color, a green bean bag chair in a corner, and two tall bookcases. A small table with two chairs sat next to the kitchenette. The doorway into the bedroom was filled with a veil of beads. Colorful posters covered the walls.

The stereo sat on what had been an end table for a higher-quality couch at one point, with the speakers situated on opposite sides of the room. Two shelves were filled with records.

"Would you like some wine?" she asked as he pulled off his coat.

This startled him. Almost never in his life had he been offered alcohol. Most of the adults in his life were part of the church, and his friends knew better.

He shook his head. "A Coke?" she asked. When he didn't answer, she crossed the room to the refrigerator.

He wandered hesitantly toward the records on the shelf. What he saw completely distracted him from everything else.

It was a treasure chest!

Derek and the Dominoes. Three Dog Night. The Allman Brothers, *Live at the Fillmore East*. The Byrds' *Greatest Hits*. *Tarkus*, Emerson Lake and Palmer. Nazareth. Frank Zappa's *Weasels Ripped My Flesh*. Elton John, *Madman Across the Water*. Floyd, *Atom Heart Mother*. Hendrix, Band of Gypsies. *All Things Must Pass*. John Lennon's *Imagine*. The new Led Zeppelin. The Guess Who.

And others, somehow more feminine, more what he might have expected: Carole King's *Tapestry*. *Bridge Over Troubled Waters*. *Pearl*, Janis Joplin.

"Is there something you'd like to listen to?" She was next to him, holding a Coke, which she handed to him.

"This is incredible," he said, immediately feeling silly. Neither Wayne nor Richard had a collection nearly as awesome as hers, but anyone who really loved music would have exactly these albums.

She slipped out a record and replaced Yes.

Sweet Baby James! Kim had played it for him last summer.

Taking his hand again, she led him to the couch. It was as comfortable as it was ugly.

She was so close, so casual, that he felt completely on edge. He realized she was probably at least five years older than he was, maybe more. She wasn't at all self-conscious, in her jeans and blouse, her breasts more exposed and within-reach than any he'd ever been right next, except possibly at a beach or swimming pool. Even her naked feet were sexy. And she smelled like flowers. He clutched his Coke as if it were a grenade.

"I bet you have most of those albums," she said, sipping her wine.

He shook his head. "My dad isn't really a rock music fan." *Meaning he doesn't allow it in the house.*

"But you know this stuff," she said. And he described his routine, listening to the latest-greatest at his friends' homes, and how he would study the music and pick up bits and pieces to play on the guitar.

"Tell me what you like," she said, refilling her wine and fetching him another Coke.

So he spent fifteen minutes describing the music he loved, that his father wouldn't allow in the house.

"Would you play for me?"

He was so startled that he didn't answer right away, and before he could protest that he hadn't brought his guitar, she was reaching behind the couch and bringing out a beautiful acoustic instrument.

An Ovation! The very best.

"You play?" he asked, surprised.

"No," she said with a smile, and handed it to him.

It was the finest guitar he'd ever touched. He fumbled with it, feeling awkward and nervous.

He started into the opening bars of "Roundabout," blew it twice, had to start over. Once he started to really play, he began to relax, and he played song after song for her, for almost an hour. His fingers went from awkward to skilled very quickly. As he played, she never took her eyes off him.

It was almost ten o'clock.

"I have to go," he said suddenly, putting down the guitar.

"That was wonderful," she said. "Thank you."

The awkwardness returned, now that he no longer had a guitar with which to defend himself. He mumbled something as he looked around for his coat. She was closer to it, and picked it up.

"Gary."

Standing in front of him, she reached a hand around his neck and drew him in, and kissed him.

It was the kiss of a woman and a man, not tentative, not shy. It was years beyond anything in his experience, firm and intentional and passionate. A French kiss, a mature kiss. Hints of wine, also new to him, and a deep sexuality that made him feel simultaneously stirred and suspended in mid-air.

With sudden horror, he realized he was totally aroused, and in this very close embrace, realized that she would notice, if she hadn't already. He began to pull away, but she was in no hurry to let him.

She let the kiss resolve gradually, remaining in control, but gently so. Their lips parted slowly.

"Tomorrow night?" she said, as she had said the night before, but this time in a whisper.

He was early to arrive and open the house for the usual Saturday morning box-sorting, having had an even earlier errand to run. The drugstore opened at 9 a.m. on Saturdays, and he had been waiting when the druggist unlocked the door, so he could get in and out before there were any other customers.

Neither the druggist nor the two clerks were people Gary knew, and as far as he could recall, neither went to his family's church. He could only hope and pray that none of them recognized him, and that they didn't know his father or mother.

And he was mortified to learn that condoms were not displayed openly on an aisle anywhere. They were kept behind the druggist's counter, and you had to ask for them. Only the urgency of getting out of there quickly, before anyone familiar wandered in, pressed Gary to action. The druggist seemed to know what he wanted before he asked. He almost choked on the word 'condom.'

He had very little to say later, during box sorting. He felt himself not looking toward the living room, not watching for her to appear. Everyone else was cheerful and noisy, and his low-key demeanor was conspicuous.

"So, Brother Gee," Richard said as he and Wayne appeared next to Gary, "Forgot to ask Thursday. You saw her." They began helping him sort cans of food into categories.

"What? Who?"

"'What? Who?'" Wayne mocked. "*Her*. The fox in the attic," he said, nodding upstairs.

"You got the door for her. Also pretty sure we saw you alone in the kitchen with her the other night."

Gary shrugged. "So?"

"So? What's her name?"

Gary felt like he'd hit a step he didn't know was there. With a surge of delayed embarrassment, he realized that at no point during the previous evening had he asked her name.

"You can't remember her name?"

"He was distracted by her other fine qualities. Both of them."

"Now Brother Gee's got somebody to ask to the Valentines Dance."

"You must be high, man. She's *wayyy* too old … "

"Old enough to be, like, his big sister … "

He let them go on. It was easier than trying to shut them up, and *way* easier than actually answering any questions.

When the care package boxes were complete and ready for the after-church stewardship team to deliver the next afternoon, everyone started cleaning up, then finding coats and jackets. Gary couldn't see his coat.

"Here you go," came Kim's voice behind him. She was already wearing hers. His was draped over her arm.

He felt himself go cold with horror, fearing that the box of condoms would fall out of the coat pocket onto the floor right in front of her. Like a striking rattlesnake, he grabbed at the collar of his coat and pulled it from her arm, careful to hold it upright.

"So, are you going to the Valentine's Dance?" Kim asked him.

Startled, he pulled on his coat, fumbling for an answer.

"Not sure," he muttered. "I might need to help my uncle, on his farm."

"On a Friday night? In winter?" The lie was so transparent, she was both surprised and hurt, and he could see it on her face.

"See you at church," he mumbled, and he fled.

Another lie, this one about a school friend his mother had only met once, covered his absence that evening. After letting himself into Harvest House, he proceeded up the stairs without announcing himself first. There were no lights on, only candles, dozens of them, in the living room and beyond. She sat on the couch with her glass of wine. He didn't know the name for the garment she was wearing, but he was pretty sure it was French. She rose, took a second glass of wine from the coffee table, and met him in the middle of the room.

"My name is Laurie," she said softly, and she kissed him.

She handed him his glass, then took his hand and led him into the bedroom.

The wine burned in his throat, almost-sweet and headier than anything he'd experienced before. His only previous encounter with alcohol had been a few sips of beer from a can offered by his youngest aunt's boyfriend two years ago, an experience that he recalled with guilt, and a sense of revulsion. Beer, he had decided, tasted horrible, and he was not anxious to try it again.

Wine was another matter. The burning was not fun, but the taste, and the warm, lazy feeling that was slowly overcoming him were sensations he realized he could get used to. His father's many sermons and speeches on the subject threatened to erupt in his conscience, but Laurie was effortlessly drawing his attention.

James Taylor played softly from the living room as he surveyed the small bedroom, sipping the wine only when she sipped hers. It wasn't so different from the living room, with its second-hand furniture and poster-covered walls. A bright red lava lamp sat on top of a dresser. It looked alien, catching little glints of candlelight from all sides.

There were little feminine touches: a hat rack holding a dozen or so colorful scarves; a stuffed bear next to the bed. They didn't come close to capturing her femininity, which overwhelmed him whenever she stepped within touching distance …

… which she did, setting down her wine glass, crossing to stand right in front of him. She still smelled like flowers, and her eyes reflected all the little fires around them. She took his wine glass and drank from it, then lifted it to his lips. He repeated the gesture, drinking more of it than he really should have, and he fought against the sudden surge of burning in his throat. She set that glass aside, too, and lifted her hands around his neck, kissing him deeply.

Her mouth was sweet and warm, and the kiss was so deep that he wasn't sure how to do it properly. A fortunate instinct took over and compelled him to simply ease into whatever happened, to follow and not try to lead, and this seemed natural, and agreeable to her. He could not understand the emotions that flowed, and could not even begin to formulate a reason why this was happening.

But he knew what happened next, and he was terrified.

As she had the night before, she took her time. Kisses were not things to be hurried. They were an exploration, her tongue and her pressures against his body encouraging him to explore as well. Her arms around his neck, and now his back, became inquiries into his muscularity, and these too were unhurried.

When she finally pulled back, it was to turn her attention to the buttons of his shirt. It was open in seconds, and the warm surface of her palms pressed against his chest as she kissed him again. Then they moved upward to his shoulders, pushing the shirt away.

His sudden self-consciousness distracted him as she kissed him a third time, one hand on the back of his neck. He didn't notice her other hand loosening his belt.

Again she stepped back, and in one swift motion shed her own garment, leaving only panties. Without taking her eyes off him, she eased back onto the bed.

Leave now! Gary's fundamentalist conscience shouted, as if perched on his shoulder. *Now nownow. While you still can!*

This isn't what he'd planned. This wasn't the way it was supposed to be. He knew the right path, he knew what was expected. He'd been hearing it since he was old enough to walk. Grow up, follow the straight-and-narrow. Let God choose someone for him, a girl who shared his beliefs. Be with that someone, in this way – *after* marriage – and no one else!

He could turn and leave. Right now.

She extended her hand, inviting him in.

At first, he couldn't take his eyes off her breasts. They were full and perfect, her nipples large and erect. In his whole life, he'd only seen breasts in the flesh twice – once when he'd walked in on his mom in the tub, at age seven (a deep and long-standing trauma), and three summers ago when he'd seen his older cousin Meredith, walking into the guest room without knocking. But these – these were *mesmerizing*.

Then he looked into those wide, chocolate eyes. And he saw so much there.

Her face, her eyes, her body, her taste, her smell – they had all completely surprised him with their sheer power. She had power, the unstoppable power of sexuality, the confidence of real womanhood, something he had never seen up close or even imagined in such intimate fullness. He'd grown up with very different ideas about the sexuality of women. He'd never considered 'power,' or sexuality-as-strength. But she had it, undeniably - power over what happens between a man and a woman, something that to Gary was nothing but a vague and hazy mystery – but which was clearly much fuller in the doing than in his fantasies.

He knew, and she knew, that she could easily command the moment – that if she wanted to force the issue, he would be powerless to deny her.

And yet there was more in her eyes.

It's up to you, they said.

And he suddenly felt closer to her than he'd ever felt to anyone.

He reached for her.

Her bed was unbelievably comfortable. Lavender sheets, a thick comforter, oversized pillows. Her body was even more comfortable, and she let him relax into what she surely knew was an unprecedented moment for him. She held him, not as aggressively as before, but instead inviting him to hold her. He did, tentatively at first, and she pressed lightly against him, her breasts with their attentive nipples making contact with his chest. Another kiss, as deep and knowing as the others, and just as long.

She rolled them over slightly, so that he was above her, and as he propped himself up, she took his face in her hands, and looked into his eyes. Her own eyes danced with joy, her smile warm and comforting. It was so surreal, it didn't even qualify as a dream. He felt like he'd fallen into some alternate universe, in some episode of The Twilight Zone.

He felt himself wanting more. He felt blood thundering through his body. He felt the flush of real heat. He was increasingly aware of her scent, more than flowers now, the scent of *woman*, utterly alien and yet completely familiar, some primal imprint in his consciousness that no teaching he'd ever had could account for. Her hands explored his arms and chest, and it was only a mildly embarrassingly long moment before it dawned on him that she was patiently urging him to do the same to her.

And he did, hesitantly, self-consciously, grateful that her eyes closed as soon as his fingertips grazed her breast.

He was so afraid he would do it wrong.

She let her hands fall away from him as he repositioned himself, lying beside her as his hand (his finger-picking hand, he idly realized) explored her. Her nipples grew harder still and her breathing quickened, her eyes clenching tighter. Relieved that she wasn't watching, he felt emboldened, a blend of desire and curiosity, and he surprised himself by leaning to one of her breasts and kissing it.

Her sharp intake of breath surprised him, and he almost backed away, but a slight moan followed, and he persisted. He gently kissed the hard nipple, while touching the other one with his hand, and she moaned again, and he went for it, taking it into his mouth.

She sighed, the most contented sigh he'd ever heard.

He couldn't believe this was happening.

And now he was completely lost. He had no idea how long he should do what he was doing, or what happened next. She didn't seem to care at all.

He pulled away after a moment, and she took the initiative, kissing him again, sliding a hand down his back and grasping the back of his jeans. He'd noticed they were loose, and with a downward motion they fell partly down. With two kicks they were gone, and he was down to his underwear, as she was. He realized, once and for all, that he was past the point of no return.

This was going to happen.

She positioned herself beside him, slightly subordinate, and without aggression but also with no-nonsense directness, she began to stroke him, through his Fruit-of-the-Looms. This was a first for him, and he fought not to flinch. The sensation was overwhelming, electric, transforming. It tore him in two, as his emotions slammed back and forth between the desire to escape and the deep need for her to give him more.

He felt himself actually squirm.

Her hand slipped around his back once again, her fingertips sliding under elastic, grabbing into the muscles there, which made him swell with excitement, and distracted him as she deftly removed the Fruit-of-the-Looms with greater ease than she'd shed his jeans.

Now he felt self-conscious.

His prayers that she not look at it were answered; that scrutiny would have snapped him completely out of the moment, so deeply would he have been embarrassed. Instead, she explored him with fingertips, and he realized that the sensations he'd thought electric before weren't even close, compared to this.

It was his turn to moan.

She kissed his neck as her fingers wrapped around him firmly, shifting the electricity so that it ran the length of him, and he felt himself swelling in her grip. She began to slowly stroke him, her grip remaining tight, and he knew he couldn't take much of this feeling.

And she seemed to know that, relaxing after a moment and releasing him completely. She leaned up, reached down and slipped her panties off.

Lying back down, she nestled into him, kissing his mouth, kissing his neck, caressing his arm. One of her legs lay against his; the other was slightly propped up. Her pose wasn't seductive or obscene. It was... inviting.

His hand slid along the smoothness of her hip, and she began another long kiss as he ventured to her thigh. Unexpectedly, her own hand gently came to rest on his wrist as he slid his fingers between her legs, not completely certain what to expect, not altogether certain what was actually there... and met with warm moisture and a soft flesh like no other flesh he had ever touched. As her tongue drew him in, he gently probed, fascinated but uncertain, and her own fingers overlapped his, guiding and pressing lightly, and he realized she was teaching him. He had no choice but to let her show him, and she did, bringing two of his fingertips to rest on a small, firm spot, and pressing down, making gentle circular motions.

He rapidly got the idea, and continued the motions as her hand left his and drifted back between his legs. Damp with traces of her own wetness, she touched him lightly, almost teasingly, and he had to fight to concentrate on his own motions.

Her arm reached around him suddenly, and she pulled him on top of her.

This was it.

He suddenly remembered what he needed next, and glanced out into the living room, where his coat was. He completely forgotten about the condoms –

She pulled him back, smiling, and shook her head. Obviously she knew what it was he was remembering, and obviously she didn't consider it important.

?

Then it dawned on him.

She's on the Pill! Of course she's on the Pill.

He'd heard quite a bit about this; his parents had strong opinions about the Pill, decidedly negative ones. *The devil's drug!* his father had declared, encouraging promiscuity and sin. *It will lead young women to ruin!* he'd heard his mother say on the phone to another mother.

This thought brought a momentary flash of conscience back to him, but she rapidly drew him back. Poised above her, propped up on his

216

arms, he felt her legs part, and felt her hand reach up and stroke him, then take hold of him.

Gently but firmly, she guided him into her, letting him take over, letting him have this moment.

He felt her body receive him, warm and tight and wet and inviting, and the feeling was transforming, far more powerful than anything he'd yet experienced this night. Somewhere in his soul he turned a corner, and new, ancient truths came within easy reach. He felt tremors in their union, as her intimate muscles caressed him, welcoming him, assuring him of her need, and the enfolding of her arms and warmth of her lips underscored the moment.

Somewhere within him, a conflicting voice began to scream. But the more ancient voice prevailed, and his instincts screamed louder, as he pulled back, relishing the feeling of their deepening, and he obeyed it, moving into the timeless rhythm.

She arched her body to meet him, moaning openly, hungry for the motion, and he felt her legs wrap around him. Her arms locked around his back, encouraging him as he began to thrust harder and faster, and after a moment she cried out loudly.

Within seconds, he felt all the torturous pressures inside him suddenly explode, and the wave of ecstasy that swept through him was almost unbearable. He buried himself within her, instinctively, hungrily, wanting the echoes to continue forever. Her embrace tightened, hot and paradoxically safe and comforting, and it felt as if she would never let him go.

The more distant voice began to rise.

He felt ashamed.

He pulled back, and saw her sweet face in candlelight. Her eyes were bright and inexplicably joyous, her arms reluctant to release him. Her smile contained no reflection of his own embarrassment and self-doubt.

He had read enough about sex to know that he had just done a very mediocre job of it, but his deeper shame was something else entirely: failure, a loss of character – sin.

This was sin.

And he had shown himself that he was, when it mattered, *unworthy*.

Within a minute, he was dressed and crossing her living room. She was not distressed or alarmed at his response. A sheet wrapped around her, she patiently stood by and watched, saying nothing as he nervously pulled himself together and departed.

As he drove home, his self-loathing rose, strangling forever his ideals about his someday-marriage and his understanding of love. Part of it was panic; he realized that he smelled like sex, and resolved to wash his hands and face with the garden hose when he got home, in case he encountered one of his parents before making it to his bedroom. He chewed a piece of gum, hoping it would cover up the wine.

He was ashamed.

And yet – some part of him also realized he'd found a whole new truth tonight, one he'd never suspected. One he'd never had believed.

The sense of wrongness that threatened to suffocate him was sweeping up against a contrasting sense of... *rightness*.

II

I remember finding out about you …

For reasons that were vague at best, Gary felt the name "Badfinger" was mildly obscene. Still, since the band's new song had appeared on WLS, he had loved it more every time he heard it.

Oddly, the song played over and over in his head as he sat in the front pew, next to his mother, immediately below the church pulpit. The words and notes of the morning's hymns flowed past him like wind in the distance, too far away to hear over the roar of Badfinger - a storm amplified by his anxiety, the disgust he felt for himself, by the overwhelming guilt.

He was fully aware, of course, that everybody else *did it*, or at least tried very hard to. Even some of the kids at church. Maybe even Richard. Wayne, not a chance. But he wasn't 'everybody else.'

He was his father's son.

And because he was his father's son, there would be punishment.

Sunday dinner was on the table in twenty-four minutes, a point of pride that Joanie announced almost defiantly. She seemed to be in that little-sister mood that demanded one-upping at least one of her brothers before the meal was over, and Gary was not in a tolerant frame of mind.

"That woman came to service," his mother said to his father, sitting down for once, in the chair at the opposite end of the dining room table.

The Reverend Riddel, intent on his slab of ham, frowned.

"Well, let's count that as progress."

218

"It just struck me as awkward."

His father looked up.

"Why so? She's only required to attend your women's study. If she comes to service, it's an extra mile for her."

"Daddy, who are you talking about?"

Joanie's question seemed to snap their parents out of the dialog, and Joanie herself out of her self-satisfied mood.

His mother and father exchanged a look, which Gary caught.

"At the church, we reach out to lost souls in our community," his mother explained in her mother voice. Their father stared at her as she spoke. "We sometimes provide food and clothes and prayers for them, and even places to live."

That grabbed Gary's attention.

"The idea is that our charity will lead them to want to know more about walking with the Lord," his mother went on. "There's a young lady that we have reached out to, and she is attending the Bible study I teach on Tuesday evenings. Since the church provides her with living quarters, we ask that she participate."

Joanie drank her milk and persisted.

"Who is she?"

Their mother looked uncomfortable. "Well, she's no one you would know, dear," she said dismissively. "She works at the hospital where I volunteer. She is a nurse's aide."

This was new information. Gary filed it away, staring at his plate, trying to seem disinterested. Behind the effort, his mind raced: *Is she talking about Laurie?* Almost certainly, with the reference to providing a place to live. If she'd been at church that morning, why hadn't he seen her? Probably because his head had been down most of the time. Why had she been there? Was she feeling as guilty as he was? Did she come to church to feel forgiven?

Based on impressions he couldn't really define, he didn't think that was very likely.

"Your friend Richard's mother spoke to me before service this morning," his mother said to Gary, mercifully changing the subject before Joanie could form another question. "She asked if I would help chaperone at the Valentine's Dance."

Gary made a non-committal sound.

"Gary, are you planning on going to the dance this time?"

His father looked up.

Gary made another non-committal sound, and reached for the potatoes.

"Gary, I asked if you are planning to go to the Valentine's Dance?"

"I hadn't really thought about it."

"He should take Kim Meyers," Joanie announced. "You should take Kim Meyers." She turned to Robbie. "She makes goo-goo eyes at him when they all sit in the back at Wednesday service."

"Cut it out, Joanie."

Robbie joined in. "Kim and Gary, sittin' in a tree –"

"Cut it out!"

"Leave the boy alone, Martha," his father said. He was even less amused than Gary.

"Well, I told her 'no,'" his mother answered. "The dance is four weeks away and we are doing orientations for new volunteers at the hospital around that time, so I will just be too busy."

"Those dances need to be properly chaperoned," his father said with a scowl. "That old school building is a maze, there are too many corners and hideaways for mischief-"

"Dad!"

A trace of a smile flitted around his mother's lips.

"Well, if you feel so strongly, I'm certain they'd be happy to have you join in as a chaperone," she answered.

His father scowled all the more.

"Well, I think that Kimberley Meyers is just such a nice girl," his mother said. "Didn't you all go out last summer, to the skating rink? Perhaps you should ask her to the dance, Gary." At this, Joanie looked very pleased with herself.

Gary made yet another non-committal sound, and wished fervently for Christ's immediate return.

There were more kids than usual for a Thursday night, and Brother Mike had gotten extra pizza to compensate. Harvest House seemed crowded, and Gary didn't much want to be there.

The previous couple of Thursday evenings and Saturday mornings had been very uncomfortable, and Gary's anxiety had shown: Richard and Wayne had gotten on his case about it. Richard had sagely speculated that what Gary needed was a girl to help him unwind. Gary had been afraid to utter a comeback, for fear of saying something that would make them suspicious.

In any universe but this, it would be obvious that the truth of what he'd done with Laurie that night weeks ago would have made him a hero, even a minor god of sorts, to his friends.

He was incredibly tense, being this close. Every time he'd been in Harvest House since that weekend, he'd been almost terrified that she would suddenly appear in whatever room he was in. And at the same time, he caught himself straining to hear above the chatter around him, hoping for some distant sound in the apartment above, some indication of her presence.

There had only been silence.

He was sequestered in a corner of the Game Room, sitting on a bean bag chair with his guitar in his lap. Richard, Wayne and Mark were shooting pool.

He strummed absently, lost in thought.

"'Looking out from my lonely room, day after day,'" came a sweet, musical voice.

It was Kim, appearing from behind Richard. She held two bottles of Coke, and knelt down beside him. He set the guitar aside.

"Don't stop," she said, "I like it when you play. I mean – you know – real songs."

She smiled, hoping he would do the same. It was a running joke that only praise and worship songs were supposed to be played during youth meetings, but that most of the youth sponsors didn't know enough pop music to know the difference.

That was actually a surprising thing for her to say.

"I like that song," she said, handing him a Coke.

"Gary," she said, her voice lowered. "Could we talk?"

He was literally cornered.

With Richard and Wayne and Mark only a dozen feet away, and undoubtedly listening in, Gary led Kim out to the front porch. They weren't wearing their jackets, so whatever she wanted, the cold air would keep it short.

"The Valentine's Dance is tomorrow night," she said, her voice as soft as it had been inside. "Are you going?"

The question was so forward that it caught him off-guard.

"Bobby Barnes asked me, but I told him no," she continued, when he didn't answer. "So did a couple of other boys. I do want to go, though."

Gary could see it coming, and there was no way to avoid it.

"I ran into your sister at service last night," she went on, "and she said you weren't going with anyone. So I was thinking – why don't we just go to the dance together?"

His mind was blank. He realized he should say something, even that it was unkind to say nothing, but no words came.

Her eyes fell away from his in embarrassment.

"It... wouldn't have to be like a date or anything, if that's what you're thinking..."

He opened his mouth to speak, but could not produce words.

She seemed so vulnerable, and he felt so inadequate, that he stepped outside of his tumbling emotions for the first time in weeks. Her cheeks were pink from cold, and her eyes shone. He had known her for... how long? Most of his life, and she had always been, well, there. She had always been there, in his life. And she'd grown prettier, and sweeter, and –

"Gary?"

She looked humiliated. And brave. And he felt so completely stupid.

"That's really nice of you," he started, trying furiously to think of a way to say it. Words didn't come. His pause began to stretch.

Her smile faded.

"Please," she said, her voice suddenly the temperature of the air around them, "Don't try to tell me you're going to be working on your uncle's farm again."

She pushed past him and went back inside.

He leaned against the ancient brick and cursed himself.

And, through a window above the porch, he heard soft music.

Sweet Baby James.

He was naked but not cold, summer breeze sighing through his bedroom window. His guitar stood in a corner of his dark room, and the Badfinger song was barely audible on his clock radio. Two glasses of red wine, as yet untouched, sat on his nightstand.

Candlelight flickered in the hallway, and she drifted into the room like a ghost. She was wearing a- he didn't know what it was called, but it was basically a very large spider web, see-thru and wispy and sort of loose and clingy at the same time. The flickering light gave him isolated glimpses of her skin beneath, and the darting shadows accentuated her potent sexuality.

222

She breathed desire and innocence in harmony, setting the candle on his dresser and crawling onto his bed, her garment open, situating herself above him. Her breasts, now shadowed, were just as he had so often imagined them in the most distant corners of his thoughts, moderate and perfect with small and communicative buds, now firm with purpose... her skin and her hair smelled of flowers... her touch almost hot, competing with the breeze sweeping through the window above.

Her eyes blazed in the window's moonlight, saying things he had imagined so many times but never believed could be, and the reality swept his old fantasies aside: Kim was as he was, some secret animal moving back and forth impatiently, somewhere beneath the surface of her very proper plans and goals and piety... sinful desires trying to break through, poisons threatening the soul, pushing irresistibly against the goodness and rightness that had been their shared birthright. And yet...

None of that mattered. Not right now.

Hesitation loomed in her eyes, her breathing, her gentle sounds, her uncertain position as she hovered above him... he understood, sympathizing with the battle that he knew must be raging within her, a battle between self and self, between want and need, between good and bad... halting, unsure, she lowered her lips to his, descending into his embrace. She tasted as she had before, like a young woman, innocence with traces of something deeper...

His arms surged with strength as they encircled her, and he took charge, paradoxically rolling them over and asserting himself in his narrow single bed.

...and she was no longer Kim, but now Laurie, her breasts suddenly magnified, her nipples much larger and darker and harder, her hips and eyes and intent no longer hesitant at all... she no longer smelled like flowers, but overwhelmed him with that mysterious, musky scent that robbed him of reason, drawing him into her hypnotic gaze with a helplessness that seemed to empower him even as it gave his power up to her.

Her lips tasted of wine... her tongue was unrestrained. Strong legs matched the force of his arms, and their embrace forged a figure wrought in iron as he fiercely entered her, and she gasped...

...and he awoke, panting and chilly from a sheet drenched in sweat. All was the same, but for the candle, the wine, and his solitude. In the corner sat his guitar, and the clock radio was silent.

He sat up, felt the breeze from the window. Impatiently, he turned and pulled it shut.

And laying back down, in his own sweat and fear and confusion, he felt ashamed.

There had been no question, none at all, over whether the usual Thursday night youth meeting would take place at Harvest House, despite it being the night before the school Valentine's Dance. Gary's father would never have entertained the idea of cancelling, despite the fact that most of the teenagers who participated would be busy with preparations for the following night.

Only four of the usual crowd, including Gary, showed up, along with Brother Mike. Kim was one of them.

Gary decided that the best way to avoid awkwardness was to place himself in the center of everything, where there could be no privacy. He packed boxes with gusto, and talked openly with Brother Mike about anything and everything.

Kim was completely silent, opening her mouth only to sing the usual praise songs, as Gary strummed, too loudly.

Kim left first, slipping out silently. Gary and Brother Mike were the last ones to leave.

"Forgot my keys," the youth pastor said, hand in coat pocket. "Let me run out to the car and get them."

"I've got mine," Gary said, pulling his set from his coat pocket. "I'll lock up."

Brother Mike nodded and hurried down the front steps of Harvest House, in the bitter cold.

"See you Saturday morning," he called out. "Have fun at the dance tomorrow!"

Gary turned out the lights in the front room, careful to leave the front porch light on.

And as he turned the key to bolt the door, he heard music above.

I remember finding out about you...

"Gary? Are you ever coming down?"

I'm going to the dance...

"In a minute, mom!"

He smoothed his hair and slipped on his sport coat, the one he'd gotten for his seventeenth birthday. His father disapproved of his wearing it to church, for reasons passing understanding.

Staring into the mirror above his dresser, Gary studied his own face. He tried to see what he felt – guilt, confusion, some undefinable loss of himself – but all he saw was the face he always saw.

Turning, he looked at his room, at his guitar in its case at the foot of the bed, at the bed itself – perfectly made – and the window above.

All as it had always been.

I'm going to the dance...

"So, ya didn't ask Kim? You're going stag?"

Joanie, behind him.

"Did ya chicken out?"

"Shut up, Joanie."

He marched out of the room and down the stairs, with his sister hot on his heels.

"Kinda humiliating to go to a Valentine's dance by yourself, isn't it?" she persisted, as he stomped through the kitchen toward the garage door. "Speaking of chickens, I'll bet you dance like one!"

"Joanie, leave your brother alone. Gary, have a nice time, dear! Remember, home by eleven-thirty!"

He closed the door behind him, stepping into the garage. Joanie didn't follow.

I'm going to the dance...

The porch light was still on at Harvest House.

Wonderful smells filled the front room as he stepped inside, slipping off his coat and letting it fall to the floor. It was food, but unfamiliar. The stereo was playing upstairs, a bit too faintly for him to make out the words of the song that was playing.

He moved slowly up the stairs.

The music came into focus. It was James Taylor again, Mud Slide Slim this time, an album he'd heard at Wayne's.

There she stood at the stove, wearing an apron over a t-shirt and the shortest pair of shorts he'd ever seen – hot pants? – swaying to the music as she stirred something very spicy-smelling.

She did not seem even remotely surprised to see him walk into the room. She even seemed to be expecting him.

"You just calllll out my name, and you knowwww wherever I am..." she half-sang, lifting a wooden spoon out of the mixture she was stirring and tasting it. She seemed pleased, and dipped out another spoonful, then scurrying over to him.

"Try this!"

He hesitantly tasted it. It was hot, hotter than anything he'd ever tasted. Hotter than Italian food. Way hotter.

"I hope you like Indian," she said, quickly kissing him on the cheek. "I figure you don't get much ethnic food at home!"

Well, that was certainly true. He couldn't remember ever having Indian food, at home or anywhere else. For that matter, he didn't know the names of any Indian food.

It was a wonderful meal, with wonderful wine, and though she must have known it was the night of the school dance, she said nothing about it, or why he was dressed up. They talked about James Taylor, about music, about ethnic food. They talked about Hair, the musical, which she had seen in New York two years earlier. He felt scandalous even discussing it.

He completely forgot about the dance.

As she began cleaning up the dinner dishes, he crossed the living room to the shelves on the far side. There were picture frames on the top of the shelves. The pictures weren't just turned down – they were empty frames, all of them.

Whose pictures had been in them? A boyfriend? Why had she taken them out? Had he left her? Did she kick him out? He wondered if there might be important information in the answers, some guide to avoiding mistakes.

Then he noticed something behind the small stack of frames. A statue.

It was small, maybe ten inches high, the figure of a naked man, formed in clay. It was a personal effort, not a thing from a store, and it was kiln-baked - to last forever. He ran his fingers over it, studying it, wondering what it could be about.

"He lost most of his left foot in Vietnam."

Her voice came from behind him, softer than he'd ever heard it before, and he was startled.

"I made that for him."

Him?

Gary's fingers strayed over the figure, and he gazed at it with a trace of amazement. It was at once lovingly detailed, muscles shaped to very precise resolution. He realized, as he appreciated what he was seeing, that he was seeing through her.

"I wanted him to know that it didn't matter to me," she said, her voice unbearably tender. "I gave it to him to show him that in my eyes, he was a whole man... a complete man."

She took it from him gently, held it and looked at it for a moment, then placed it back on the shelf. It was the first time he'd seen her embarrassed.

He had known, on some level, he would end up here. He had insisted to himself that nothing would happen.

And he had known, on some level, that it would. He wanted that, and he hated himself for wanting it.

After another album and a second glass of wine, he had followed her into the bedroom without hesitation, and had found her playfulness relaxing. Her total lack of self-consciousness at her own nakedness helped dissipate his own awkwardness, and he felt completely comfortable, sliding onto the bed next to her. The seriousness of the moment by the bookshelf had evaporated, and she wrapped her arms intensely around one of the pillows at the top of the bed, inviting him closer with her eyes.

The best stuff, she whispered playfully, *is always under the pillow!*

He slid a hand under the pillow she was holding and pulled out a handful of foil-wrapped chocolates, expensive ones by the look of them. Releasing the pillow, she grabbed one and unwrapped it, put it halfway into her mouth, then leaned forward to offer him the other half. The chocolate melted in the kiss, messy but tantalizing. Her tongue felt different in the warm, sweet moisture, and she made a sound she'd never made before.

He was exhausted.

They had made love over and over, in ways he had never imagined – in ways he felt might even be indecent. She was forceful while still being playful, not letting him rest, not taking no for an answer. When he wondered whether he would face the humiliation of being unable to provide for her any further, she had anticipated him, and stirred him to further action using her hands and her mouth in ways he'd heard other guys talk about, but never even dared to imagine in his most private thoughts.

Her scent was as it had been in his dream, feminine and powerful but in an animal way, not at all girlish - filled with lust and madness and some deep rightness that surged in his blood like molten fire, making all of these wrong things seem right...

He excused himself to go into the bathroom, but he was really just taking the opportunity to take a few deep breaths and recover. Maybe she'll fall asleep while I'm in here…

Stepping back out into the bedroom, in the glow of blacklight, he found her sprawled across the bed, her pillow laying across her stomach and what was below. She grinned.

The best stuff is always under the pillow…

When he awoke, it was almost two in the morning.

He bolted upright, realizing the situation, realizing the trouble he was in. Whatever spell he'd been under, Indian food, James Taylor, blacklight, her smell - it was broken, and so was he.

He leapt out of the bed and began gathering up his clothes in the dark. She stirred, confused.

"Gary…?"

"I am in so much trouble! I should have been home hours ago!"

She sat up as he pulled on his shorts and pants, and turned on the light next to the bed, to help him find the rest of his clothes.

"Oh, I am so sorry! We both fell asleep… it must have been the wine –"

"No!"

He almost shouted, and she shrank back.

"This is wrong!"he heard himself say, as he pulled on his shirt. "This isn't something I should be doing! This isn't how it should be!"

For the first time since he'd met her, he saw confusion in her eyes.

"The things we've done – I can't do this! I shouldn't be here!"

She clutched a sheet around her breasts.

"Oh, Gary, honey, I didn't mean – "

"This isn't who I am!" He shouted it, then realized he'd shouted. "I shouldn't have done any of these things! Now there's no way to go back, no way to change it!"

He pulled on his shoes. She moved to get out of the bed, to come to him.

He stood at the bedroom door.

"Now I'm broken," he said, and he actually felt hot tears gathering. "I'm *broken!*"

"Gary, sweetheart – "

He fled.

They would be waiting in the living room.

They would be sitting there, his mother's eyes soaked with tears, his father tense with barely-contained rage, clutching an accumulation of minutes-turned-to-hours - the air thick with ghostly images of Gary's broken body in a ditch somewhere, especially after what had happened on the interstate last November.

He stopped at the twenty-four-hour convenience store and washed up, afraid he'd be caught if he used the garden hose this time.

The house was dark.

Of course, he thought. They trusted him. Where he'd gone, what he'd been doing – none of it would ever have entered his parents' minds.

They trusted him!

That made everything much, much worse.

III

Gary stumbled out of bed the next morning, having had almost no sleep, and lingered in the hot shower. He went to Harvest House, as always, to help distribute the week's food and clothes, because he had to.

Kim did not appear.

Neither did Richard, Wayne, Mark or any of Gary's other friends who had been at the dance the previous evening.

The following morning at church, Kim was there, but did not meet his eye. Richard and Wayne were at church, full of stories about the dance and peripheral events, and razzing for Gary over not showing up. Gary was more concerned that Laurie would be there, as his mother had said she had been recently, and he dreaded seeing her in front of everyone. But he didn't see her.

Sunday dinner was leisurely. Gary's mother and sister took a relaxed forty-two minutes getting the food to table, and once it was there, the tone was indifferent. It wasn't until dessert that his mother dropped her bombshell.

"Richard's mother had quite a piece of news for me this morning, Gary," she said. "Apparently, no one saw you at the Valentine's dance Friday night."

Everyone froze, including Gary.

He felt his cheeks and ears burning as their stares fixed on him.

229

There was a long pause.

"Gary?" It was his mother's voice, but all Gary could think of was his father's eyes on him, eyes he would not meet.

"Gary, do you have an explanation?"

Joanie's triumphant grin gave him an out.

He hung his head briefly, frowning, then looked straight at Joanie.

"I was embarrassed, mom."

His mother's mouth dropped open, this not being an answer she had expected.

"Embarrassed? Gary, whatever for?"

"I..."

Joanie and his little brother were mesmerized. His father was frowning.

"I can't dance!"

The younger children erupted with laughter, his father let out a sigh, and Gary let his face and ears glow red in relative safety. He stared at his plate.

His mother's attention shifted to Joanie and Robbie, and she vented her annoyance freely, shooing them from the table to eat their dessert on the back porch.

"Gary, this won't do at all," his mother said when they had gone. "Why didn't you say anything?"

He shifted uncomfortably.

"Mom, it's really not the kind of thing you talk about. Especially not with your own mother."

"Why, I never realized! Now I understand why you didn't ask that Kimberly Myers to go with you. Oh, it all makes sense now. I'm surprised you even made an effort."

He was terrified that she would raise the question of where he had actually been.

"Well, we must do something about this. You have your senior prom coming up, after all."

Oh, dear god, no...

"We'll get this all taken care of! We have almost three months."

His father finally spoke.

"Martha, what in the world are you talking about?"

She smiled a smile of pure joy.

"Between now and the prom... I will teach Gary to dance!"

Oh, Jesus, take me now...

Something like sympathy flickered across his father's face, but the frown persisted.

Gary smiled weakly at his mother, who busied herself with clearing the table, bustling with happy energy.

"Finish your ice cream," his father said as she vanished into the kitchen. "Then I'll see you in my study."

Gary's spine ran cold as he nodded and sat alone at the table, staring at his ice cream. His father hadn't missed what his mother had missed – his actual accounting for his absence from the dance Friday night. His mind raced, searching for plausible excused. But all of his best friends, everyone known to his parents, had been at the dance. Any lie he told now would be caught. And yet... telling the truth would be far, far worse.

He closed the door to his father's study behind him and took his place in the chair in front of his father's desk. His father was still frowning, and Gary felt almost light-headed.

"Son, we've needed to talk for a while now," his father began, and Gary felt immediate confusion. This didn't sound like the beginning of a conversation about Friday night.

"I know from the things you've said these past few months that you may be having doubts about Trinity," his father continued. "For so long, we've just assumed it would be the best thing, and it seems to me we should have discussed it more than we did."

He paused, and Gary simply stared at him, clearly not understanding. He was so surprised at the change of subject that it did not occur to him to be relieved.

"I've arranged for Mr. Price from the school to pay us a call when he passes through in two weeks," his father continued. "He'll be able to give you a better idea of what will be involved in getting your application together, and he'll answer any questions you might have. And your mother and I have decided it would be a good idea to take vacation in Tennessee this summer, so we can spend a day on campus and have a look around. You haven't seen the school since you were small, I don't think."

Gary could do nothing but nod.

"What I need for you to do is to give this some thought over the next couple of weeks, and have some questions in your mind that we can discuss then. How does that sound?"

"That sounds okay," he said, even though it didn't, and he resisted the impulse to add "sir."

As he opened the door of the study to leave, his father called out behind him.

"Oh, one other thing," he said. "You're not the only one Mr. Price will be seeing. Your friend Kimberly has an interview, too."

Gary turned and looked at his father.

"But Kim is going to state?" he said blankly.

"Perhaps," his father said, "but I was told that she has an interest in attending Trinity now, and she'll be meeting with the recruiter, just as you will be."

Gary nodded, then closed the door behind him.

This can't really be happening ...

The recruiter from Trinity came and went, and Gary gave the meeting more sincerity and effort than he had originally planned. There was a part of him that felt guilt and shame gnawing away within, amid feelings that he had let Kim down, let Laurie down, his parents, and mostly himself. The fix for that must be, he decided, to get back on the path he'd been on all his life. The path to Trinity.

And yet there was another part of him, some deeper part he'd never been able to hear until these recent months, that was speaking to him with a clarity that was unsettling, presenting thoughts and ideas that had always been out of reach. Thoughts and ideas that now threatened to change him.

He would not be seeing Laurie again, he had decided. He didn't want these choices.

The recruiter mentioned having met with Kim before meeting with him. Maybe it was time to talk to her.

"Kim?"

She was headed out the front door of Harvest House, into the moderate chill of a mid-March evening, one of the last to leave. Gary had waited two weeks to make the attempt to talk to her, and a Thursday evening offered the greatest opportunity for privacy.

Once again, they stood together on the cold front porch, under an evening sky. She did not seem anxious to hear from him.

"Hey," he said, hesitantly but warmly. She said nothing.

"Thanks for waiting," he began. "I've wanted to say something for a while now."

She still said nothing, but she turned to look at him.

"I want to say that I'm really sorry," he said, and he meant it, and looked directly at her to let her know it. "I wish we had gone to the Valentine's dance together. I didn't mean to be rude to you, and I think if we'd gone together, we'd have had a great time."

Her expression softened. She took a step closer to him.

"I went to the dance alone," she said. The way she said it made clear to him that it had been embarrassing. "I think we'd have had a great time, too."

"Gary," she said, looking into his face with a puzzled expression. "Why didn't you come? Where were you?"

Panic swept over him. He had not expected that question, especially not that directly.

If I lie to her, will she be able to see it in my face?

"I... can't dance," he said.

She stepped closer, uncomfortably close. Close enough that he picked up her scent, even in the cold.

"Gary," she said quietly, "I know better."

It was different. The scent was her scent, which he'd known for years. But now he was more aware of it than ever before, and it communicated something different, something... new.

"Gary," she persisted, "Why weren't you at the dance?"

He wasn't sure he could lie to her outright. Kim had known him since they'd both been small. He wasn't sure he wanted to lie to her. But, as with his father, he couldn't possibly tell her the whole truth.

He settled on partial truth.

"I've had some stuff lately that I've needed to think about," he said, "Stuff I have to work out for myself."

She nodded, sympathetic, in a way that utterly surprised him.

"I know what you mean," she said. "I guess you talked to the man from Trinity College."

Bless her.

"Yeah," he said. "That's what I wanted to talk to you about."

She said nothing, waiting for him to continue.

"It looks like I'll be sending my application in soon," he continued, "and I was surprised when I found out you were thinking about going to Trinity. I thought you were going to state."

She hesitated.

"I am," she said. "Since last summer, when you told me you were going to Trinity, I thought a lot about going there, too. My mom set up the appointment with that recruiter from the school. I had already changed my mind."

"You're not going to Trinity?"

She hesitated again, as if taking a moment to argue with herself.

"No," she answered. "I'm going to state, like I had planned before."

"What changed your mind?"

Now she really hesitated, biting her lower lip.

He waited, resisting the cold, resisting the urge to prod her.

"Gary," she said slowly, "When we went out last summer, when we talked... I don't know how to say this. Please be patient with me. I... since we were kids... "

Her eyes watered. Suddenly he felt very, very vulnerable, very guilty.

"Gary, I have believed for a long time that we were meant to be together," she said, her voice steady and calm in spite of the tears. "You and I... we have a connection. We've always had it, since we were little kids. We know each other's moods, we know each other's thoughts... we understand each other. When you and I talk... it's like when I listen to my parents talk in the kitchen, at night when the rest of us are supposed to be asleep."

He had no response.

"We've been friends all our lives, but we both feel... we're more than..." She blinked tears away.

"I love you, Gary," she said, even more bravely, and she looked right into his eyes as she said it. "And *I believe that you love me*. I don't know what's going on with you right now, and I don't know any way to ask you... but I can see that things have changed."

A tear spilled down her cold, red cheek. But her eyes never wavered, and her voice didn't break.

"Gary, I have to go where I'm going, and so do you. And if we're going to different places, then that has to be okay."

He met her gaze, and felt two inches tall, ashamed and embarrassed. There was something new in her face, along with her scent - no longer the scent of a girl – and he felt humiliated, looking into the eyes of a woman, yet unable to feel like a man.

"I really do love you, Gary," she said, and she reached forward and embraced him, hard.

"And I'll miss you." She stepped back, hesitating for a moment.

He said nothing.

And she was gone.

Feelings welled up in him like floodwaters, and he bolted back into the now-empty living room. He pulled his coat away and flung it to the floor.

Somewhere inside him, there was Kim. It had always been Kim. He had felt himself growing past her, these recent weeks, and now he realized that she had grown past him.

He was unworthy of her. He had ruined himself, ruined what they had.

He burst into tears, and sobbed.

Thinking he was alone, he did not see or hear Laurie, sitting at the top of the steps.

Gary was headed for the school, to the basketball game. Richard, Wayne, Mark – everyone would be there.

Kim would be there.

He drove in silence. And reached for the radio.

You just call out my name... and you know wherever I am, I'll come runnin'...

It felt like the radio was speaking to him. His first impulse was to ignore it, but after last night... after talking to Kim... no, he was done with that.

It had been two months since that first night.

Four weeks, now, since the second night.

He didn't fully understand the voice calling out to him now.

The car made its own way back, not toward the school, but toward the ancient brick house in town.

There was no porch light. If there was light in the windows above, he couldn't see it.

The front room of Harvest House was dark and still, but he knew she was here. There was light, very dim, at the top of the stairs.

Leaving his coat behind, he went quietly up.

A candle burned on the coffee table. A half-empty wine glass sat next to it. Music, almost too low to be heard clearly, played on the record player.

He looked up and saw her in the bedroom doorway, her eyes wet and red. She ran to him.

He held her tightly as she began to sob. No longer strong and in control, no longer playful, no longer all the things she had been, she burrowed into him, weeping uncontrollably. He tightened his arms around her, not understanding, but willing, in spite of himself, to do this for her.

Had he done this?

Had she been like this, hurt by his rejection, by his fleeing from her as he had those four weeks ago?

Had he been that insensitive, so totally focused on himself, on his own feelings?

Her muscles went slack, as if she were collapsing, held up only by his arms. He held her as if he would never let her go, and she sobbed into his chest, her tears soaking his shirt.

I'm here... I'm so sorry!

He found strength he didn't know he had, encircling her with a new tenderness he'd never known he could express. Moments passed, as the record played, and his arms did not grow tired. When her sobbing began to soften, he kissed her forehead, and she pulled back a bit, looking up at him through the flood of tears, and all the love and compassion he'd ever felt in his life were there for him now, accessible, when he needed to offer them most.

It felt like what he was giving her right now was everything in the world to her. She trembled in his arms, drawing strength from him, and he found himself happy to give it.

As the moments passed, a calm descended, and her trembling was stilled, though their embrace remained firm. She began to sway lightly to the music, and he joined in.

They danced, bodies entwined, her wet face on his chest, his arms enfolding her with strength and gentleness.

What have I done?

They danced, slowly, until the record stopped.

He was not sure who led who into the other room, but it was not the playful, passionate exchange it had been before. He eased her onto the bed with him, holding her as he had been held, allowing her to curl up into him for comfort and warmth, embracing her as if she was all there was in the world. He felt her breathing, warm and light on his wet chest, and stroked her hair, reaching into himself for everything he could give to her.

He stroked her wet cheek, looking into her eyes in dim moonlight, and kissed her... not with lust, not with intent... but with warmth and strength and a connection that was almost spiritual. His arms tightened around her, and what flowed between them was healing, not passion, still charged with manhood and womanhood, but with depth and understanding. He gave something he had never given, something he hadn't known he possessed to give, something new... and as she received it, she opened herself to him in a way he'd never have thought to expect.

When he thought back later, he could not remember where their clothes had gone, or how, but it didn't matter. It had been no torrid strip-down filled with tease and play as before, but the motions of man and woman simply being man and woman, merging more out of need than desire. His hands had explored her with warmth and firmness and respect and comfort, out of some instinct suddenly surfacing, and their kiss had been a wordless exchange between souls, full and lingering.

Her body was something new, no longer intimidating and enticing, but now vulnerable and intimate and familiar in a way that he felt deep in the cells of his own body. Their joining was a perfect duet, firm and rhythmic and natural, lasting far longer than it had before, and when her tears began to flow again he simply accepted them, confident in their shared solace.

Giving and taking in equal measure, he felt like a man, and revered her as a woman.

Through her tears her body tightened around him, needing him, drawing life from the moment, and when ecstasy finally swept over her, it was simply part of the flow, not a goal. And when he surged into her, moments later, full and powerful and almost overwhelming, it didn't feel like an ending...

They lay there together, still entangled, still joined, breathing the same air, feeling each other's heartbeat, until he finally leaned to one side and gathered her up in his arms again.

They fell asleep in moonlight, as they had a month before... and when he awoke, he slipped out quietly, letting her sleep, unconcerned with coming home late or the possibility of being caught sneaking in this time.

He no longer cared. He had faced his failures and made peace with his tangled feelings.

Kim was out of reach now. Laurie needed him, and he had passed through that place of putting his own feelings first. He understood what was required of him, if he was to really love someone.

He needed to confront his own brokenness, and work it out, somehow. Only then could he present himself to Laurie, and ask her to marry him.

No, I can't forget this evening, or your face as you were leaving …
Late to the dinner table, he passed Joanie and Robbie, who had
already been excused and were off to their rooms to do homework.
Pot roast with carrots and potatoes passed before him and he scooped
out a modest helping as his mother poured coffee for herself and his
father.

"I'll need your help down at Harvest this weekend," his father told
him idly, dumping a spoonful of sugar into his coffee. "We need to do
some work in that upstairs kitchen."

He looked up, startled.

"With that Laurie girl moved out, you all can nice it up to charge a
rent," his mother said as she ducked into the kitchen.

An icy fist squeezed Gary's heart.

"Moved out?"

As he asked the question, he tried too hard to sound indifferent. He
stuffed food into his mouth.

"Without a word of notice," his father replied. "Up and gone."

"Try to help a body," said his mother, returning. A plate bearing a
piece of cake was set before her husband, another to the side of
Gary's dinner. "After all the church did for her. Not even a thank you."

Chewing his food, he felt dizzy, like he needed air. His face felt red.

Up and gone???

He noticed that his mother was staring at him.

"After all the church did for her?" he asked.

His mother looked at his father, who stared back for a moment, then
turned to him.

"The elders didn't want anything said unless she chose to tell folks
herself," his father explained. "We took her in after the crash."

The crash!

"You remember the Chevy van with that man and the baby?"

Cold terror hit Gary, like a blast of icy wind in the face. The contents
of his stomach turned to lead.

"The baby was her son," his father said, his voice lowered. "The man
was his daddy."

"Not her husband," added his mother, her tone carrying a grim little
condemnation.

"Weren't sure how she'd get by after that," his father said. "The
church took her in, to look after her until she got her bearings."

"We tried to get her to talk at Bible group," his mother said. "She would never speak of it. We gave her plenty of chances." She sighed. "In all these months, she never let down for anybody, not that I know of."

His insides were a bottomless canyon, cold and dark and filled with unintelligible echoes. Sweeping over him was a sense of loss so vast, so deep, he was suddenly afraid he would vanish into it forever.

Had that been what he was to her? Filling up some empty space? Taking her mind off something too terrible to bear? He felt confused and ashamed. How many days had passed since they had last been together, that time that had changed him so much? What was his excuse?

"Did she give notice at the hospital?" his father asked his mother.

She took on a knowing look, and shook her head.

"Oh, that's the place she needed out of most," his mother answered, lowering her voice as his father had. "Word got around quick. She didn't much care. Even seemed... pleased with herself."

"Word of what?" his father frowned.

His mother leaned in toward them, hesitant to reveal the gossip but deciding he was old enough.

"Well," his mother said, "She was *with child*... "

Can't live, if living is without you...

Soft morning light trickled through the ancient curtains, illuminating lazy wisps of dust he had stirred up by entering. The silence was like a blanket smothering him – or it might have been the maddening tension inside him, feelings pressing in on him from all directions relentlessly.

Had she used him? Had it all been some kind of deception? Had she taken something from him, something so sacred and important and permanent, with planning and purpose - knowing he could never follow, because of who he was?

Is that why she had chosen him?

Or had he really touched her as she had touched him? Had the things he sensed been true, had something lasting happened here?

He felt helpless and stupid, and there was a misery in his sense of having failed himself, and failed her, and the incommutable sentence of never knowing whether he had let her down.

On the other side of the tension was an inexplicable calm, an awareness of thoughts he hadn't yet voiced to himself, but which lived fully formed inside him...

The certainty that he would not go to Trinity, but to state; that the dread he had carried so long had lifted.

That he would see Kim.

He would see Kim, and he would apologize, and he would mean it, and he would get her to see that he meant it. They would go to the senior prom together, if she was willing.

And then, he would say new things.

He climbed the wooden stairs slowly, hesitantly, unnerved at their creaking.

The little rooms were alien.

There was nothing of her here, no trace of her passage. No sign that she had ever existed. Dark wood and musty smells, in ruddy sunlight, made it seem a room for a visiting grandparent. No beads hung in the doorway. The tables and shelves were empty. The bed was naked mattress and uncased pillow.

He sat on the edge of the bed, his eyes moist, almost holding his breath. He hoped for some ghost, some visitation, some trace of her. He lay down on the mattress, breathing deeply, aching for her scent. He had never needed anything so badly. He had to have something, anything, to guide him, to show him what it had meant, what he had been to her. The holes inside him could be patched, but he would rather have them filled.

After all that had happened, how could she have left without a word? How could she have reached into him so deeply, and allowed him reach into her, and taken what she had from him, without leaving anything? Couldn't she have at least written a goodbye note?

A confusion as great as the night sky hovered over him as he lay there, remembering, shifting to become a vast stillness... like mist over a battlefield, the battle between who he had been and who he could feel himself becoming. The irreconcilability of this brokenness he now felt, self-doubt he could not resolve on his own, a burden he had not invited, was a heavy wooden door trapping him inside himself. He had walked into this room, and confronted the fears within, at her beckoning – he had trusted her to provide a key. And now she was forever beyond his reach.

His old faith was gone, and he needed something – *anything!* - that he could build upon, in pursuing a new faith.

A tear spilled onto the mattress, and his hand touched the pillow.

Suddenly it dawned on him, and his heart raced.
The best stuff is always under the pillow!
And under the pillow - he found the statue.

Robin Scott is a journalist and public speaker, living in the Midwest.

Made in the USA
Middletown, DE
14 December 2020